PRAISE FOR THE NOVELS OF CHRISTINA LAUREN

"*In a Holidaze* is everything I've ever wanted in a wintry love story. As hilarious as it is sweet, as sexy as it is tender, this story is pure, irresistible magic from start to finish. I couldn't possibly love this book any more—my favorite Christina Lauren novel yet!"

—Emily Henry, *New York Times* bestselling author of *Beach Read*, on *In a Holidaze*

"Christina Lauren's *In a Holidaze* is the perfect fresh take on finding your joy and falling in love. One page in and you want to put up your tree at all times of the year, sip hot cocoa, and dive into a marvelous cast of characters while staying on your toes wondering what will happen next."

—Carrie Ann Ryan, *New York Times* bestselling author of *Forever Only Once*, on *In a Holidaze*

"An absolutely dazzling holiday romance: clever and cozy and deliciously sexy, with a cast of characters and a spirit-of-the-season lesson you won't soon forget."

—Kate Clayborn, author of *Love Lettering*, on *In a Holidaze*

"A toxic workplace nurtures an intoxicating romance in Lauren's latest, supplying readers with all the drama and wit of the enemies-to-lovers trope. When a book has such great comic timing, it's easy to finish the story in one sitting."

—*Kirkus Reviews* on *The Honey-Don't List* (starred review)

"Lauren (*The Unhoneymooners*) delivers a breezy, tongue-in-cheek rom-com as insightful as it is irreverent. Readers will laugh out loud."

—*Publishers Weekly* on *The Honey-Don't List*

"[The] story . . . is worth the wait, and the rich family back-stories add sweetness . . . [with] a twist that offers readers something unexpected and new."

—*Kirkus Reviews* on *Twice in a Blue Moon*

"What a joyful, warm, touching book! I laughed so hard I cried more than once, I felt the embrace of Olive's huge, loving, complicated, hilarious family, and my heart soared at the ending. This is the book to read if you want to smile so hard your face hurts."

—Jasmine Guillory, *New York Times* bestselling author of *The Wedding Party*, on *The Unhoneymooners*

"Witty and downright hilarious, with just the right amount of heart, *The Unhoneymooners* is a perfect feel-good romantic comedy. Prepare to laugh and smile from cover to cover."

—Helen Hoang, author of *The Bride Test*, on *The Unhoneymooners*

"This is a messy and sexy look at digital dating that feels fresh and exciting."

—*Publishers Weekly* on *My Favorite Half-Night Stand* (starred review)

"You can never go wrong with a Christina Lauren novel . . . a delectable, moving take on modern dating reminding us all that when it comes to intoxicating, sexy, playful romance that has its finger on the pulse of contemporary love, this duo always swipes right."

—*Entertainment Weekly* on *My Favorite Half-Night Stand*

"The story skips along . . . propelled by rom-com momentum and charm."

—*The New York Times Book Review* on *Josh and Hazel's Guide to Not Dating*

"With exuberant humor and unforgettable characters, this romantic comedy is a standout."

—*Kirkus Reviews* on *Josh and Hazel's Guide to Not Dating* (starred review)

"From Lauren's wit to her love of wordplay and literature to swoony love scenes to heroines who learn to set aside their own self-doubts . . . Lauren writes of the bittersweet pangs of love and loss with piercing clarity."

—*Entertainment Weekly* on *Love and Other Words*

"A triumph . . . a true joy from start to finish."

—Kristin Harmel, internationally bestselling author of *The Room on Rue Amélie*, on *Love and Other Words*

"Lauren's standalone brims with authentic characters and a captivating plot."

—*Publishers Weekly* on *Roomies* (starred review)

"Delightful."

—*People* on *Roomies*

"At turns hilarious and gut-wrenching, this is a tremendously fun slow burn."

—*The Washington Post* on *Dating You / Hating You* (a Best Romance of 2017 selection)

"Christina Lauren hilariously depicts modern dating."

—*Us Weekly* on *Dating You / Hating You*

In a
Holidaze

CHRISTINA LAUREN

GALLERY BOOKS

New York   London   Toronto   Sydney   New Delhi

Gallery Books
An Imprint of Simon & Schuster, Inc.
1230 Avenue of the Americas
New York, NY 10020

First Gallery Books trade paperback edition October 2020

GALLERY BOOKS and colophon are registered trademarks of Simon & Schuster, Inc.

For information about special discounts for bulk purchases, please contact Simon & Schuster Special Sales at 1-866-506-1949 or business@simonandschuster.com.

The Simon & Schuster Speakers Bureau can bring authors to your live event. For more information or to book an event, contact the Simon & Schuster Speakers Bureau at 1-866-248-3049 or visit our website at www.simonspeakers.com.

Interior design by Erika R. Genova

Manufactured in the United States of America

10 9 8 7 6 5 4 3 2 1

Library of Congress Cataloging-in-Publication Data
Names: Lauren, Christina, author.
Title: In a holidaze / Christina Lauren.
Description: First Gallery Books trade paperback edition. | New York : Gallery Books, 2020.
Identifiers: LCCN 2020008256 (print) | LCCN 2020008257 (ebook) | ISBN 9781982123949 (trade paperback) | ISBN 9781982123956 (ebook)
Subjects: LCSH: Christmas stories. | GSAFD: Love stories.
Classification: LCC PS3612.A9442273 I5 2020 (print) | LCC PS3612.A9442273 (ebook) | DDC 813/.6—dc23
LC record available at https://lccn.loc.gov/2020008256
LC ebook record available at https://lccn.loc.gov/2020008257

ISBN 978-1-9821-2394-9
ISBN 978-1-9821-2395-6 (ebook)

In a
Holidaze

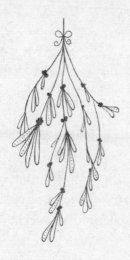

chapter one

Call me harlot. Call me impulsive. Call me hungover.

No one ever has before, but someone absolutely should this morning. Last night was a disaster.

As quietly as I can, I slip out of the bottom bunk and tip-toe across the freezing floor to the stairs. My heart is beating so hard I wonder if it's audible outside of my body. The last thing I want is to wake Theo and have to look him in the eye before my brain is warmed up and my thoughts are cohesive.

The second step from the bottom always creaks like something out of a haunted house; it's been victimized by nearly three decades of us "kids" run-stomping our way up for meals and down for games and bed in the basement. I stretch to carefully put my foot on the one just above it, exhaling when I land with no sound. Not everyone is so lucky;

that loose board has busted Theo sneaking in late—or early, depending on how you look at it—more times than I can count.

Once I'm in the kitchen, I worry less about stealth and go for speed. It's still dark; the house is quiet, but Uncle Ricky will be up soon. This cabin is full of early risers. My window of opportunity to figure out how to fix this is narrowing quickly.

With a barrage of memories from last night rolling like a mortifying flip book through my head, I jog up the wide stairway to the second floor, ignore the mistletoe hanging above the landing, round the banister in my candy cane socks, sneak quietly down the hallway, and open the door to the narrower set of stairs leading to the attic. At the top, I nudge open Benny's door.

"Benny," I whisper into the chilly blackness. "Benny, wake up. It's an emergency."

A gravelly groan comes from across the room, and I warn him, "I'm turning on the light."

"No—"

"*Yes.*" I reach over, flicking the switch and illuminating the room. While we offspring have long been relegated to bunk beds in the basement, this attic is Benny's bedroom every December, and I think it's the best one in the house. It has pitched ceilings and a long stained-glass window at the far end that projects sunlight across the walls in brilliant stripes of blue, red, green, and orange. The narrow twin bed up here shares the space with the organized clutter of family heirlooms, boxes of decorations for various holidays, and a wardrobe full of Grandma and Grandpa Hollis's old winter clothes, from back when buying a cabin in Park City wasn't a laughable financial prospect for a high school principal from Salt Lake. Since none of the other families had girls when I was a kid, I would play dress-up all alone up here, or sometimes with Benny as my audience.

But now I don't need an audience, I need a kind ear and a cold, hard shot of advice because I am on the verge of hysteria.

"Benny. *Wake up.*"

He pushes up onto an elbow and, with his other hand, wipes the sleep from his eyes. His Aussie accent comes out hoarse: "What time is it?"

I look at the phone I have gripped in my clammy palm. "Five thirty."

He stares at me with squinty, incredulous eyes. "Is somebody dead?"

"No."

"Missing?"

"No."

"Bleeding profusely?"

"Mentally bleeding, yes." I step deeper into the room, wrap myself up in an old afghan, and sit in a wicker chair that faces the bed. "Help."

At fifty-five years old, Benny still has the same fluffy sandy-brown hair he's sported my entire life. It reaches just past his chin, wavy like it was permed for years and at some point decided to stay that way. I used to imagine he was a roadie for some aging eighties rock band, or an adventurer who led rich tourists to their doom out in the bush. The reality—he's a Portland locksmith—is less exciting, but his jangle of turquoise bracelets and beaded necklaces at least lets me pretend.

Right now that hair is mostly a tangled halo of chaos around his head.

With each of the twelve other bodies in this house, I've got deep history, but Benny is special. He's a college friend of my parents—all of the grown-ups in this house attended the University of Utah together, except Kyle, who married into the group—but Benny has always been more friend than parent figure. He's from Melbourne, even-tempered and open-minded. Benny is the eternal bachelor, the wise adviser, and the one person in my life I know I can count on to give me perspective when my own thoughts are swerving out of control.

When I was a kid, I would save up my gossip until I saw him over the Fourth of July weekend or Christmas break, and then unload everything the moment I had him to my-self. Benny has a way of listening and giving the simplest, most judgment-free advice without lecturing. I'm just hop-ing his level head can save me now.

"Okay." He clears some of the gravel out of his throat with a cough and brushes a few wayward strands of hair out of his face. "Let's have it."

"Right. So." Despite my panic and the ticking clock, I decide it's best to ease him in gently to this conversation. "Theo, Miles, Andrew, and I were playing board games last night in the basement," I start.

A low "Mm-hm" rumbles out of him. "A standard night."

"Clue," I stall, tugging my dark hair over my shoulder.

"Okay." Benny, as ever, is blissfully patient.

"Miles fell asleep on the floor," I say. My younger brother is seventeen and, like most teenagers, can sleep on a pointy rock. "Andrew went out to the Boathouse."

This "Mm-hm" is a chuckle because Benny still finds it hilarious that Andrew Hollis—Theo's older brother—finally put his foot down with his father and found a way out of the infantilizing bunk bed situation: he moved into the Boathouse for the duration of the Christmas holiday. The Boathouse is a small, drafty old building about twenty yards from the main cabin. What cracks me up is that the Boathouse isn't anywhere near a body of water. It's most frequently used as an extension of the backyard in the summer and most assuredly not set up for overnight guests to the Rocky Mountains in December.

And as much as I hated not seeing Andrew Hollis in the top bunk across the room, I honestly can't blame him.

No one sleeping in the basement is actually a kid anymore. It's been well established that Theo can (*ahem*) sleep anywhere, my brother, Miles, idolizes Theo and will go wherever Theo is, and I put up with it because my mother would murder me barehanded if I ever complained about the Hollis family's abundant hospitality. But Andrew, nearly thirty years old, was apparently done placating the parents, and took a camping cot and sleeping bag and strolled his way out of the cabin our first night here.

"We'd all had a couple drinks by then," I say, then amend, "Well, not Miles, obviously, but the rest of us."

Benny's brows lift.

"Two." I grimace. "Eggnog."

I wonder if Benny knows where this is going. I am a

notoriously wussy drinker and Theo is a notoriously horny one. Though, to be fair, Theo is just notoriously horny.

"Theo and I went upstairs to grab some water." I lick my lips and swallow, suddenly parched. "Um, and then we were like, 'Let's drunkenly go for a walk in the snow!' but instead . . ." I hold my breath, strangling my words. "We made out in the mudroom."

Benny goes still, and then turns his suddenly-wide-awake hazel eyes on me. "You're talking about Andrew, right? You and Andrew?"

And there it is. With that gentle question, Benny has hit the nail on the head. "No," I say finally. "Not Andrew. Theo." That's me: harlot.

With the benefit of sobriety and the jarring clarity of the morning after, last night's brief, frantic scramble feels like a blur. Did I initiate things, or did Theo? All I know is that it was surprisingly clumsy. Not at all seductive: teeth clashing, some feverish moans and kisses. His hand basically latched onto my chest in a move that felt more breast-exam than passionate-embrace. That's when I pushed him away, and, with a flailing apology, ducked under his arm and ran down to the basement.

I want to smother myself with Benny's pillow. This is what I get for finally saying yes to Ricky Hollis's boozy eggnog.

"Hold on." Bending, Benny pulls a backpack up from the floor near the side of the bed and retrieves a long, thin one-hitter.

"Seriously, Benedict? It's not even light out."

"Listen, *Mayhem*, you're telling me you made out with

Theo Hollis last night. You don't get to give me shit for taking a hit before I hear the rest of this."

Fair enough. I sigh, closing my eyes and tilting my face to the ceiling, sending a silent wish to the universe to obliterate last night from existence. Unfortunately, when I open them again, I'm still here in the attic with Benny—who's taking a deep inhale of weed before sunrise—and a bucketful of regret settling in my gut.

Benny exhales a skunky plume and sets the pipe back in the bag. "Okay," he says, squinting over at me. "You and Theo."

I blow my bangs out of my face. "Please don't say it like that."

He raises his eyebrows like, *Well?* "You know your mom and Lisa have been joking all these years . . . right?"

"Yeah. I know."

"I mean, you're a people-pleaser," he says, studying me, "but this goes above and beyond."

"I didn't do it to make anyone happy!" I pause, considering. "I don't think."

It's a long-standing joke that, since we were kids, our parents hoped Theo and I would someday end up together. Then we'd officially be family. And I suppose, on paper, we make sense. We were born exactly two weeks apart. We were baptized on the same day. We slept together in the bottom bunk until Theo was big enough to be trusted not to jump off the top. He cut my hair with kitchen scissors when we were four. I covered his face and arms with Band-Aids each time we were left alone together until our parents got smart and started hiding the Band-Aids. So that we could be excused from the table, I used to eat his green beans and he'd eat my cooked carrots.

But all of that is kid stuff, and we aren't kids anymore. Theo is a nice guy, and I love him because we're practically family and I sort of have to, but we've grown into such different people that sometimes it seems like the only things we have in common happened more than a decade ago.

More importantly (read: pathetically), I've never been into Theo, primarily because I've had a crazy, silent, soul-crushing crush on his older brother for what feels like my whole life. Andrew is kind, warm, gorgeous, and hilarious. He is playful, flirty, creative, and affectionate. He is also deeply principled and private, and I'm pretty sure there's nothing that would turn him off a woman faster than knowing she made out with his younger, womanizing brother while under the influence of eggnog.

Benny, the only other person in this house who knows about my feelings for Andrew, watches me expectantly. "So, what happened?"

"We were tipsy. We ended up in the mudroom, the three of us: me and Theo and his tongue." I shove the tip of my thumb into my mouth, biting it. "Tell me what you're thinking."

"I'm trying to understand how this happened—this isn't like you at all, Noodle."

Defensiveness flares briefly but is almost immediately extinguished by self-loathing. Benny's my Jiminy Cricket, and he's right: that isn't like me. "Maybe it was a subconscious shove: I need to get over this stupid Andrew thing."

"You sure about that?" Benny asks gently.

Nope. ". . . Yes?" I'm twenty-six. Andrew is twenty-nine. Even I have to admit that if anything was ever going to happen between us, it would have happened by now.

"So you figured, why not Theo?" Benny asks, reading my thoughts.

"It wasn't that calculated, okay? I mean, he's not exactly hard to look at."

"Are you attracted to him, though?" Benny scratches his stubbly chin. "That feels like an important question."

"I mean, lots of women seem to be?"

He laughs. "That isn't what I asked."

"I guess I must have been last night, right?"

"And?" he asks, grimacing like he isn't sure he wants to know.

"And . . ." I wrinkle my nose.

"Your expression is telling me it was terrible."

I exhale, deflating. "So bad." I pause. "He licked my face. Like, my entire face." Benny's wince deepens, and I point a finger at him. "You are sworn to secrecy."

He holds up a hand. "Who would I tell? His parents? *Yours*?"

"Have I ruined everything?"

Benny gives me an amused smile. "You are not the first two people in history to have drunkenly made out. But maybe this was a catalyst in a way. The universe is telling you to move on, one way or another, where Andrew is concerned."

I laugh because this feels genuinely impossible. How does one move on from a man so kind of heart and fine of ass? It's not like I haven't tried to get over Andrew for, oh, the past thirteen years. "Any idea how?"

"I don't know, Noodle."

"Do I pretend like nothing happened? Do I talk about it with Theo?"

"Definitely don't ignore it," Benny says, and as much as I was hoping to get permission to put my head in the sand, I know he's right. Avoiding confrontation is the Jones family's biggest vice. My parents could probably count on one hand the number of times they've maturely discussed their feelings with each other—which is probably what their divorce lawyer would tell you. "Go wake him up before the day gets rolling. Clear the air."

He glances out the window, at the sky that is reluctantly brightening, and then back to me. Panic must be bleeding into my expression, because he puts a calming hand on mine. "I know it's your nature to smooth out problems by avoiding confrontation, but it's our last day here. You don't want to leave with that lingering between you. Imagine coming back to that next Christmas."

"You're the most emotionally intuitive locksmith alive, you know."

He laughs. "You're deflecting."

I nod, tucking my hands between my knees and staring down at the worn wood floor. "One more question."

"Mm-hm?" His hum tells me he knows exactly what's coming.

"Do I tell Andrew?"

He rebounds a question right back: "Why would Andrew need to know?"

I blink up to his face and catch the gentle sympathy there. *Oof.* He's right. Andrew doesn't need to know, because he wouldn't care one way or another.

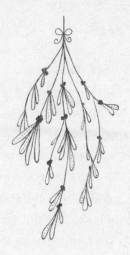

chapter two

I'm praying that everyone is still asleep when I sneak back out of Benny's room, and for the most part, the house is silent and still. My plan: Wake up Theo, ask him to come talk to me in the kitchen—no, not the kitchen, too close to the mudroom—before anyone else is up. Clear the air. Make sure we know it was a fluke, nothing to be weird about. It was the eggnog kissing! Definitely nothing anyone else needs to know about.

Am I being too paranoid about a sloppy kiss and a boob grope? Without a doubt. But Theo is like family, and these things tend to get messy. Let me not be the proverbial stick of dynamite in this comfortable chosen-family dynamic.

Look back on a hundred other mornings here, and I'm usually awake in the kitchen, quietly cheating at solitaire while Ricky, Andrew and Theo's dad, munches on cookies and zombie-sips his coffee, slowly coming to life. *Maelyn*

Jones, you and me are two peas in a pod, he'll say once he's verbal. *We both wake up with the sun*. But this particular morning, Ricky isn't up yet. In his place is Theo, bent over a giant bowl of Lucky Charms.

It's still disorienting to see him with short hair. For as long as I can remember Theo had dark, wavy surfer hair he'd sometimes pull into a short ponytail, but it's gone, cut off only days before we all arrived at the cabin. Now I stand in the doorway, surrounded by strands of metallic garland and tissue paper holly the twins and Andrew hung up yesterday morning, staring at the top of Theo's short-haired head and thinking he looks like a stranger.

I know he knows I'm here, but he doesn't acknowledge me; he's feigning a deep fascination with the nutritional information on the cereal box in front of him. Milk drips from his chin, and he swipes it away with the back of his hand.

My stomach turns to stone. "Hey," I say, folding a stray dish towel.

He still doesn't look up. "Hey."

"You sleep okay?"

"Sure."

I cross my arms in front of me and am reminded that I'm braless, in pajamas. The linoleum floor is freezing beneath my bare feet. "You're up early."

One bulky shoulder lifts and drops. "Yeah."

When I blink, I suddenly see what's happening with clear eyes. I'm not dealing with Lifelong Friend Theo right now. This is Next Morning Theo. This is the Theo most girls see. My mistake was in assuming that I'm not *most girls*.

I move to the coffeepot, stuffing a filter in, filling it with dark roast, setting it to brew. The deep headiness of coffee fills my head, and, for only a breath, it distracts me from my angst.

I glance at the empty Advent calendar on the counter—empty not because yesterday was Christmas but because Andrew loves chocolate and finished it five days ago. His and Theo's mom, Lisa, made some sort of cookie bars on the first day of vacation, but they've barely been touched because nobody is willing to risk a tooth after watching Dad crack one of his.

I know every dish in this kitchen, know each potholder, towel, and place mat. This place is more precious to me than even my own childhood home, and I don't want to tarnish it with stupid, eggnog-soaked decisions.

I take a deep breath and think of why we come here: To spend quality time with our chosen family. To celebrate togetherness. We drive each other crazy sometimes, but I love this place; I look forward to coming here all year.

Theo drops his spoon onto the table, clattering me back into this tense, loaded room. He shakes the cereal box over his bowl, refilling it.

I try to engage again: "Hungry?"

He grunts. "Yeah."

I give him the benefit of the doubt. Maybe he's embarrassed. Lord knows I am. Maybe I should apologize, make sure we're on the same page. "Listen, Theo. About last night . . ."

He laughs into a bite of cereal. "Last night was nothing, Mae. I should have known you'd make a huge deal out of it."

I blink. A huge deal?

Briefly, I imagine hurling the closest object within reach

at his head. "What the hell is that—" I begin, but footsteps stop my tirade and save Theo from getting brained by a cast-iron trivet.

Ricky comes into the room, letting out a gravelly "Mornin'."

He grabs a mug, and I grab the pot, filling his cup when he reaches out expectantly, and we shuffle toward the table: our familiar little dance. But then Ricky falters, unsure where to sit with an unexpected Theo in his chair, and he pulls out another one, sitting with a relieved groan, inhaling his coffee.

I wait for Ricky to say it. Wait for it. *Maelyn Jones, you and me are two peas in a pod.* But the words don't come. Theo's created a pocket of cold silence in the ordinarily warm space, and a tiny flicker of panic sparks beneath my ribs. Ricky is the King of Tradition, and I am the obvious heir to his throne. This is the one place in the world where I've never questioned what I'm doing or who I am, but last night Theo and I went off-script, and now everything is weird.

I glare across the table at him, but he doesn't look up. He tucks into his Lucky Charms like a hungover frat boy.

Theo is a dick.

I am suddenly blindingly furious. How can he not even have the balls to look at me this morning? A few drunken kisses should be nothing to Theo Hollis, a scratch that's easily polished. Instead, it feels like he's deliberately gouging deeper.

Ricky slowly turns to look at me, and his questioning expression penetrates my peripheral vision. Maybe Theo is right. Maybe I am making too big a deal out of this. With effort, I blink and push back from the table to stand.

"Think I'll take my coffee outside and enjoy the last morning here."

There. If Theo has half a brain—which is presently up for debate—he'll take the hint and follow me outside to talk.

But once I'm sitting on the porch swing, bundled up in a down coat, thick socks, boots, and a blanket, I'm cold from the inside out. I don't want to shake the foundation of this special place, which is why I've never been tempted by Theo's flirtation, or admitted to anyone but Benny that I have real and tender feelings for Andrew. Our parents' bedrock friendship is far older than any of us kids.

Lisa and Mom were roommates in college. Dad, Aaron, Ricky, and Benny all lived together in a ramshackle rental off campus; they gave the old Victorian the incredibly creative name of International House of Beer, and from photos it looked like something out of *Animal House*. After graduation, Aaron moved to Manhattan, where he met and married Kyle Liang and they eventually adopted twins. Ricky and Lisa stayed in Utah, Benny roamed the West Coast before settling in Portland. My parents put down roots in California, where I was born and, eventually, Miles—the Surprise Baby—when I was nine. They divorced three years ago, and Mom is happily remarried. Dad . . . not so much.

Aaron has often said that these friendships saved his life when his mom and brother died unexpectedly in a car accident during junior year, and the group rallied around him to celebrate the holidays together. Even with all these ups and downs in life, the tradition stuck: every December twentieth we give ourselves over to Ricky's highly specific and detailed Christmas itinerary. We haven't missed a single year as long as I've been alive, even the year my parents divorced. That year wasn't comfortable—*strained* is an understatement—but somehow spending time with our non-blood family helped soften the dislocation within our blood family.

The vacation has always been the celebratory red circle on my calendar countdown. The cabin is my oasis not only because Andrew Hollis is here, but also because it's the perfect winter cabin, the perfect amount of snow, the perfect people, and the perfect level of comfort. The perfect Christmas, and I don't want to change a thing.

So did I just completely ruin everything?

I lean forward and hug my knees. *I am a mess.*

"You're not a mess."

I startle, looking up to find Andrew standing over me, grinning and holding a steaming mug of coffee. With a view of his face in the bright morning light—mischievous green eyes, the shadowy hint of stubble, and pillow creases on his left cheek—my body reacts predictably: heart takes a flying leap off a cliff and stomach sinks warm and low in my belly. He is both exactly who I wanted to see right now and the last person I want to know what's bothering me.

Trying to remember what my hair looks like, I pull the blanket up to my chin, wishing I'd taken the time to put on a bra. "Was I talking to myself?"

"You sure were." He smiles, and Lord, if the sun doesn't come out from behind the clouds. Dimples so deep I could lose all my hopes and dreams inside them. I swear his teeth sparkle. As if on cue, a perfect brown curl falls over his forehead. You have got to be kidding me.

And oh my God, I made out with his brother. Guilt and regret mix sourly in the back of my throat.

"Did I reveal my plans to overthrow the government and install Beyoncé in her rightful place as our fearless leader?" I ask, deflecting.

"I must have come in after that part." Andrew gazes at me with amusement. "I just heard you say that you're a mess." Something's in his expression, some playful twinkle I can't quite translate. Dread gives me a swift kick to the solar plexus.

I point to his face. "What's happening here?"

"Oh, nothing." He sits down beside me, puts his arm around my shoulders, and plants a kiss on the top of my head. The kiss is distracting enough for the dread to dissolve, and I work to not grab for him as he pulls away. If I could ever be on the receiving end of a long, tight Andrew Hollis hug, it would be the affection equivalent of chugging down a tall glass of water on a scorching day. I know I've never deserved him—he's too good for any mortal—but it never stopped me from wanting him anyway.

A film of unease settles back over me when he laughs out my name against my hair.

"You're awfully chipper this morning," I say.

"And you are *not*," he remarks, leaning forward to playfully study my face. The headphones around his neck fall forward slightly, and I can tell he never bothered to turn off the music; "She Sells Sanctuary" by the Cult filters tinnily through them. "What's going on, Maisie?"

This is what we do together; we become our old-person characters Mandrew and Maisie. We make our voices shaky and high-pitched—to play, to confide, to tease—but I'm too freaked out to play along. "Nothing." I shrug. "Didn't sleep well." The lie feels oily on my tongue.

"Rough night?"

"Um . . ." My internal organs disintegrate "Sort of?"

"So you and my brother, huh?"

Everything in my head is incinerated. Brain ash blows out onto the snow. "Oh my God."

Andrew's shoulders lift when he laughs. "You two kids! Sneaking around!"

"Andrew—it's not a thing—I don't—"

"No, no. It's okay. I mean, no one is surprised, right?" He pulls back to get a look at my expression. "Hey, relax, you're both adults."

I groan, burying my face in my arms. He doesn't get it, and worse—he really *doesn't* care.

His tone softens, instantly apologetic. "I didn't realize you'd be so freaked out. I was just messing with you. I mean, to be honest I figured it was just a matter of time before you and Theo—"

"Andrew, no." I look around, desperate now. A surprise escape hatch would be a great discovery. Instead, a glint of silver catches my eye—the sleeve of Andrew's hilariously awful holiday sweater hanging over the edge of the trash can. Miso, the Hollises' corgi, got ahold of it on Christmas Eve and Lisa must've decided it was beyond saving. I wouldn't mind joining it in the trash right now. "It's not like that between us."

"Hey. It's fine, Maisie." I can tell he's surprised at the degree of my alarm, and he puts a reassuring hand on my arm, misinterpreting my meltdown: "I won't tell anyone else."

Mortification and guilt surge in my throat. "I—I can't believe he told you."

"He didn't," Andrew says. "I came back to the house last night because I left my phone in the kitchen, and saw you two."

Andrew *saw* us? Please, let me die here.

"Come on, don't make such a big deal about a little kissing. You're talking to the guy whose mom moves the mistletoe around the house every day. Half this group has kissed each other at some point." He gives me a noogie and, if possible, my mortification deepens. "Dad sent me out here to call you in for breakfast." He playfully jabs my shoulder, like a pal. "I just wanted to give you some shit."

With a little wink, Andrew turns and heads back into the house, and I am left trying to find my sanity.

• • •

Inside, holiday music still tinkles silvery through the air. The living room is now home to the remnants of Christmas: a stack of broken-down boxes, trash bags stuffed with wrapping paper, and storage bins full of folded ribbons to reuse next year. Suitcases have been lined up near the front door. While I was freaking out on the porch, the kitchen filled, and I've apparently just missed the hilarity of Dad and Aaron getting caught on the landing together under Lisa's location-hopping mistletoe.

Breakfast is already in full swing: Mom has added the last bit of ham to eggs and potatoes and whatever else was still in the fridge for a casserole. Lisa pulls some Danish *sigtebrød* out of the pantry, and Ricky piles plates with pancakes and bacon. We're a sluggish bunch, full of the months' worth of calories we each ingested in the past two days, but I know, too, that we're shuffling around morosely because it's our last morning together. I'm not the only person in this room dreading returning to the humdrum of a nine-to-five life.

In a few hours Mom, Dad, Miles, and I will load up and drive to the airport. We'll fly back to Oakland together, and then separate at arrivals. Mom's new husband, Victor, will be back from his annual trip with his two grown daughters and will have flowers and kisses for Mom. Dad will drive alone back to his condo near UCSF. We probably won't see him for weeks.

And on Monday, I'll return to a job I don't have the guts to quit. The life I *want* to enjoy. I just don't. In a twist of stellar timing, my phone chimes brightly with a reminder to email a profit-and-loss spreadsheet to my boss by tomorrow morning. I haven't even opened my laptop since we arrived. Guess I know what I'll be doing on the drive to the airport. Every cell in my body feels droopy when I think about it.

We all find our seats around steaming platters of food.

Phones are supposed to be off-limits during meals, but Miles and his enormous brown eyes always manage to get away with murder, and nobody wants the hassle of arguing with Theo, who is now nose-deep in Instagram, liking photo after photo of models, muscle cars, and golden retrievers. He still won't look at me. Won't talk to me. As far as he's concerned, I'm not even here.

I can feel Benny watching me with that gentle, perceptive way of his, and I meet his eyes briefly. I hope he reads the skywriting there: ANDREW SAW ME AND THEO MAKING OUT AND I WOULD VERY MUCH LIKE TO DISSOLVE THROUGH THE FLOORBOARDS NOW.

Kyle hums while he pours a mug of coffee. He must have a Hangover Jesus somewhere, suffering for his sins, because even after the cocktailpalooza last night, Kyle still looks like he could glide onto any Broadway stage and dance his way into next week. By contrast, his husband, Aaron, didn't drink a drop but looks haggard anyway: He's been going through a bit of a midlife crisis.

Apparently it started when one of their friends commented that Aaron's hair was mostly gray but *looks good for a guy his age.* Kyle swears it was said with the best of intentions, but Aaron didn't care; his hair is now dyed so black it looks like a hole in whatever room he's in. He's spent most of this trip working out like a madman and frowning into mirrors. Aaron's not suffering from a hangover; he can barely lift a cup to his mouth because he did so many push-ups yesterday.

Now Kyle turns and surveys the room. "What's with the weird vibe?" he asks, taking his usual seat.

"Well, I've got an idea," Andrew says with a wide grin at his brother, and I almost choke on my coffee. Benny flicks his ear.

Finally, Theo's eyes swing to mine and then guiltily away. *That's right, jackass, I'm right here.*

Ricky clears his throat before taking Lisa's hand. Oh my God. Do they know, too? If Lisa tells my parents, my mom will be naming her grandchildren before we're even out of the driveway.

"Maybe it's us," Ricky says slowly. "Lisa and I have some news."

It's the small, nervous quiver in his voice that catches my frayed pulse and sends it hammering in a different direction. Is Lisa's melanoma back?

Suddenly, a bad mudroom hookup feels like very small potatoes.

Ricky picks up the platter of bacon and gets it moving around the table. Lisa does the same with the casserole. But no one takes anything. Instead, we all vacantly pass the dishes around, unwilling to commit to eating until we know what level of devastation we're facing.

"Business is fine," Ricky reassures us, looking at each of our faces. "And no one is sick. So it isn't that, don't worry."

We exhale collectively, but then I see Dad instinctively place his hand over Mom's, and that's when I know. There's only one thing we value as much as we value each other's health.

"But this cabin, see, it's old," Ricky says. "It's old and seems to need something new each month."

A hot tangle forms in my chest.

"We wanted to let you know that we sure do hope we can continue spending the holidays together, just like we have for the last thirty years or so." He takes the full bacon platter as it comes back to him and gently sets it down, untouched. We all remain still, even Aaron and Kyle's five-year-old twins—Kennedy with her legs tucked to her chest, a dirty *Care Bears* Band-Aid still clinging valiantly to her scabbed knee, and Zachary clutching his sister's arm— dreading what we all know is coming next: "But we'll have to figure out a new plan. Lisa and I have decided that we're selling the cabin."

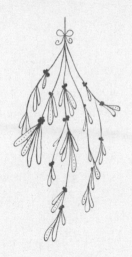

chapter three

Cue the most depressing music ever. I'd prefer that, actually, to the morbid silence in the rental car as Mom, Dad, Miles, and I make our way down the snow-dusted gravel driveway to the main road.

Mom cries quietly in the passenger seat. Dad's hands fidget on the steering wheel like he's not sure where to put them. I think he wants to comfort her, but he looks like he could use some comfort of his own. If it feels like the cabin means everything to me, it's nothing compared to the memories they must have. They came here as newly-weds, brought me and Miles as babies.

"Mom." I lean forward, putting my hand on her shoulder. "It's going to be okay. We'll still see everyone next year."

Her quiet sobs turn into a wail, and Dad grinds the steering wheel in his grip. They divorced after nearly a quarter century of marriage; the cabin is the only place they get along anymore. It's the only place they've ever gotten along, really. Lisa is Mom's closest friend; Ricky, Aaron, and Benny are Dad's only friends outside of the hospital. Dad was willing to forfeit the house, primary custody of Miles, and a chunk of his income every month, but he was unwilling to give up Christmas at the cabin. Mom held her ground, too. Victor's daughters were thrilled to be able to keep their time with their dad, and we've somehow managed to maintain a fragile peace. Is that going to last if we have to go somewhere new, without any happy memories or nostalgic anchors?

I glance at my brother and wonder what it must be like to float through life so happily oblivious. He's got his headphones on and is mildly bopping along to something perky and optimistic.

"I didn't want to fall apart in front of Lisa," Mom hiccups, digging in her purse for a Kleenex. "She was so devastated, couldn't you see it, Dan?"

"I—well, yes," he hedges, "but she was probably also relieved to have made the hard decision."

"No, no. This is awful." Mom blows her nose. "Oh, my poor friend."

I reach over and flick Miles's ear.

He flinches away from me. "What the hell?"

I tilt my head toward our mother, as in, *Give her some support, you idiot.*

"Hey, Mom. It's okay." He blandly pats her shoulder once but doesn't even turn down his music. He barely looks up from his phone screen to give me a look in return that says, *Happy now?*

I turn back to the window and let out a controlled breath, working to keep it from being audible.

Before we left, Lisa took what will probably be our last group photo on the porch—somehow managing to cut the tops off the back row of heads—and then there were tears and hugs, promises that nothing would change. But we all know that's a lie. Even though we've pledged to still spend the holiday together, where will we go? To Aaron and Kyle's two-bedroom Manhattan apartment? To Andrew's Denver condo? To Mom and Victor's house, which used to be Mom and Dad's house? Awkward! Or maybe we'll all squeeze into Benny's camper in Portland?

My brain takes off on a hysterical tear.

So we'll rent a house somewhere, and we'll all arrive with suitcases and smiles but everything will feel different. There won't be enough snow, or the yard won't be big enough, or there won't even be a yard. Will we decorate a tree? Will we go sledding? Will we even all sleep in the same house? I imagined my childhood would end gradually, not with this full sprint into a brick wall starkly labeled *End of an Era*.

Mom sucks in a breath and quickly swivels to face us, interrupting my mental spiral. She places a hand on Miles's leg, gives him an affectionate pat. "Thank you, baby." And then mine. Her nails are painted fuchsia; her wedding ring glints in the midmorning light. "Mae, I'm sorry. I'm fine. You don't have to take care of me."

I know she's trying to be more conscious of how much of her emotional burden I tend to take on, but her vulnerability lances my chest. "I know, Mom, but it's okay to be sad."

"I know you're sad, too."

"I'm sad as well," Dad mumbles, "in case anyone was wondering."

The silence that follows this statement is the size of a crater on the moon.

Mom's eyes spring fresh tears. "So many years we spent there."

Dad echoes hollowly, "So many years."

"To think we'll never be back." Mom presses a hand to her heart and looks over her shoulder at me. "Whatever happens, happens." She reaches for my hand, and I feel like a traitor to Dad if I take it, and a traitor to Mom if I don't. So I take it, but briefly meet his eyes in the rearview mirror. "Mae, I see the wheels turning up there, and I want you to know it's not your job to make sure that we are all happy next year and the transition is smooth."

I know she believes that, but it's easier said than done. I've lived my entire life trying to keep every tenuous peace we can find.

I squeeze her hand and release it so she can turn back around.

"Life is good," Mom reassures herself aloud. "Victor is well, his girls are grown, with kids of their own. Look at our friends." She spreads her hands. "Thriving. My two children—thriving." Is that what I'm doing? *Thriving?* Wow, a mother's love really is blind. "And you're doing fine, right, Dan?"

Dad shrugs, but she isn't looking at him.

Beside me, Miles nods in time to the music.

"Maybe it's time to try something new," Dad says carefully. I meet his eyes in the rearview mirror again. "Change can be good."

What? Change is never good. Change is Dad switching medical practices when I was five and never being home again during daylight. Change is my best friend moving away in eighth grade. Change is a terribly advised pixie cut sophomore year. Change is relocating to LA, realizing I couldn't afford it, and having to move back home. Change is kissing one of my oldest friends when I was drunk.

"It's all about perspective, right?" he says. "Yes, the holidays may look different, but the important parts will stay the same."

The cabin is the important part, I think, and then take a deep breath.

Perspective. Right. We have our health. We have each other. We are comfortable financially. Perspective is a good thing.

But perspective is slippery and wiggles out of my grip. The cabin! It's being sold! I made out with Theo but I want Andrew! I hate my job! I'm twenty-six and had to move home! Miles applied to schools all over the country, and will probably be a homeowner before I've moved out of my childhood bedroom!

If I died today, what would be written about me? That I'm an obsessive peacekeeper? That I put together a serviceable spreadsheet? That I also loved art? That I couldn't ever figure out what it was that I truly wanted?

Tuning out the sounds of Judy Garland on the radio, I close my eyes and make a silent plea: Universe. *What am I doing with my life? Please. I want . . .*

I'm not even sure how to finish the sentence. I want to be happy, and I'm petrified that the path I'm on now is going to leave me bored and alone.

So I ask the universe, simply: *Can you show me what will make me happy?*

I lean my head against the window, my breath fogging up the glass. When I reach up to clear it away with my sleeve, I'm startled to see a grimy Christmas wreath decorated with an equally grimy bow. A blaring horn, a blur of shaggy green hurtling toward our car.

"Dad!" I shriek.

It's too late. My seat belt locks, and we're hit from the side. Metal screams and glass shatters in a sickening crunch. Whatever was loose in the car is airborne, and I somehow watch the contents of my purse escape and float with surreal slowness as we roll. The radio is still playing: *Through the years, we all will be together, if the fates allow . . .*

Everything goes black.

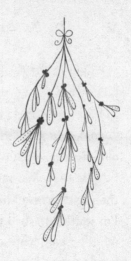

chapter four

Shooting an arm out to the side to brace against the impact of the collision, I come to with a gasp. But there's no car door there, no window; I smack my brother directly in the face.

He lets out a rough *oof* and catches my arm. "Dude. What the hell, Mae?"

I bolt upright against a lap belt, clutching my head and expecting to find blood. It's dry. I suck in another deep, jagged breath. My heart feels like it's going to jackhammer its way up my throat and out of my body.

Wait. Miles is on my right. He was on my left in the car. I reach for him, holding his face in my hands, and jerk him closer.

"What are you doing?" he mumbles into my shoulder.

I don't even mind his heavy-handed Axe body spray right now, I am so intensely relieved that he's not dead. That I'm not dead. That we're all . . .

"Not in the car," I say, releasing him abruptly.

I whip my head left to right, wildly searching. Confusion is a startling, bright light. It's the white noise of an engine, of a vent overhead. It's the dry, overheated recycled air. It's rows and rows of heads in front of me, some of them turning to look at the commotion behind them.

I'm the commotion behind them.

We aren't in the car, we're on an airplane. I'm in the middle seat, Miles in the aisle, and the stranger in the window seat is trying to pretend like I didn't just wake up and flip out.

Disorientation makes my temples throb.

"Where *are* we?" I turn to Miles. I have never in my life been so off-kilter. "We were just in the car. There was a wreck. Have I been unconscious? Was I in a coma?"

And if I was, who put me here? I'm trying to picture my parents carting me, unconscious, through the airport and loading me into this seat. I just cannot imagine it. My dad, the meticulous physician; my mom, the overprotective worrier.

Miles looks at me and slowly pulls his headphones off one ear. "What?"

With a growl, I give up on him and lean toward where Dad is unfastening his seat belt across the aisle. "Dad, what happened?"

He stands and crouches next to Miles's seat. "What happened when?"

"The car accident?"

He glances at my brother, and then back at me. His hair and beard are white, but his brows are still dark, and they slowly rise on his forehead. He looks fine, not a scratch anywhere. "What car accident, Noodle?"

What car accident?

I lean back and close my eyes, taking a deep breath. *What is going on?*

Trying again, I pull Miles's headphones all the way off. "Miles. Don't you remember the car accident? When we left the cabin?"

He rears back, giving my barely restrained hysteria a semidisgusted look. "We're on a plane, on our way to Salt Lake. What do you mean 'when we left the cabin'? We haven't gone yet." He turns to Dad, hands up. "I swear she's only had ginger ale."

We're on our way to Salt Lake?

"There was a truck," I say, straining to remember. "I think the back was filled with . . . Christmas trees."

"Probably just a weird dream," Dad says to Miles, like I'm not sitting right here, and returns to his seat.

• • •

A dream. I nod, like that makes sense, even though it doesn't. It does not. I did not dream an entire vacation. But Miles isn't going to be a font of information even under normal circumstances, and Dad has gone back to his crossword puzzle. Mom is asleep in the aisle seat in front of Dad, and from where I'm sitting I can see that her mouth is softly open, her neck at an odd angle.

What had I been thinking about just before the crash? It was about Christmas, I think. Or my job? I was looking out the car window.

The car.

Which we apparently aren't in anymore.

Or weren't in ever, maybe?

I dig in my bag under the seat in front of me, pulling out my phone and waking up the screen.

The display says that today is December 20. But this morning was December 26.

"Wow." I lean back, looking around. Panic presses in at the edges of my vision, turning the world black and fuzzy.

Breathe, Mae.

You have a level head. You've dealt with crises before. You manage the finances for a struggling nonprofit, for crying out loud. Crisis IS your job. THINK. What are some possible explanations for this?

One: I died, and this is purgatory. A possibility lights up in my mind: Maybe we're all like the characters on *Lost*, a show Dad and Benny drunkenly complained about for at least two hours a few years ago. If this plane never lands, then I guess I'll know why. Or if it lands on an island, I guess that's also an answer. Or if it explodes midair . . .

Not helping calm me down. Next theory.

Two, Dad is right, and I've had some monster nap and somehow dreamed up everything that happened last week at the cabin. Upside: I never kissed Theo. Downside: . . . Is there a downside? Not having to return to work on Monday, getting to repeat my favorite week of vacation, minus the mistakes? And maybe the Hollises aren't selling the cabin! But the thing is, it doesn't feel like a dream. Dreams are fuzzy and oblong, and the faces aren't quite right, or the details don't track in any linear way. This feels like six days of actual memories, crammed with complete clarity into my head. And besides, if I were going to dream-make-out with anyone, wouldn't it be Andrew? I guess not even Dream Mae is that lucky.

Miles looks over when I snort out a laugh, and his frown deepens. "What's with you?"

"I have no idea how to answer that."

He looks back at his phone, already over it.

"Just to confirm," I say, "we're headed to Salt Lake, right?"

My brother offers up a skeptical smile. "You are so weird."

"I'm serious. We're headed to Salt Lake City?"

He frowns. "Yeah."

"And then to Park City?"

"Yes."

"For Christmas?"

He nods slowly, as if interacting with a very impaired creature. "Yes. For Christmas. *Was* there something in that cup besides ginger ale?"

"Wow," I say again, and laugh. "Maybe?"

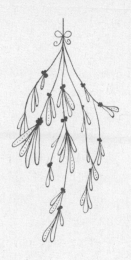

chapter five

I lag behind my family from the Jetway to baggage claim. It earns me more than one impatient look, but everything seems to grab my attention. A crying baby at the adjacent gate. A middle-aged businessman speaking too loudly on his phone. A couple bickering in line for coffee. A young boy wrestling to get out of his heavy blue coat.

I can't shake the feeling of déjà vu, like I've been here before. Not just here in the airport, but *here*—in this exact same moment. At the base of the escalator to baggage claim, a man drops his soda in front of me, and I stop just in time, almost like I knew it was going to happen. A family with a WELCOME HOME banner passes by, and I turn to watch them for several paces.

"I swear I've seen that before," I say to Miles. "The family back there with the sign?"

His attention moves past me briefly and disinterestedly

back ahead. "This is Utah. Every family down here has a 'Welcome Home' sign. Missionaries, remember?"

"Right," I say to his retreating form. Right.

Because I've been so slow on our trek from the arrival gate to baggage claim, our suitcases are the only ones left, patiently circling around and around the carousel. Dad collects them, stacking them onto a cart while Mom cups my face.

Her dark hair is curled into waves and pulled back on one side. Her eyes are tight with worry. "What's with you, honey?"

"I don't know."

"You hungry?" She searches my eyes. "Need an Advil?"

I don't know what to tell her. I'm not hungry. I'm not anything. I half feel like I'm floating through the terminal, staring at things I swear are already memories inside my head.

● ● ●

My stomach drops when I see everyone already on the porch at the cabin, waving us down the driveway. I'm sure I saw this same view only six days ago, on December 20. I remember being the last to arrive. Flight schedules had been tricky, so Kyle, Aaron, and their twins came in on Friday night. Theo and Andrew, I remember, drove up earlier than usual, too.

Our tires come to a crunching stop beside Theo's giant orange truck, and we clamber out of the same Toyota RAV4 that was most certainly totaled in the Car Crash That Didn't Happen. We are immediately engulfed by hugs from all sides. Kyle and Aaron make a sandwich out of me. Their twins, Kennedy and Zachary, gently wind themselves around my legs. Lisa finds a window of space and wiggles in close. In the distance, Benny waits patiently for his hug, and I send him a nonverbal cry for help.

My brain can't seem to process what's going on. Have I lost a year somehow? Honestly, what are the odds that I'm actually dead? My version of heaven would be at the cabin, so how would I know? If I was in a coma, would I feel the frigid winter air on my bare face?

I peek past Lisa into the trees, searching for a hidden camera crew. *Surprise!* they'll shout in unison. Everyone will laugh at the elaborate prank. *We totally had you fooled, didn't we, Mae?*

All this mental fracas means that I've barely considered what it will be like to see Theo before I'm lifted off my feet in a bear hug. I experience this like I'm watching from a few paces away.

"Smile!" Bright light momentarily blinds me as Lisa snaps a picture. "Oh shoot," she mutters, frowning down at the image on the tiny screen. I'm sure only half of my face ended up in the photo, but she seems to think it's good enough because she tucks her phone back in her pocket.

When Theo puts me down, his grin slowly straightens. Did the mudroom make-out even happen? And what is my expression doing right now? I want to reach up and feel my face just to know.

"What's up, weirdo?" he says, laughing. "You look like you forgot my name."

Finally, a small smile breaks free. "Ha. Hi, Theo."

"She's probably in shock about your hair." My attention is pulled over Theo's shoulder to where Andrew stands, waiting patiently for his own hug. Oh yes. This is definitely my version of heaven.

But then Andrew's words sink in, and I realize everyone else is seeing Theo's haircut for the first time. I saw it nearly a week ago.

"Yeah, *wow*," I stammer, "look at you. When did you cut it?"

Absently, I pull Andrew into my arms, squeezing. My head is spinning so hard that at first I don't register the bliss of having his body pressed against mine. Andrew is all long limbs and hard, sinewy muscle. His torso is a flat, firm plane, but it molds to me as he squeezes closer, giving me a hit of eucalyptus and laundry soap.

"Hey." He laughs quietly into my hair. "You okay?"

I shake my head, holding on longer than is strictly necessary for a greeting, but he doesn't seem to fight it, and I can't locate the correct brain-to-muscle command to loosen my grip.

I need this warm, physical anchor.

Slowly, my chest relaxes, my pulse steadies, and I release him, narrowing my eyes in surprise when he steps back and I see splotches of pink on his cheeks.

"Last week." Theo runs a palm over the top of his head, grinning his wide, big-toothed smile.

"Last week what?" I drag my gaze away from Andrew's blush.

"My hair," Theo says, laughing at me. "I cut it last week. You like?"

And there's zero trace of weirdness in his voice. Zero awareness in his expression that we, you know, had our tongues down each other's throats. "Yeah, yeah, it's great." I am doing a terrible job being convincing here. "*Totally* great."

Theo frowns. He runs on praise.

I glance up at Benny, who is drawing something with Zachary in the snow with a branch. My voice wobbles: "Hey, Benny Boo."

He grins, jogging over to me and sweeping me up in his arms. "There's my Noodle."

Yes. Benny. This is who I need. I grip him like he's a deeply rooted vine and I am dangling over a cliff, whispering urgently into his ear, "I need to talk to you."

"Now?" His hair brushes my cheek, and it's soft and smells like the herby hippie shampoo he's used my entire life.

"Yeah, *now*."

Benny puts me down and disorientation spins at the edges of my vision, making me dizzy. I don't realize I'm leaning to the side until he catches me. "Hey, hey. You all right?"

Mom rushes over, pressing a palm to my forehead. "You're not hot." She gently touches beneath my jaw, searching for swollen glands. "Have you had any water today?"

Lisa moves closer and they share a look of concern. "She's lost all her color."

My brother glances up from his phone. "She was being weird on the plane, too."

"She had a *nightmare* on the plane," Dad corrects,

admonishing. "Let's get her inside." He comes up behind me and wraps an arm around my waist.

"Can you stop talking about me like I'm not standing right here?"

As we make our way up the broad front steps, I look back over my shoulder at Andrew. Our eyes snag and he gives me a half-playful, half-worried grin. He's wearing that terrible silver sparkly sweater he loves so much, the one he wears on the first day of the holidays every year.

The one Miso ruined only a couple of days ago.

Just as I have the thought, Miso races forward. In a flash of déjà vu, I shout, "Watch out, Kennedy!" But I'm too late: the dog barrels between her feet, knocking her over the threshold and into the entryway. Kennedy bursts into tears.

I stare numbly down, watching Aaron and Kyle check her chin, her elbow. This happened before. My ears ring. Just this morning, I stared at Kennedy at the kitchen table with a well-worn *Care Bears* Band-Aid covering her cut knee.

"Her knee." I am freaking the hell out right now. "She scraped her . . ."

Kyle rolls one pant leg up and then glances over his shoulder at me, impressed. The blood hadn't soaked through the fabric yet, but the cut erupts with bright red drops. "How'd you even know that?"

The laugh that rolls out of me is bordering on hysterical. "I have no idea!"

We walk into the house. Kyle takes Kennedy to the bathroom to clean her up, and I'm led to a seat at the kitchen table.

"Get her some water," Lisa whispers to Andrew, who brings me a glass and sets it down like the table might shatter. Staring down, I notice he put extra ice in it, just like I would've if I'd done it myself.

I lift it, hand shaking, ice tinkling, and take a sip. "Okay, you guys, stop staring at me."

No one moves. Mom comes closer and starts massaging my free hand.

"Seriously, you're freaking me out." When everyone tries to find something else to do in the small kitchen, I catch Benny's eye, and then widen my own: *We need to talk.*

Like a heat-seeking missile, my attention shifts to Andrew when he crosses the room and sneaks chocolate from the Advent calendar. He looks over at me just as he pops a piece into his mouth and offers a faux-guilty shrug. Nearby, Dad leans against the counter, watching me with Worried Parent eyes until his gaze is caught by the plate full of beautiful cookie bars beside him.

My stomach drops. He's going to get one, and he's going to bite it, and—

A sickening crack echoes through the room.

"Oh my God," he says, sticking a finger in his mouth. "I cracked my molar."

OH MY GOD.

Lisa goes ashen. "Dan! No. Oh no. Was it—?"

Everyone rushes to reassure her that *Of course it wasn't the cookie that broke his tooth* and *Oh, they're a little hard, but they're delicious.* Andrew grabs another piece of chocolate. And I use the commotion to sneak out of the kitchen to catch a giant gulp of fresh air outside.

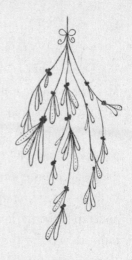

chapter six

O utside, I can breathe.
      Inhale, exhale.

Deep inhale, slow exhale.

It wasn't a dream.

I traveled through time, backward six days.

I've seen things like this in books and movies: Someone has an accident and comes out of it with superpowers. Flight, superstrength, super-vision.

Man, I wish I'd paid attention to lotto numbers last week.

The thought makes me laugh out loud, and my breath puffs in the cold air. *Mae, you are losing it.*

Staring at the tree line and the glittering snow is nature's perfect shock absorber. It really is gorgeous up here, in the outskirts of Park City at Christmastime. I should pull out my notebook and sketch it; maybe that would calm these frazzled nerves of mine.

The neighbors' house is more hidden by foliage than it was when I was younger, and gives the Hollis cabin a lovely feel of wintry isolation. A split rail fence runs down both sides of the property line, and the thicket of pines that were once as tall as Dad now tower over the driveway. Theo dared me to pee in there once, then got so mad when I managed to do it—standing up, I might add—that he stole my pants and ran into the house. That same winter, Andrew and I built an igloo in the side yard and swore we were going to sleep inside, but only made it ten minutes before giving up.

The view helps slow my pulse and clear the fog of my brain until I can take a final deep breath, count to ten, and then exhale in a long, warm puff of fog.

"What the actual *fuck*," I whisper to myself, and then burst out laughing again.

"I was just going to say the same thing."

I startle so violently that when my left arm swings to the side, I manage to launch Andrew's mug of hot toddy out of his hand, over the side of the porch. We both track it as it arcs and lands in a snowbank; the warm liquid melts the fluffy powder in a puff of steam, causing the white unicorn mug I made him when I was fifteen—his go-to mug at the cabin—to sink out of sight. Little does he know I painted the words *Mae + Andrew* on the bottom of the mug in white before coating the entire bottom with a bubblegum pink.

"Wow. Okay." He turns around, leaning back against the porch railing to look at me. "I was coming out here to ask why you were acting so weird, but I see I need to keep things present tense."

I have so many questions about what the hell is going

on that my thought stream has just turned into static white noise.

"You're staring at me like you don't know where you are." Andrew takes a step forward. "I was going to give you some shit, but I'm genuinely worried that you're suffering some sort of head injury and not telling us."

"I'm just a little foggy today."

He grins, and his matching set of dimples make a delightful entrance. Pressing his steepled fingers to his chest, he says, "I'm Andrew Polley Hollis, which was the worst combination of middle and last names for a seventh grader. You call me 'Mandrew.' I fiddle with sound equipment at Red Rocks for a living. My little brother is kind of an asshole. I am the one man alive who likes neither scotch nor beer. You and I used to play vampires when we were kids and didn't realize the marks we were leaving on each other's necks were hickeys." He gestures to his body. "Six two. About one eighty. Aries. This"—he points to his head of curls—"is natural, and a constant mess."

"The hair has a mind of its own?" I grin. *Are we flirting? This feels like flirting.*

Shut up, brain.

"Inside you'll find your father, Daniel Jones, obstetrician, owner of a newly broken tooth. He is notoriously uptight about his hands, and tells a lot of very disturbing stories about childbirth. Your mother, the one who keeps feeling your forehead, is Elise—you look a lot like her, I might add. She is a worrier, but actually pretty funny, and someday her paintings are going to sell for more than this place is worth, mark my words."

I nod, impressed alongside him that Mom's career is flourishing. He waits for me to say something, but I gesture for him to continue because Andrew's voice is hypnotic. It has a honeyed depth with just the barest scratch around the edges. Honestly, I'd gladly listen to him read me the dictionary.

"My parents, Ricky and Lisa, are also inside." He grins wolfishly at me. "Dad is the guy taking your father to the dentist. The most important thing to remember is that none of us should eat anything Mom bakes. My mom, Scandinavian in heritage and temperament, is a brilliant writer. But unlike Elise, who is a cooking goddess, Lisa is not, as we say, skilled in the kitchen."

I grin. "Or with a camera."

Andrew laughs at this. "Kyle and Aaron Amir-Liang are the two perfectly groomed gentlemen with the genius five-year-olds. I'm not exactly sure what's happening with Aaron's hair this year—it seems to have disappeared and been replaced by a permanent black space above his head." He pauses, lowering his voice. "And was he wearing leggings?"

A bursting laugh escapes me. "I think he was. I guess we can be glad he's moved out of the designer sweatpants phase? That was . . . a lot of information about Uncle Aaron that teenage Mae did not need."

Andrew snaps. "It's a good sign you remember that, though. Now, I don't need to tell you that Kyle is an award-winning Broadway performer and used to be a back-up dancer for Janet Jackson, because he'll undoubtedly mention it himself sometime tonight."

I laugh again, biting my lip. I'm sure I'm exhibiting the wild-eyed bliss of a contestant on a game show who's just won a million dollars. My memory never gets Andrew right. My brain doesn't know how to make that green of his eyes, doesn't believe cheekbones can be so sculpted, dimples so deep and playful. Andrew, in the flesh, is always such a shock to the system.

"Last year Zachary learned about death when his gold-fish kicked the bucket. He walked around like a tiny grim reaper telling us we're all going to die someday. Kennedy knows the capital of every state or country in the world," he says confidentially. "She says some of the smartest things to ever come out of this group, and we don't let anyone give that little girl any crap. She's going to be the first president on the spectrum, mark my words. But hopefully not the first woman."

"I think you're right."

"Let's see . . . your brother, Miles, though . . ." He winces playfully. "He's smart, but I'm not sure he's looked up from his phone in the past two years. If you want to have a conversation with him, you might want to consider strapping his phone to your forehead." Leaning in, Andrew searches my eyes, and my heart drops through the porch. "Does any of this ring a bell?"

I reach to smack him. "Stop it. I really am fine. I'm sure it's just the altitude messing with me."

Andrew looks like he hadn't considered this, and to be fair I hadn't, either, before the words came out, so I mentally high-five the handful of remaining neurons that appear to be doing their job up there. Footsteps rumble behind us, and Benny's shaggy head pokes out onto the porch. He steps out to join us, shivering in only a thin bike shop T-shirt.

"Hey, Noodle," he says, brows up expectantly. "Sorry to interrupt. Can I grab you for a second?"

● ● ●

I guess I can't fault Benny for pulling me aside when I've given him at least ten pleading SOS looks since our arrival. We head inside, and I melt in pleasure at the heat of the entryway relative to the brilliant chill of the winter twilight. With the voices of everyone filtering down the hall, and Andrew's proximity fading, reality descends: somehow, I think I'm here again.

My brain screams, *This isn't normal!*

Intent on getting us as far away from everyone else as I can, I head for the stairs leading to the upper floor of the house. Turning to Benny, I put my index finger over my lips, urging him to be quiet as we tiptoe upstairs. In silence, we round the banister, shuffle down the hall, and climb the steep, narrow steps to his attic room. When I was little, I was afraid to come up here alone. The stairs creaked, and the landing was dark. But Benny explained that if the stairs leading up to the attic were as pretty as the rest of the house, everyone would find the treasures hidden up there.

With my heart pounding out a thunderstorm in my throat, I jerk him inside and close the door.

His turquoise bracelets rattle together when he comes to a stumbling stop, brows raised. "You all right?" he asks, genuine concern making his accent bleed the words together.

For the second time today—*How long is today?*—I wonder what my face looks like.

"No, I don't think so." I listen for a few seconds, making sure no one has followed us up here. When I'm satisfied we're alone, I whisper, "Listen. Some crazy stuff is going on."

He gives me a knowing wink. "I'll say. You and Andrew seemed pretty flirty out there. Is that what you wanted to talk about? Has something happened?"

"What? No. I wish." I point to the chair in the far corner by the windows and flap my hand until he takes the hint and sits down.

He leans forward, elbows on his knees, and fixes his attention on my face. The calm assurance of Benny's focus is like a numbing salve to my frazzled nerves.

"Okay," I begin, pulling up another folding chair and sitting across from him, knee to knee. "Have I ever given you the impression that I am—how should I put this? Mentally impaired?"

"Before today?" he jokes. "No."

"Emotionally unbalanced?"

"A few moments when you were thirteen to fifteen, but since then? No."

"Okay, then please believe that when I say what I'm about to say, I am being totally serious."

He takes a deep breath, bracing himself. "Okay. Hit me."

"I think it's possible I'm in the past, repeating the same holiday, and I'm the only one who knows it."

It sounds even crazier once I say it aloud. His bushy brows push together, and he shoves his too-long hair out of his eyes. "You mean the nightmare your dad mentioned?"

"No, I mean for real." I look around the room, wishing there was something here that could help me. Lisa's old Ouija board? Too creepy. Theo's old Magic 8 Ball? Too desperate. "Things that happened six days ago are happening over again."

He reaches into his pocket, pulls out a mint, and pops it in his mouth. "Start from the beginning."

I run a hand down my face. "Okay. So, earlier today for *me* was December twenty-sixth. Dad, Mom, Miles, and I were in a car headed to the airport—from here. This truck ran a red light—" I pause, piecing the fragments together. "A truck carrying Christmas trees, I think. Everyone was distracted, and it hit us. I woke up on the plane." I look up, making sure he's following. "A plane *back here*, today. December twentieth."

He lets out a quiet "Whoa." And then, "I don't get it."

I lean closer, trying to sort my words into order. "Maybe I'm not actually talking to you right now. Maybe I'm in a coma in the hospital, or maybe I really am dreaming this. All I know is that I already lived through this Christmas, managed to mess it all up, got creamed by a Christmas tree truck, and now I'm back, and it's the beginning of the holiday all over again."

"You sure about this?"

"Not even a little bit."

He nods slowly. "Cool. Okay. Keep going."

"Before we left, Ricky and Lisa told us that they were going to sell the cabin."

Benny's hazel eyes go wide. "They *what?*"

"Right?" I nod emphatically. "So obviously we were all really upset when we left. Plus my panic about making out with Theo, and getting busted by Andrew—"

Benny cuts me off. "Uh, back up."

"You knew about it, don't worry." I try to casually wave this detail to the side. "What I—"

He holds up a hand. "I can assure you I did not know that you made out with Theo because this conversation would have started there."

"Well, I told you this morning, but like everything else—everyone else—you've forgotten." I take a deep, calming breath. "For the record, you were much more helpful last time."

He considers this. "Was I also high?"

"Actually, yes."

He holds his hands palms-up as if to say *There you go*. "Start there, then tell me everything."

I groan in renewed mortification. "Last night there was eggnog."

He lets out a little "Ah" of understanding. Benny loves his weed, but, like me, he is easily knocked over by a cup of Ricky's eggnog. That stuff should come with an octane rating.

"It was brief and awkward," I tell him. "You told me to go talk to him the next morning, but he totally ignored me. *Then* I found out that Andrew saw us kissing. *Then* we found out that the Hollises are selling the cabin, and we left. Boom—car accident. Boom—back on plane. Boom—here we are."

Benny whistles. "I'm going to have some words with Theo."

"Seriously, Benny? That's what you're taking away from this? The primary redeeming thing about starting this holiday all over again is *not* having to process any of this with Theo!"

Benny seems to think on this. "I feel like I'm following you down this road pretty easily, friend. Are you sure you're not having some sort of altitude-poisoning thing?"

I snap my fingers with a memory. "Dad's tooth? I knew that was going to happen."

"If you knew, why didn't you warn him?"

"I was freaking out!" I yell, and then wince, hoping no one downstairs heard me. Lowering my voice, I continue, "And what would he have said? 'No way, this cookie bar looks delicious'? I'd already seen Theo's haircut, which is why I acted like a robot. And remember how I knew Kennedy's knee was bleeding?" I point to the door, like Benny can see the kitchen from here.

"You didn't, by chance, get into my little blue bag, did you?" he asks.

"No, of course not!"

"Okay, good. Because I had this friend who grows mushrooms in his closet, and he gave me—"

"Benny, I'm not high, I'm not drunk, I'm not on mushrooms! I'm being serious. This is freaking me out!"

"I know it is, Mae. Okay, I'm thinking."

Downstairs, I hear the faint sounds of everyone making their way to the living room for welcome cocktails. I screw my eyes shut, trying to pull forward all the tiny details that

I never expected to be important, but which are the difference now between Benny believing me or not. Kyle's round, theatrical voice carries upstairs, followed by Ricky's deep, booming laugh.

"Oh. Oh." I snap, pointing at the door. "Kyle just showed Ricky his new tattoo."

Benny stretches, listening. "Did you hear that all the way up here? Wow."

"No," I say. "I remembered it."

I can tell he doesn't totally buy that.

Zachary's elated laughter reaches us, and I can't help it—despite all the chaos in my head, I'm smiling. "Okay. Miso is licking Zacky's toes. Listen to him laughing."

"A pretty safe guess," Benny hedges. "That dog loves the twins."

I sigh. "Come on. Believe me."

"I want to, but you know how this sounds."

The problem is, I do.

"Let's say you're right," he whispers, "and what you're telling me is really happening. It's sort of like *Back to the Future*, except the past. Wait." He shakes his head. "He went to the past in that one, didn't he?"

I nod, and then keep nodding because exhaustion drags through me so heavily that I could honestly pass out right now.

"Does that make me Doc?" he asks.

I laugh. "Sure." But my amusement quickly fades. "But what do I do? Is this happening so I don't kiss Theo again? This seems like a pretty lame flex, Universe."

"But without kissing Theo you wouldn't be here," he reasons.

"No. Kissing Theo is where I messed things up . . . right?"

"No. It's like in *Avengers*, where they want to go back and kill the guy with the stones, but if they *had* killed him then they wouldn't be having the conversation to begin with." He pauses. "Holy shit, time travel is confusing."

I rub my temples. "Benny."

He gazes at me, and I stick the tip of my thumb in my mouth, chewing. "I think you should go talk to Dan," he finally says.

"*Dad?* He's the most literal and scientific person I've ever met. He would not for a second believe that I'm either a time traveler, a superhero, or clairvoyant."

Benny laughs. "I mean because he's a doctor."

"Yes, a doctor who knows birth canals and umbilical cords."

His voice is gentler now, because I'm clearly not following along. "I'm sure he remembers the basics enough to check your pupils and reflexes."

Oh.

"Like for a head injury? That's really what you think this is?"

Benny squares his hands on my shoulders. "I believe that something's going on with you. But that's all I'm qualified to do—believe you. I'm not sure I'm qualified to help. Your dad can tell you if everything seems to be working the way it should."

Maybe that's the ideal situation—something neurological happening. I mean, otherwise this is impossible, right?

"Okay." I kiss Benny's cheek and step back, nodding. "Plan A: assume I'm injured or crazy."

Benny's sweet smile crashes. "I did *not* say that."

"I'm kidding. I'll go talk to Dad."

With a little wave, I turn to the attic steps but I miss the first one. My leg comes out from under me and instead of falling backward, I pitch forward, slip, and—

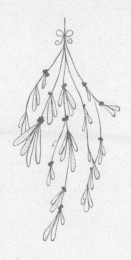

chapter seven

"AHHHHHHHH!" I wake up shouting loudly, startling from the sensation of falling down a steep flight of stairs. My arm shoots out to the side to catch the banister. But there's no banister there, no stairs. I smack my brother directly in the face again.

He lets out a rough *oof* and catches my arm. "Dude. What the hell, Mae?"

Bolting upright, I'm already sweating. I reach for my neck. Do I look like a corkscrew? Is my head on the right way? *Can I see my own butt?* I slump with relief until I notice the same white-noise hum of an engine, the same dry, recirculated air. The same *everything*.

"*No,*" I whisper, heart pounding. *Not again.*

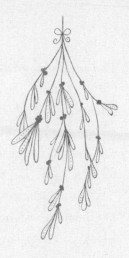

chapter eight

Benny stares at me. He blinks slowly, and I silently watch him try to process all of this. Again.

"I feel like I'm following you down this road pretty easily, friend." He frowns, worried. "Are you sure you're not having some sort of altitude-poisoning thing?"

Taking a deep breath, I rub my temples and remind myself to be patient; Benny doesn't know he's been through this before. He doesn't know he just asked me this same question. Whatever time loop I've tripped into isn't his fault.

"This is the third time I've lived this day," I say. "It's the second time I've had this conversation with you."

"So you saw your dad crack a tooth," he says slowly. "Three times?"

"Yeah."

"And you didn't think to warn him?"

I slump down, covering my face, and let out a groan.

The airport was exactly the same. The drive was identical. Only this time, my arrival at the cabin was even more disorienting than before. Panic kept my throat tight and fragile as I realized that yes, I *had* done this before—whether it was only in my head or was actually happening, I'm living this day again. I just don't know how or why.

The only thing that calmed me down once we arrived was my time with Andrew on the porch again. Maybe because I looked even paler and more vulnerable, he seemed to put more effort into his ridiculous introductions.

We gather here in December to build snow creatures, sled down huge mountains, make piles of cookies, and watch our parents get day-drunk . . .

We used to pretend to be in a rock band and you'd be David Bowie and I'd be Janis Joplin . . .

You talk in your sleep but unfortunately never say anything scandalous or interesting, it's mostly about food and spreadsheets . . .

"What else happens tonight?" Benny asks now, bringing my attention back to the present. He reaches for my hands to gently pry them away from my face. "What are some things you remember that . . ."

I pick up where he trails off. "That might help you believe me?"

Sweet Benny gives an apologetic wince and a shrug, but I don't blame him. I haven't caught my reflection anywhere, but I'm sure I look like a complete maniac. I'm clammy, breathless, feeling frayed at the edges. Oddly stiff, I stretch my neck from one side to the other, and a loud crack reverberates through the room. Huh. Better.

Voices move from the kitchen down the hall to the living room.

Abruptly, I stand and pull Benny after me. "Oh. Oh. Kyle is about to show everyone his new tattoo."

We move across the room to the door. I swear Benny moves with this weird tiptoe step that makes him look like Shaggy from *Scooby-Doo* as we carefully make our way down the attic steps and peer around the corner. Ricky's voice carries through the house from the living room. "Guys, come here!" Ricky calls. "Kyle got a cool new tattoo!"

When the words reach us, Benny grips my arm so hard I can feel each one of his fingertips.

I close my eyes, listening carefully. "Ricky's gonna give himself a hard time for forgetting to get Hendrick's for Aaron. Miso is going to lick Zachary's toes, and he'll laugh hysterically. Lisa is going to put on a Bob Dylan Christmas album that is legitimately *terrible*, and Theo is going to have a sip of beer go down the wrong pipe and will start coughing for, like, ten minutes straight." I look at Benny and nod, resolute. "Just wait."

We turn our quiet attention back to the living room, out of sight but within earshot.

"I don't know what I'm going to think if you're right," Benny whispers.

"Yeah. Same."

• • •

Twenty minutes later, we're back in the attic and Benny is pacing the length of the floor, back and forth. His bracelets jingle with every step. I'm on the bed, staring up at the ceiling. He's freaking out because everything I said would happen happened. Finally, he stops near me and lets out a reverently whispered "Whoa. I'm not even high right now."

I know I should feel vindicated, but given that it's no surprise to me that I was right, I have to wonder: *Is this my life now? Am I doomed to live this day over and over? Should I try to leave the attic again, or will I fall down the stairs?*

And the biggest question of all: Does it even matter what I do, or is time—for me—just . . . broken?

Well, worst-case scenario, I guess, is I relive this day over and over and keep flirting with Andrew on the porch.

I push up onto an elbow. "Okay. So: What do I do?"

"I think you should talk to your dad," Benny says with firm resolve.

"Nope." I roll onto my back again. "You said that last time. I Peter Pan'd it down the stairs and woke up on the plane."

"Ouch," he whispers, rubbing his neck guiltily. "I'm sorry, Noodle."

His tone makes my heart ache, and I sit up, pulling him to sit next to me so I can smooch his cheek. "Wasn't your fault."

"Maybe just . . ." He holds his hands up, unsure. "Just try to make it through tonight? Maybe tomorrow it will become clear what you're supposed to do. Maybe it's about Theo. Maybe it's about the cabin. I bet you'll figure it out. My motto is 'Go with the flow,' so I think that's what you need to do here." He pats my knee. "She'll be right, mate."

Go with the flow. Of course that's Benny's motto.

It's not like there's a guidebook to time jumping, or

some obvious portal in the attic wall—at least in Narnia they knew to get back to the wardrobe. So I guess our only clear option is to go downstairs and rejoin the festivities—*go with the flow* it is.

I stand up and Benny takes my arm protectively. "Besides all that," he says, "everything else okay? Work? Social life? Romance updates?"

I pause with my hand on the door. "Work?" A fist of dread squeezes my lungs. "Meh. Social life is fine. Mira— remember my college roommate? She moved back to Berkeley, so it's basically just the two of us scrolling Yelp for new restaurants where we can go eat our feelings."

Benny laughs, and then goes silent, waiting for me to answer the last looming question. Finally, he prompts: "And?"

"What is romance again?" I ask rhetorically. "I've had three dates in a year. On two of them it was immediately obvious we were not a good fit, and I used the very old and very tired 'My friend has an emergency and needs me' excuse."

"Oof."

"The third guy was good-looking, gainfully employed, easy to talk to—"

"Nice."

"—but on date two admitted that although he and his wife still live together, he *swears* they're separated and totally plans to move out soon."

Benny groans. "No."

"Eh, there's not much game to be had when you're still living with your mommy." I wave my hand, saying, "So yeah. Romance is on hold."

He kisses my temple. "Life ain't easy."

"You can say that again." I grin over my shoulder at him as I turn. "I mean, you probably will say that again, you just won't know it."

Benny laughs, insisting on walking ahead of me down the stairs, and I take them as slowly and painstakingly as I can. When I make it to the bottom, he gives me a genuine high five—which I gladly take. We are now celebrating the small victories.

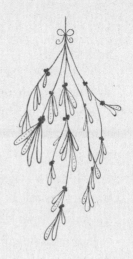

chapter nine

My eyes open to the dark, and the view of blank nothingness is so familiar it sends a spike of relief through me. I know exactly where I am: bottom bunk, basement room, the cabin. What I don't know is *when.*

When I fumble for my phone, I don't honestly know what I'm hoping for—whether I want to go back to the present or stay here in the past. It's moot anyway: one look at my home screen and I see it's December 21. I made it to the next morning, but who knows if I'll make it through the rest of the day? Still, I give myself a mental high five. Remember? Small victories.

I roll onto my back to let it sink in. I want to understand not only *what* is going on, but *why.* Did I make this happen somehow? If so, how? What was happening right before the crash?

Mom was crying over the sale of the cabin.

Dad was advocating for some change in our lives.

Miles was in his own little world, so the usual. And I . . . well, I was falling down a mental rabbit hole of dread, panicking about losing the one thing in my life that always made sense before—

I stop, bolting upright in the darkness, remembering. *Universe*, I'd asked. *What am I doing with my life? Please. Can you show me what will make me happy?*

Is it even possible? I take a deep breath and make myself answer the question anyway: *What makes me happy?*

This cabin, of course. And my family and our chosen family here with us every December. But also . . . Andrew's laugh. A quiet afternoon spent drawing in my backyard. Watching Miles try to breakdance. Building snow creatures at the cabin. My mother's cooking. Sledding. Aaron's cheese blintzes. The feeling of drifting off to sleep with a window open in the springtime.

But I was sent back here, specifically. Not ahead to the spring or summer. Not home to the backyard with a sketchbook. *Here*. And I need to know why.

Eyes closed, I let a flurry of images take over until one hits the brakes, coming into focus in my mind.

Theo and I were thirteen, Andrew was sixteen, and it was the first time that I registered that he was objectively gorgeous. Before then, the Hollis boys were firmly rooted in the *family* category and I noticed them in the way that I noticed my own reflection: both dispassionately and obliviously. But that winter, Ricky was having a bunch of electrical issues at the cabin, and he kept sending Andrew down to the fuse box to reset the breakers. When he wasn't helping his dad, Andrew was playing War with me and Kyle, and it was getting pretty intense. I thought Andrew was pulling high cards from the bottom of his deck. He calmly insisted he wasn't. I followed him down to the basement, yelling at the side of his face while he aimed a flashlight on the fuse box and calmly told me to "be quiet for two seconds, Mae" and then the lights went back on and his profile was illuminated and it felt like a boulder rolled over inside me.

For the first time, I really *noticed* him—the soft hair at his temples, the increasingly masculine shape of his neck, the perfect line of his nose, how big his hands suddenly seemed. From that moment on it felt like my adolescence was split into two halves: before I fell for Andrew, and after.

We went back upstairs, but I didn't want to play anymore. Not because I would be mad if I lost, but because I wanted him to win. I wanted him to win because I wanted him to be happy. Andrew wouldn't ever be just a family friend again; he would always be a little bit more, a little bit mine, even if he didn't know it.

But the feeling was unsettling: I didn't like that sensation of being a lightweight screen door in a heavy wind.

The rest of the holiday was a torment. Andrew in his pajama pants, no shirt, obliviously scratching his stomach as he helped a four-year-old Miles hang origami cranes. Andrew sitting next to me at the table, watching me draw and swearing, with loving wonder, that he thought I had a gift for art, just like my mom. Andrew in jeans and a thick wool sweater, helping Dad and Benny bring in firewood. Andrew earnestly playing song after song on his guitar for me and Theo, trying to introduce us to the wonder of Tom Petty. Andrew half-asleep on the sofa in front of the fire, with Miles asleep on him. When we all played Sardines, and I hid, I would pray that Andrew would find me first, that we would get time alone in an enclosed, hidden space together. That we would "accidentally" make out.

Andrew was enthusiastically musical, reluctantly athletic, quiet, and unattainable. Generous with time and compliments, selfless with family. Adorably messy hair, shy smile, and the kind of teenage monster who never needed braces. Imagine sleeping in a bunk bed across the room from that every night, with the new awareness that Andrew might have a girlfriend, that he had body parts I hadn't ever considered before, that he was probably already having S-E-X.

Although it would make sense for the grown-ups to eventually worry that something scandalous would happen between me and one of the Hollis boys down in the secluded basement, no one batted a lash. My mother was normally incredibly strict about boundaries, but we were family, after all. Maybe Andrew was so obviously uninterested in me, and I was so obviously uninterested in Theo, that it never pinged their parental radar, even when we were old enough to drink alcohol and make terrible decisions.

I grew up going to church every Sunday but decided a long time ago that Catholicism wasn't for me. Now, in the darkness, I'm starting to believe that something has given me a true do-over. A bullet dodged at the most wonderful time of the year. But in this world full of people who need much bigger things than to have avoided a stupid, drunken kiss, I wish I understood why me.

• • •

I climb out of bed, careful not to wake Theo or Miles. Cautiously entering the kitchen, I'm not sure what I'll find.

But everything seems normal. Aside from the missing holly garland that the twins haven't yet put up in the kitchen, everything looks exactly like it did when we left only five days from now. Or is it two days ago? Who the hell knows.

Ricky shuffles in just after I do. His salt-and-pepper hair is tidy up front but a holy mess in the back. His eyes are still squinty, but he beams so brightly at me it causes an actual ache in my chest. I give myself a second to celebrate that I'm really *here*, in this kitchen. I thought I'd lost this.

"Maelyn Jones," he says hoarsely, "you and me are two peas in a pod."

Inside, I am glowing, waiting.

He sits down with a groan. "We both wake up with the sun."

Ahhhhh. There it is.

"You know the worst thing in the world would be never hearing you say that again?" I kiss the top of his head and then pour him a cup of coffee in his favorite reindeer mug.

"Why would you even worry about that?"

I don't answer. *Hard to explain, Ricky.*

But the thought lands again, heavier now, like a stone in a river: *I thought I'd lost this.* I thought I would never have this moment again with Ricky, in this kitchen, and here I am. Does he have any idea what a gift this place is to all of us? The cabin makes me more than happy, it makes me feel *grounded*. Am I getting a chance to keep them from selling?

He takes a long sip and sets his mug down. "How're you feeling this morning, Noodle?"

Me? How I'm feeling is suddenly the least of my worries. With clarity about a possible purpose comes an exhilaration so profound it can only mean that I'm on the right track. After all, the ceiling didn't fall and the floor didn't open up to send me back to the plane.

"I'm fine." I lean back against the counter. I'm smiling at Ricky over my coffee, but my thoughts are a cyclone of recollecting, plan making, playing it cool. "Better than ever, actually."

I turn to the sound of feet on the stairs to see a sleep-rumpled Benny peeking around the corner. He holds a finger up to his mouth and motions for me to come toward him. A glance over my shoulder shows Ricky happily sipping his coffee and already at least three cookies deep into the shortbread tin, so I push off the counter and quietly make my way into the hall.

With a hand on each shoulder, Benny bends at the knees, peering into my eyes.

I wait for an explanation. None comes. "Yes?"

"Just looking."

"For?"

"Not sure. Trying to remember the signs of a concussion."

I roll my eyes and pull him up. His cardigan is shockingly soft. "Is this *cashmere*?"

He stares down at it like he doesn't remember putting it on. "Maybe?" He looks back up at me. "Focus, Mae."

Blinking my eyes, I remember why we're here. "Do you remember our conversation last night?"

"Yes?"

I exhale, relieved. "Okay," I say, mentally working this out. "We're doing this over again, but I'm the only one who realizes it. I haven't been sent back, so I must be doing something right?"

"Is there another explanation?"

I chew on my lip. "That I'm crazy? That this is all random? That I'm actually in a coma in a hospital in Salt Lake?"

"I don't like any of those options," he admits.

"Uh, yeah," I scoff, grinning wryly. "I'm not wild about them, either."

"I'm here," he reasons. "I mean—I'm *real*. I'm in this with you, and so it can't just be happening to you, right?"

A thought occurs to me: "Quick. Tell me something I wouldn't possibly know about you—other than your stash of mushrooms, too obvious. Just in case I reboot all over again."

"You know about the mushrooms?"

"Benny."

He frowns as he thinks. And then he leans in and whispers a rushed string of words.

When he pulls back, I stare at him. "*Benny.*"

He laughs, shaking his head. "I know."

I shudder. "I meant something like, 'My first dog's name was Lady.' Not like, 'I lived a strange double life as a nude waiter in Arizona.'"

He shrugs. "It's the first thing that came to mind."

Closing my eyes, I shake my head to clear the image.

"Do we tell the others?" Benny asks. "I mean, this whole situation is pretty wild. Maybe one of them has experienced this before and managed to get to the other side of it? Maybe you're right, and this place really is magic."

"I like your thinking, but I might have a better idea. I mean, Ricky and Lisa deciding to sell the cabin was the catalyst for my whole wish in the first place. Do you think it's possible we're supposed to convince them to keep it? Maybe if we all pitch in and show them what it means to us?"

He looks past me to where Ricky is cuddling his coffee. "Never hurts to try, I suppose."

"Everyone is always complaining about all the traditions," I whisper, "but Ricky really does so much for us. What if we're all just very gung-ho about things? What if we offer to help with the upkeep? Repairs?"

"You think you can get everyone on board?" he asks.

I look out the window and grimace. Today's tradition was once about building snowmen, but then younger Mae apparently asked why we couldn't build snow*girls*, and then tiny Miles came along and asked why he couldn't build a snow monkey. Now, December 21 is Snow Creature Day, and that seems to work for everyone.

That is, unless it's terrible outside. Ricky doesn't adjust the itinerary for inclement weather, and we've all grown so competitive about this activity that we're usually out there for a good two or three hours before we've picked a winner. A glance out the window reveals an intimidating gray-blue sky. Thick, daggerlike icicles hang menacingly from the eaves. There's no way we'll get a complaint-free group out there today.

I gulp as I look back at him. "I'll try."

Benny sucks in a breath between his teeth. "Man, changing the future, though. Like, have you ever heard of the butterfly effect? What if you change one tiny thing and something terrible happens?"

"Listen," I say, "if the universe wants to drop a cursed ring in my lap that I'm supposed to throw into a lava-filled mountain, I'm all for it. But right now this is all I've got."

● ● ●

I follow Benny into the kitchen just as the back door opens. Andrew steps inside and brings with him a sharp streak of ice-cold air, as well as a shot of adrenaline straight into my heart.

I shout out a bright "Hey!"

In my head, I've said it with easy composure, James Dean leaning against the doorframe. In reality, I've hollered it with odd aggression, and everyone else flinches.

Benny puts a calming hand on my back.

Andrew pulls out an earbud and grins at me, unfazed because he is a magical creature. "Hey yourself."

He's shivering, wearing a down jacket, scarf, gloves, and a blanket as a shawl. This human tangle of hot + adorable is usually hidden in the audio tech booth during shows at Red Rocks but should absolutely be onstage for everyone to enjoy.

"So, the Boathouse was toasty warm?" I ask, at normal volume now.

He pushes a mess of brown curls out of his eyes. "Even freezing out there is better than sleeping in the bunk bed downstairs."

What an adorable liar. The bunk beds might be in a basement, but it's at least insulated down there, and the beds themselves are cozy and warm and covered in fluffy down comforters. The Boathouse is a twelve-by-twelve box with one entire wall of windows that overlook the back side of the mountain, and not even a wood-burning stove to keep it heated. It's gorgeous but barely a step above snow camping. Andrew will die in this battle of wills with his dad.

Smug now, Ricky studies his shivering oldest son over the rim of his coffee mug. "You sure about that?"

Behind us, Benny snorts.

A memory bubble pops in my brain. "Why not use those big sleeping bags in the basement storage area?"

Three pairs of eyes swing to me and I realize I've just messed up.

Andrew's interest is definitely piqued. "Sleeping bags?"

"How on earth did you know about those?" Ricky asks with an astonished smile. "*I* didn't even remember we had them. We haven't used 'em in years."

"Yes, Mae. How did you know about those?" Benny says, and then gives me a covert thumbs-up.

I know about them because on Christmas morning, Ricky remembered that they were there. He aired them out and gave them to Andrew after he came in shivering for the fifth day in a row. They're these enormous army-green canvas bags that each weigh about forty pounds. The insides are a thick red flannel with a weird deer-hunting motif that honestly makes the bags look like bloody carcasses when they're unzipped, but who am I to judge if Andrew's warm? I remember he bundled himself in one and said it was the best night's sleep he'd had all year. I just got him an extra four nights of blissful slumber.

I look skyward. Bonus points, Universe?

Bonus points or not, remembering the sleeping bags is how I end up outside in the freezing cold, wearing an enormous parka, holding a baseball bat at eight in the morning and beating an unzipped bag where it hangs over a clothesline. I steer clear of the icicles.

Farther down the line, Andrew swings his tennis racket at the other green-and-red canvas-and-flannel carcass. He gives it a good *whack* and sends plumes of dust flying everywhere. "Oh, Maisie, this was a clutch idea."

"You should know by now where to come for the big brain."

Andrew squints at me in the cold morning air. "I haven't seen these in at least a decade."

The implied question—the same one Benny and Ricky asked aloud only minutes ago—is plainly expressed in his eyes. "I was looking for a roasting pan for Mom," I lie. "They were back there in the storage area." Blinking down to the garish red interior, I mumble, "They're so gory. It's almost disturbing."

"I remember camping in these as a kid," he tells me, "and pretending I was Luke Skywalker sleeping in a tauntaun."

"A-plus nerd reference."

"'Snug as a Luke in a tauntaun' isn't a saying yet, but we could make it happen."

"You know," I say, taking a swing, "you *could* go into town and buy a space heater."

Andrew smacks his sleeping bag several times, clearing an impressive amount of dirt. "That would be admitting defeat."

"Ah. Definitely worth dying to avoid."

"Where my dad is concerned, that is correct. But thank you for being so smart." His smile crinkles his eyes and a tiny, mighty voice screams in my cranium: LOOK HOW HAPPY THAT SMILE MAKES YOU. "Speaking of defeat," he says, "you ready for today?"

Freezing as it is, snow has also fallen and there is a gorgeous layer of fresh, fluffy powder for our next adventure. "Oh, hell yes."

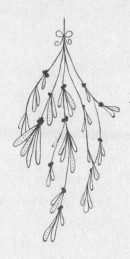

chapter ten

It surprises no one who knows the Hollis family that they take their snow-creature building very seriously. Set out for us when we all emerge onto the front porch after breakfast are implements ranging from large shovels to tiny garden spades, rakes to squeegees. At the base of the stairs, a table is covered in cups, plates, buckets, knives, spoons, ice cream scoops, and even handheld torches to help us shape, mold, and carve out the perfect features of our creations. Beside the table are a wood box and a large wicker basket; the box holds fresh carrots, turnips, potatoes, and a variety of squash for noses and limbs. The basket has mittens, wigs, hats, and scarves.

As is tradition, we team up, work to build the best sculpture, and then vote on which should win. The stakes are high: for our dinner tonight, Ricky intentionally picks a wide range of steaks, from hammered chuck to filet mignon. Everyone drops their anonymous paper vote for best sculpture in a box—honor code says you can't vote for yourself—and the winning team gets to pick their dinner and everyone else's. On Snow Creature Day, I've never eaten filet mignon.

Only a few days ago, Andrew and I built a snow monkey but didn't happen upon brilliance until the very end, when we had to rush to finish and lost to Mom and Ricky's grizzly bear. Theo started trash talking; he and Andrew ended up wrestling. Things turned competitive, I hopped into the mix, and Theo tackled me and then seemed to take an awfully long time getting up.

Was that the start of something I didn't see coming? I shudder.

I will not be letting that happen again.

The twins bound down the steps and dive into the fresh powder; as has been true every year of their short lives, they will be enthusiastic participants for about fifteen minutes, then will lose interest.

Aaron made his bubbe's famous cheese blintzes this morning, but didn't eat a single one, choosing instead to sip on a protein shake and insist he was "perfectly content without all that dairy" and has "never felt better." Now he's on the porch in ripped skinny jeans, a floral bomber jacket, and a pair of trendy thick-soled sneakers that look better suited to walking around in a spaceship than in six inches of fresh snow.

"This is . . . different," Andrew says, looking him up and down.

"Doesn't Papa look cool?" Zachary says, and tugs on the

end of Aaron's Burberry scarf. "He has the same shoes as Mr. Tyler."

"Who is Mr. Tyler?" I ask.

Kyle looks on with the long-suffering smile of a spouse who has endured his husband's shenanigans for months and is all too happy to share the joy. "That's the twins' twenty-four-year-old Instagram-famous soccer coach."

Aaron jogs in place. "They're super comfortable."

Andrew is a delightful sweetheart: "I'm sure they are."

By this point in our lives, we all know the routine: Partners split off and get to strategizing, then building. It might make more sense for me to pair up with Theo because we're practically twins but 1) Miles would murder anyone who dared steal quality time with his idol; 2) Andrew and I are both easily distracted as well as only marginally invested in winning, so nobody else wants us on their team, and 3) I just really want to be with Andrew. Not the most noble reason, but here we are.

As for the rest, Benny is only occasionally interested in the event, and mostly just acts as a judge and/or cheerleader. Lisa works with Kyle. Aaron works with Dad, who, to Dad's credit, takes a long look at Aaron's outfit but refrains from commenting. Theo and Miles team up, obviously, and Ricky and Mom are a team. Nine times out of ten, they win. I guess that's what happens when you pair a landscape architect with an artist.

When Kennedy and Zachary started kindergarten last year, we instituted a Swimsuit Rule: Nothing can be carved that would be hidden by a swimsuit. Without the guideline, Theo cannot be trusted. There were a number of years there in our early twenties when even Theo's snow lizards had boobs.

Out of the corner of my eye, I catch him the precise moment he spots the thick curved branch that inspires him and Miles to make the snow elephant. The adrenaline of this discovery kicks his energy into high gear and the two guys high-five like fraternity pledges who've just tapped their first keg.

Benny sidles up to me at the table. "What's your plan?"

I watch as Andrew sifts through the box of veggies, waiting for inspiration. A few days ago, we'd started making a panda and then aborted that option when we realized it really just looked like a bear—which Mom and Ricky were already doing and better. We pivoted to the monkey, and I think it would have been amazing if we'd started on that from the get-go.

"I'm going to use what I learned last time and win."

Benny nods for a few quiet seconds before muttering dryly, "That seems altruistic."

I glare half-heartedly at him. "Originally, Ricky and Mom won—like they always do—and everyone complained," I whisper. "We don't want people complaining, we want people having fun! Project Save the Cabin, right? So, if Andrew and I win, we can make a big deal that it's our first steak-pick ever. Rah-rah traditions!"

Benny stares at me. "Everyone knows you don't care about the steak."

I stare back at him. "Maybe I'm hungry."

He lifts a brow.

"Or maybe I'm tired of losing."

Benny snorts into his coffee. "There it is."

Andrew approaches. I bump my shoulder against his and pretend to give him a vote. "What are you thinking?"

"A panda bear?" he says, holding his hands out to indicate a big, round belly.

I give this five seconds of fake consideration, tapping my chin.

"I think your dad and my mom are already making a bear." I tilt my head, subtly gesturing, before realizing that of course they're still gathering materials and I'd have no way of knowing what they're doing; all they have is a shape- less mound of snow.

Andrew frowns at me quizzically, green eyes narrowing.

"I heard Mom talking about it earlier," I lie. "I bet it'll be amazing."

He buys this—*Thank you, Universe*—and I walk over to the side porch to locate the two perfect pieces of bark that will become our monkey's ears. "Maybe we do a monkey?" I hold them to the sides of my head, demonstrating.

With a smile, he digs into the box and brandishes the two arm-shaped squash that will fit our monkey perfectly. We grin wildly at each other. We are geniuses!

"Be cool," he whispers quickly, wrangling his smile under control. We share a subtle fist-bump.

At first, we're all working in our respective areas, ignor- ing what everyone else is doing because it takes a while for the lumps of snow to start looking like anything specific. But as time goes on—around when the twins get bored and start making snowballs nearby—we get more competitive. Each team glances over their shoulders more frequently. We all start to whisper and point. No one is eager for a dinner of sinewy chuck, and we have to know which team we'll need to beat.

Nearly forty-five minutes in, the monkey is coming out even better than I could have imagined—even better than she did last time. Her ears are just big enough to make her look cartoonish and cuddly. I managed to snag some beautiful tortoiseshell buttons that make her eyes look dark and luminous. Andrew is gifted with the butter knife, apparently, because he's alternating between heating it up with a lighter and carefully carving out her features. Her nose and mouth are perfect. Look what we can do when we actually put in effort!

And maybe cheat. Just a little.

"It's too wet."

I look up at Andrew when he says this. "What's too wet?"

Swallowing audibly, Andrew uses the butter knife to point to where I'm struggling to get the monkey's tail to curl up and back over itself. It crumbles every time I dig out the extra snow. "You have a moisture problem."

The words bounce back and forth between us, growing louder somehow in the ringing silence. His eyes twinkle with repressed laughter, and finally, unable to hold it in anymore, we both break.

"Did you just tell me I have a *moisture problem*?"

He can't stop laughing. "No—yes."

"Are you broken, Andrew Polley Hollis?"

He doubles over. "I promise I've never said that to a woman before."

Pressing my hand to my chest, I say, "What an absolute honor to be the first." I wave him over. "Come help me with this."

"With your moisture problem?"

"Andrew."

He crawls over, eyes glimmering as they meet mine. I want to capture this moment. I want to put it in a snow globe and be able to see it just like this, forever.

We decide to name our monkey Thea, because we want to reach peak trolling levels with Theo when we win. I make sure to stand to the side often, looking like I'm thinking really hard about my next step. Andrew catches what I'm doing and gives me an approving smirk.

Our bait works beautifully. Ricky meanders over, eyes Thea. "What is that?"

I see his trash talk and knock it down, coyly running a finger beneath her artistically sculpted jaw. "You know exactly what it is. Her name is Thea, but I like to think of her as filet mignon."

He tilts his head, walking in a wide circle around her. I can tell he's shocked and impressed; Andrew and I are bringing our A-game.

Finally Ricky speaks, but it comes out with a jealous edge. "I don't know, Mae. Have you seen our bear?"

Giving it a brief glance, Andrew says, "Oh, that bark-covered lump of snow over there?"

"Hey, that's going to be my masterpiece!" With a laugh, Mom throws a loose snowball in Andrew's direction.

Unfortunately, at that exact moment, Dad stands up about halfway between them and the snowball hits him with a thud, squarely on the side of his neck. The ice slides under his collar, and I see a big puff of it disappear beneath his sweater.

My stomach drops. Mom is lighthearted and fun-loving. Dad is . . . well, he is not. He is kind but sensitive, and never good at being the butt of a joke.

Please, I think. *Don't fight. Don't derail this day.*

Mom playfully singsongs, "Oops! Did I hit you, Dan?"

The group holds its collective breath. Mom, unfazed, does a saucy little dance. This woman is playing with fire.

Holding eye contact, Dad bends to collect and form a perfect—and terrifyingly compact—snowball. I deflate in relief when he stands and I see that he's grinning. When he tosses the snowball at her, I swear it whistles ominously through the air, missing her by only inches.

Mom screeches in delight. Dad laughs, bending to make another one, calling out, "Oh, you're in for it now."

This is new.

But my nerves are growing frayed again; Andrew and I are doing so well with Thea, and for a few blissful seconds, I actually forgot that I've lived this day before and just let myself enjoy it. But being in snow with this crowd is a bit like walking around in a pool of gasoline with a lit match. Snowball fights are always a possibility.

The twins, who have been stockpiling a monster number of snowballs themselves, take Dad's act as a sign that they are good to launch, and before I realize what's happening, the entire scene is devolving into a huge war. Match to gasoline: Zachary pelts his dad Aaron in the back of the leg, who blows out the crotch of his designer jeans as he attempts to tuck and roll for cover. Standing again, he pelts Kyle in the stomach, who pelts Dad on the arm. Dad aims for Kyle but hits Lisa in the shoulder, and she retaliates with a vicious snow bullet that hits him squarely between the shoulder blades. Apparently her aim with a snowball is much better than her aim with a camera.

"Guys, stop!" I hold my arms out, but no one is paying attention. Not even Ricky seems fazed at this breach of tradition; he's beaming snowballs at his sons with a laugh that seems to echo off the cabin, the trees, the mountains.

People are running, diving, dodging behind snow creations and—to my immense shock—knocking them over. With a flash of Aaron's hot-pink briefs, he and Dad charge, and Mom and Ricky's snow bear goes down in a powdery crumble. With the twins' enthusiasm, Theo and Miles's elephant is reduced to a sad, lumpy mound, and in retaliation, they take out Lisa and Kyle's giraffe—already an overly ambitious project. By the time Theo stands, the giraffe has lost its head and now looks like a white boulder. Only an hour ago, the lawn was a perfect, thick sheet of fluffy, wet snow. Now patches of dirt peek through. Blades of grass are mixed with broken, muddy snowballs. It is unbridled, wintry chaos.

"What is happening?" I shout to Andrew through the commotion.

"At last, tradition is crumbling!" He wears a maniacal grin as he runs to take a bracing stance in front of Thea, arms wide, adding gallantly, *"They can take this day, but they cannot take our monkey!"*

Panic climbs like a vine in my throat. Sure, snowball fights are a blast, but this isn't how today is supposed to go.

We can have a snowball fight tomorrow, or even Christmas Eve. I mean, if we're willing to throw this tradition away, what happens later tonight when Dad and Ricky go to pick out the Christmas tree? Will they ignore the tradition of hunting for the best one, and instead bring home the first one they see? Are we going to disregard everything that makes this vacation perfect?

Throwing my arms out wide, I protect Thea as long as I can, through what feels like an insane flurry of flying snowballs. But out of the corner of my eye, just as Andrew nails Miles with a perfect shot right to the groin, I see Theo making a swan dive in our direction.

Andrew tackles his brother, but it's too late. Thea, the final animal, goes down in an explosion of snow and wrestling limbs just as Benny steps outside.

The chaos clears, and the view before me is reduced to a gathering of panting, snow-dusted idiots.

Benny stops at the bottom of the stairs and looks around, confused. "I was gone for, like, two minutes, you guys."

With everything destroyed, they finally take a few moments to survey the destruction on the front lawn. I expect devastation and remorse. I expect Ricky to let out a wailing, heartbroken *What have we done?!*

. . . But it never comes. Instead, he's grinning at what a mess we all are, and then throws his head back and lets out a delighted, booming laugh.

"What is wrong with you?" I cry out. "Don't you get it? This is special! What about tradition? We won't be able to keep doing this together if we don't respect what we've all built!"

Andrew puts a gentling hand on my arm. "Mae," he says, but we're all distracted by a groaning crack overhead. I look up just in time to see a large snow-covered branch buckle beneath the weight and plummet, almost in slow motion. Straight for me.

chapter eleven

This time I wake up screaming in betrayal, clutching my face and my head, searching for blood or brains, or God knows what. But, of course, there's nothing.

I don't have to look to know exactly where I am, and I honestly have no more shits to give.

"I DO NOT UNDERSTAND WHAT IS GOING ON," I shout to the plane around me. Sure, 219 other people have to deal with a crazy woman yelling in an enclosed space with them, but hopefully the universe hears me, too, because I have *had* it.

I didn't ask my dad if I had a head injury.

I made a pledge to save the cabin.

I was absolutely on track to never kiss Theo Hollis again.

What the hell else am I supposed to be doing?

A hush falls over the entire plane, and I feel the press of

my family's stunned attention on the side of my face. Even Mom woke up for this.

A flight attendant leans over Miles to whisper to me. Tiny silver bells pinned to her sweater jingle in the deafening silence. "Ma'am, is everything okay?"

"I'm fine," I say, irritably and clearly not fine at all. But who cares? Nobody! They're not going to remember this anyway! "Just been living the same freaking day over and over again, but whatever. Let's just land and get on with it."

"Can I get you a beverage?" she asks, sotto voce.

"Is that code for 'You're scaring other passengers; can I give you some wine?'"

She just smiles.

"I'm good. Thanks." Leaning forward, I catch my father's eye. "Dad, when we get to the cabin, don't eat the goddamn cookie."

•   •   •

We climb out of the car, and it's lovely and everyone is excited and yes, this is normally my favorite moment of the year with my favorite people, but Lord, I can't do it again. I am so tired.

I give advice as I quickly deliver hugs. "Kennedy, watch out for Miso on your way inside. Dad, once again, don't eat the cookies. Everyone? Kyle has a new tattoo. It's on his arm—a music note—and it's very cool but don't touch it, it's healing. Ricky," I continue, "don't worry about the Hendrick's, everyone is fine with Bombay—and Aaron isn't drinking anyway because he's middle-aged and stressed about getting old. Speaking of hair, Theo, your haircut is great, but your hair wasn't ever the problem. And Lisa?" I say, and a twinge of guilt worms through me because they're all staring at me with wide, worried eyes. "I love you—so much—but maybe let Aaron pick the music tonight." I pause. "And let Mom take the photos."

If it weren't so cold out, we'd be able to hear crickets chirping in the confused silence.

"I really don't mean to sound like an asshole," I say, adding, "Oops, earmuffs, kids! I've just had a day." This makes me laugh—*a day!*—and it takes me a few awkward seconds to get the cackling under control. "It's well established that I'm a terrible drinker, but if anyone is mixing drinks, I'd love something fruity with vodka. No eggnog."

Andrew snaps his fingers, and I look over at him. His eyes are wide, but his mouth is smiling. My eternally unflappable hero. "Coming right up, Crazy Maisie."

Do I want to follow him inside? Do I want to flirt with him on the porch? Yes. But it won't matter; it will only get my hopes up.

I stare at the sky and let out a long, exhausted groan. "What is even the *poooooint*?"

A hand comes around my upper arm. "Maelyn?" It's Dad. "Honey, what's going on?"

"I'd say it's a long story, but it's actually not. I'm stuck here. In time." I let out an unhinged cackle. "Do I want to visit this cabin every year? Yes. But do I *really* want to keep reliving December twentieth forever in order to do it? No. No, I do not."

He and Mom share a worried look. "Maybe we should take her to a doctor," Mom says.

Dad turns to look at her incredulously. "I *am* a doctor."

She sighs. "You know what I mean."

"I don't, actually."

The tide of guilt rises higher in me—they're already bickering, and I'm the reason—but I can't fix that right now. They'll have to figure this out on their own.

Turning my pleading eyes on Benny, I say, "We need to talk."

I look back to Mom, sending her a silent *Just give me a minute*, before Benny and I head up to the porch. I love my mother, but right now I need Benny's even temper.

I try to undo my turbulent arrival with some quick, gentle kisses to the tops of Kennedy and Zachary's heads, but they go still and nervous under my touch.

At least Kennedy pays attention to where the dog is when she walks inside.

And Dad doesn't eat a cookie.

But no one is going to remember this anyway.

• • •

Benny sits next to me on the porch swing, and we rock back and forth in aware silence. I can barely make out the shape of the house next door through the trees but can see the smoke curling from the chimney, the glow of their outdoor Christmas lights through the branches.

The branches.

I look up warily. Across the yard, I think I spot the snow-covered branch that cracked me on the head, and I point at it, growling, "You will not get me tomorrow, you fucker."

Benny goes still. "Are you gonna tell me what's going on?"

"It won't matter."

He studies me. "Why not?"

"Because this is the fourth time I've been in this day, and no matter what I try to do differently, I keep coming back."

"Like *Groundhog Day*?"

"Is that a movie?"

He scrubs a hand down his face. "God, you're young. I still think it's one of the weirdest traditions, believing spring is determined by a groundhog's shadow. Spring starts on the same day every year where I'm from."

I must be staring at him in bewilderment, because he nods. "Yes, Maelyn, *Groundhog Day* is a movie."

"Then yes. No matter what I do, I keep getting clobbered and waking up on the plane."

"Maybe you should talk to your—"

"My dad?" I say, and shake my head. "Nope. We tried that two go-arounds back, but I fell down the attic stairs, and—" I make a splat motion and he winces. I gesture for him to finish the sentence.

"You started over again?"

"Bingo. Apparently, it's not my head," I say, aiming my voice to the sky. "And apparently it's not about saving the cabin?"

No answer. The universe is profoundly unhelpful.

Benny frowns. "Saving the cabin from what?"

Inhaling deeply, I decide to tell him everything again. Even if I only make it to tomorrow, I need someone here with me who knows. Eggnog. Face licking. Traitor Theo.

Adorable Andrew. Regret, regret, regret. Cabin. Accident. Purgatory. Whatever.

"Oh," I say, "And I asked you to tell me something that only you know so you'd believe me if this happened again."

"And?"

"And you told me about the club in Sedona."

His eyes go wide. "I *did*?"

"Yup." I shiver. "So I have to live with that information now."

Benny lets out a quiet "Whoa."

"As crazy as it sounds, I think this is all happening because I asked the universe to show me what would make me happy and it's just sending me here over and over again *with no instruction booklet*," I shout upward. "Like, yes, I love it here. I get it. And now I shall live here forever. Eternal Christmas. Be careful what you wish for, am I right?" I laugh a little maniacally.

After a long pause, Benny finally asks, "Okay, but let's say that you have no limits on what you can wish for, what—in this whole enormous world—would make you truly happy?"

As if on cue, footsteps pad quietly from the front door across the porch. And there, walking outside holding a sparkling tumbler full of orange juice, vodka, and extra ice, is Andrew. "Screwdriver. Heavy on the juice," he says with a sweet smile. "Because, no offense, you're a lightweight, Maisie."

He sits down on the porch swing, sandwiching me between his warm body and Benny's. My emotions are on fire, and the lust of my life looks back and forth between me and Benny. "So. What were we talking about?"

Don't trust the universe.

We were talking about what in the whole wide world I'd wish for, and you appeared. Funny, right?

A glance at Benny tells me he's not coming to my rescue here. Damn him for choosing this moment to make me face my feelings.

"We were talking about my crazy day," I say, "and Benny asked what would make me happy, and you walked out with a drink." I take it from him, adding, "So thank you. I am happy now."

I take a deep drink and *wow*, Andrew does not mess around—this is not "heavy on the juice." I'm surprised that flames don't flicker off my tongue when I exhale. Next reboot, I'll have to ask him to make one that tastes slightly less like fire.

"That's strong," I gasp, handing it to Benny, who sets it down on the table to his right.

"You are in rare form today, Maisie," Andrew says, laughing.

I cough harshly, wincing through the burn. "Just living my truth."

"I'm getting that." I feel him look at Benny over the top of my head. "As long as you're not upset with us for some reason?"

Guilt pierces through my reckless mood. Whether they're figments of my imagination or pawns in the universe's game, I love these people desperately. I'll have to be kinder next time I lose my mind. "I hope I didn't hurt your mom's feelings."

He laughs. "According to Dad, she's been playing that

Bob Dylan Christmas album for three weeks now and we've all told her it's terrible. Maybe hearing it from someone who isn't her son or husband will make a difference." Andrew's dark brows pull together. "But how did you know Dad forgot the Hendrick's?"

"Weird hunch," I say.

Andrew pushes out his bottom lip, sweetly considering this, and then nods like he's totally satisfied with my non-explanation. He rolls with weird, surreal stuff almost as well as Benny does. "That must have been one hell of a dream you had on the plane. Last week I had a dream I worked at a carnival," he says conversationally. "For, like, a week afterward I kept feeling like I was constantly late to work at the cotton candy booth. It was crazy stressful."

This makes me laugh, and the three of us fall silent. The wind whistling through the tree line is the only sound until I can't help it: "Why the cotton candy booth, though?"

"Are you kidding?" Andrew looks at me, incredulous. "That would be, like, the *best* carnival job."

"The stickiest job," I correct.

Benny hums in agreement. "I'd work the Tilt-A-Whirl."

I grimace deeply. "That's a lot of puke to clean up." Andrew shivers in response, and I look at him. "What? You think people won't be hurling around the cotton candy booth?"

Benny laughs and closes his eyes, tilting his face to the sky. "What are we even talking about anymore?"

The sun has long since disappeared behind the mountains, and I'm so deeply tired that it feels like gravity's pulling more heavily on me. "Andrew," I say, "it's gonna be really cold out in the Boathouse."

Beside me, he goes still. "How'd you kn—"

"Another hunch."

He sits with this for a second, then says, "Still better than a bunk bed."

"I guess," I concede. "But let's beat out those old sleeping bags in the basement before you head out there tonight. I don't want you to freeze. Let's save you and the protruding parts of your body."

"I . . ." He stares at me. "Sleeping bags?" At my silence, he adds quietly, "Another hunch?"

"Yup."

Two dimples dive into his cheeks. "You worried about me out there, Maisie?"

"I'm always worried about you," I say.

"And my protruding body parts?"

Next to me, I sense Benny is valiantly trying to disappear into the swing.

"Always," I say, adding with unbridled honesty: "I love you massively. Let's get you set up out there, and then I can take a nap."

When I look over at him, the moment elongates; he isn't laughing, teasing, or playing. He's just staring at me. Our gazes don't break, and for just a breath, Andrew's attention dips to my mouth and I see his lips make a small, surprised pout. Like he's seeing something new on my face that wasn't there before.

If only this were *his* fuse box moment, a boulder rolling over. A girl can dream.

Still, the sensation of his attention is a drug, and when I try to stand up, I weave in place, nearly falling. Both Benny and Andrew bolt up to catch me. But Andrew has me first and more securely—his hands come up to my forearms, steadying me as I crowd into his space.

I can't help it; my defenses are down. That Andrew hug I've always wanted? It's happening now. I step forward into his arms.

I only need it for a second. I just want to be held, to be hugged by him in a moment that isn't about saying hello or goodbye. I can tell he's surprised at first, but then his arms come around my waist as mine come around his neck, and I pull him closer, so tight.

I crack open an eye, waiting to be jerked back to the plane. I know it's coming because here I am, being greedy and making this about me instead of something much, much bigger.

But my feet stay rooted on the porch.

"I'm just gonna—" Benny quickly fades into the background, unobtrusively making his way to the front door. Bless you, Benny.

"Hey. You okay?" Andrew asks against my hair.

"Yeah." I close my eyes and turn my face into his neck. With a hit of the warm, soft smell of him, I try to swallow down the affection swelling in my throat. But it sticks there, like a pill swallowed without water.

"Just needed a hug?" There's a smile in his scratchy voice, and I nod. The Cure's "Just Like Heaven" filters out from his headphones; the sound is muffled by the press of our bodies, but the melody is clear enough to push an ache of nostalgia between my ribs. I've heard Andrew sing this song a hundred times. Music is entwined with his DNA, it is the bedrock of his gentle happiness, and right now this hug feels like a lullaby, like a calming melody hummed at bedtime.

Frankly, I could stay like this forever, but deep inside I know this isn't what the universe is asking me to do. I squeeze him closer one last time, and then step back. "That was just what the doctor ordered. You give good hug, Mandrew."

"Well, thanks, ma'am." His hair falls like wild brambles over his forehead. Eyes so bright and green I've always found the color mesmerizing. He licks his lips, and I stare at a mouth that is full and flirty and pointed at me. He pushes his hair off his forehead, only to have it fall forward again.

My filter is momentarily broken. "What is *up* with you?" I ask quietly.

He laughs. "What's up with me? What's up with you? Who is this demanding new Mae who needs drinks and hugs?"

"You wouldn't believe me if I told you," I say.

"Well, whatever it is, I like her," he tells me. "You're making me feel a little drunk, out of the blue. Which isn't a bad thing, by the way."

Before I can think too much on what he means, his mouth curves into a grin and Andrew tugs my knit cap over my eyes so all I get of his retreat is a laugh.

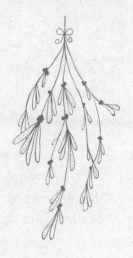

chapter twelve

Even though, if I do the math, I've eaten this same breakfast twice in forty-eight hours, I still go to town the following morning. Do I usually try to ensure that there's enough food to make it around the table? Of course. But I also know that there's twice as many blintzes in the warming oven, and that we never finish, and what are we here for, anyway? To leave perfectly good food on the table? No way. Not on my unpredictable watch.

Andrew takes the suddenly-much-lighter platter from me, laughing. "I see that we're still getting rambunctious Mae this morning. I approve."

"Listen," I say. "There's enough for a crowd of fifty. Let's stop pretending we don't want to put our whole faces in this plate and pick up the slack."

Game for this, Andrew takes a heaping pile of blintzes,

and then loads up his plate with more bacon and eggs when they come around. "I'll regret this."

I stick a big bite in my mouth, speaking around it. "Will you, though?"

He gives me a smile that reads, *You're right, I won't.*

"If you bring this same energy to building snow creatures this morning," Aaron says, letting the meat platter pass him by, "it could be either very good or very bad for your chances of winning." He's still in his pajamas, and I feel like I should warn him about the wardrobe malfunction he'll experience in a few hours, but I'm not sure there's a way to sanely explain how I know that.

"What's that supposed to mean?" I ask instead.

"I think what he's saying," Kyle says, taking the platter from his husband, "is that your vibe this year feels a little . . ."

"Unpredictable," Dad finishes, carefully.

"He means 'nuts,'" Miles corrects.

"That is not what I meant, actually."

Kennedy smashes her pancakes with a fork. "What kind of nuts?"

Miles looks up from his phone. "The crazy kind."

Zachary stands up on his chair. "I don't like walnuts."

"Miles," Mom chides.

"What?"

"It's Christmas. Be nice to your sister," she says.

Kyle wrestles Zachary into his seat. "When I was a backup dancer for Janet Jackson," he continues, "we called this sort of mood 'frizzly.'"

Andrew meets my eyes as if to say *Please note Janet Jackson backup dancer mention, number one.*

"'Frizzly' is a good description for how I'm feeling." I don't add that even though I'm the one whose *vibe is unpredictable*, everyone but Aaron has taken twice as much food as they usually do, too.

Kyle hands the empty platter to Theo, who complains that he has to go refill it.

"Mae." I look up to see Theo standing back from the table, giving me the boy chin lift to indicate that I should come with him. To help him open the oven? To hold the platter while he fills it?

Instead, I gesture how busy I am, thwack a giant dollop of jam on my blintzes, mumble, "Why the hell not?" and follow with an enormous spoonful of applesauce.

But with this masterpiece in front of me, it is easy to ignore the gaping stares around the table.

"Honey," Mom says gently, "are you sure you want to eat all that?"

I never argue with my mother, but since none of this matters anyway—

"My eyes say yes," I tell her. "My stomach says probably not. But these are the best blintzes I'll have all year, and who knows when I'll get them again?" I look at Benny and wink. "Well, except me. For sure I'll get them again." I nose-dive my fork, spearing a bite of food.

Benny gives me a gentle warning look. "Take it easy, kiddo. Why don't you keep the condiments moving?"

With a frown, I hand them to Andrew, who gamely smothers his own breakfast.

"Mae," Kennedy says from the far end of the table, "if you eat all of that, you will throw up."

"I ate four chocolate chip pancakes once and threw up in Papa's car," Zachary says.

Kennedy closes her eyes. "It smelled bad for a long time."

"Like the subway," Zachary adds enthusiastically.

"Kennedy, Zachary," Aaron begins, "no vomit talk at the table."

"That's right," Ricky says, helpfully redirecting. "Let's talk about building. Everyone know what they're making this year?"

Andrew leans in, whispering in my ear. "I was thinking we could do a panda."

I shake my head and turn my face to his. We're only a few inches apart. He has a tiny dot of applesauce just below his lip. In my head, I lick it off, and a voice inside me purrs, *Just do it. He won't remember anyway.*

"We're going to build a snow monkey," I tell him. "Her name is going to be Thea, and we're going to win."

• • •

Andrew bends, carefully sculpting Thea's face. All around us, everyone works in focused silence. Not a snowball in sight.

"So, we never really talked about this stuff, but you're still in Berkeley, right? Not back in LA?"

I look over at him, surprised by the question. I mean, I'm not surprised that he asked it—it's an obvious thing to talk about with someone you only see a few times a year. What surprises me is how Real Life Mae feels like someone who existed a long, long time ago. I am now Cabin Mae. Time

Loop Utah Mae. Apparently she spends all her time with Cabin Andrew. For all I know, I might never go back home again. If this time jump keeps happening, I might never leave Utah, and the real world will never know I ever left.

Exhaling slowly, I say, "Yeah, LA wasn't really working." In truth, LA didn't work because I shouldn't have taken the job to begin with. I was fresh out of college and it was a graphic designer job at a tiny startup that could barely pay me a living wage in one of the most expensive and least accessible cities in the country. The shame of moving back in with my mother—and her new husband—was immediately outweighed by the relief of not having to use a credit card to pay my bills. But two years later, I feel less money-smart and more failure-to-launch.

"But life is good?"

"I mean," I say, "I don't have to pay rent, and I get to hang out with Miles whenever he'll have me. But I also sleep in my childhood twin bed and know what it sounds like when my mother and her new husband have sex, so . . . define 'good.'"

He winces deeply, groaning, "*Why?*"

"Listen, if I suffer, you suffer."

"How's work, then?"

I pack a bit more snow onto Thea's abdomen. "It's okay."

"Easy," he says, and his deep voice vibrates down my spine, "don't get overexcited on me."

This makes me laugh. "Sorry. It's just that when I took the job, I thought I'd be doing more of the fun stuff and less of the soul-sucking computer stuff."

"I thought you were doing something with kids?"

I shrug, oddly detached. "The program didn't turn out exactly how I expected."

An understatement if I've ever made one. When I moved home, I applied for a job at a Berkeley-based nonprofit whose goal is to bring free, innovative programs to disadvantaged and low-income kids. Having double majored in graphic arts (Mom told me to chase my dreams) and finance (Dad told me to be practical), I proposed building free afternoon programs in downtown Berkeley where kids could learn graphic art and design. In a perfect world, I'd teach the classes, and the kids would build their résumés *and* earn money for college by offering low-cost graphic design services to local businesses.

"Your boss didn't go for your plan?" he asks, and uses his thumb to carefully swipe away a line of loose snow.

"Oh, she loved the idea," I tell him. "We spent over a year mapping out how it could work, determining what funds would need to be raised and how to raise them, working out the licensing, and debating how to staff the site."

"Right, okay, I remember that bit."

"And she did. Staff the site, that is. This past summer she hired a friend of hers to teach the course."

He lets out a low, sympathetic groan. "Wait, so after all that setup, you're not even running it?"

I shake my head. "Neda—my boss—figured with my accounting degree, it would be better for 'the team' if I managed the books."

"You're doing the *accounting*?"

"I do some of the website stuff, too, but yeah. The accounting takes up most of my time." I crouch near

Thea's legs and pack in a bit more snow at her haunches. "I've never even met one of the students, because the way we—or I should say *I*—carefully worded the licensing, we protect the kids by not having adults in the classroom who aren't part of the curriculum. I love what we do, I just don't love my part in it."

"This may be overstepping, but what if you quit? The great thing about being at home is you have a safety net if you need it."

He isn't the first person to suggest it. My closest friend from college, Mira, has been trying to convince me to leave this job for months now. I'm notoriously terrible at jumping without a parachute, so I face the interminable chicken-and-egg problem: if I found another job, I could quit, but finding another job means admitting that I'm going to quit. The entire loop is paralyzing.

"Eh," I say, eloquently.

Andrew frowns sympathetically. "That sucks, Maisie. I'm sorry."

It does, but my attention is suddenly drawn to what's happening elsewhere. Or, rather, to what's not happening. Everyone is still so focused, so silent. Andrew and I are the only two people talking. I'm not seeing any of the open-mouthed laughs or hearing any of the excited screams of the snowball fight. I can tell how hard we're all working on our projects, but we're doing it because that's what we do. That's the routine. But no one—not even Ricky—is relishing it.

The snowball fight was spontaneous, it was hilarious. It made everyone laugh and feel connected. I shouldn't have ever tried to stop it.

"This isn't right," I say.

Andrew looks at me, and then out at our families. "What isn't right?"

"They're all moving like cyborgs. What are we even doing this for?"

"Because it's tradition," Andrew says, like it's obvious—and it is—but how many of us really care anymore? He follows my attention to the other groups, working with grim determination.

I stand, grinning over at him, before bending to scoop up a big ball of snow. Packing it tight in my palms, I scan my eyes across the potential victims. "The question is who deserves *this*."

Without hesitation, Andrew bends, packing his own snowball. "Theo."

"Maybe Miles."

"Maybe your dad."

"*Definitely* my dad," I agree.

"My mom chose that horrible music even though you told her not to," he counters.

"Kyle never gets hungover. It's unfair," I say.

Andrew hums. "Do you think the snowball would disappear into the black hole of Aaron's dye job?"

"Worth testing," I agree. "Science depends on us."

"But then there's Benny," he says. "He's been chilling on the front steps with a warm cup of coffee this whole time."

"Because he's smart."

"Damn him and his good decisions." Andrew tosses the snowball back and forth between his hands.

"Benny, then. On the count of three," I say. "One."

"Two."

"Three."

We launch our snowballs directly at an unsuspecting Benny. Mine hits him in the shoulder. Andrew's hits him squarely in the chest. At first, he looks at us with deep and immediate betrayal. But something shifts in his expression when he sees me and Andrew standing here together, bending to pack fresh snowballs. Maybe he sees the dynamite in my gaze, or maybe he can tell how much Andrew needs this change in the routine—maybe he even sees how much I need this to happen—but he picks up a clump of snow himself, packs it, and hurls it directly at Ricky.

Within only a handful of seconds, I lose track of who's hit me, who's hit Andrew, when Thea gets crushed, and what's even happening amid the flurry of flying snow. All I know is that the sound of my loved ones' laughter bouncing off the hillside is the best sound I've ever heard.

Another small victory.

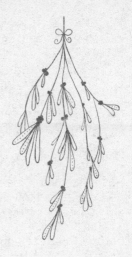

chapter thirteen

The Park City Nursery is a traditional nursery most of the year, but in the winter it's transformed into a twinkling, sparkling wonderland. The little green building that usually houses gardening tools is covered in a selection of fresh wreaths and filled with holiday decorations and gifts. Strands of lights stretch overhead, and instead of pots of brightly colored summer blossoms, there are holly garlands, poinsettias, and tiny fir trees everywhere. There's even a giant firepit ringed with seating, and employees handing out spiced cider.

Usually Dad and Ricky brave the masses, but tonight I needed to get out of the house. Since just doing what I want hasn't failed me yet, I told Andrew he should come with me. Happy to avoid navigating this mess, the dads dropped us at the curb, headed to a coffee shop, and told us to call them when we had a tree ready to load up.

I can feel Andrew watching me as we maneuver through the crowd, and it has the odd effect of making me feel both overheated and shivery. "I should have asked *you* about work," I say, stepping around a couple crouching to check the price of a tree.

"You were too busy starting a snowball war."

I laugh. "How are things in Denver?"

"I'm in that strange position," he says, "of having the utterly perfect job, but absolutely no opportunity for advancement. The only other position above mine is lead sound engineer, and the guy in that job is only five years older than me and is never going to leave Red Rocks."

Andrew has always been what we affectionately refer to as a sound geek. He took every music class he could find in school and went to every show that came through town. I envy his love for what he does; he'd probably do the work for free.

"Have you ever thought about getting into music production?"

He shakes his head. "I don't have the mental intensity for that life."

"Want me to knock this coworker off? Maybe my career problem is that I haven't found my true calling as an assassin."

Andrew grins. "I wanted to say, you will figure things out, Mae. You're so talented. The artistic apple doesn't fall far from the artistic tree."

His perennial confidence in me is bolstering. "Thanks, Mandrew."

"This is random, but have you ever had your tarot cards read?" he asks.

"Is that a serious question?"

He laughs. "Yes?"

"I haven't," I admit, "partly because I never want to hear bad news."

"I had mine done," he says, and immediately holds up his hands. "I know, it sounds crazy—believe me, I thought it was a joke—but a woman was reading them at a party. She says only assholes do tragic readings."

"You think I should have my tarot cards read to find out my true career path?" The last thing I need, I think, is to play with more cosmic energy.

"I'm just saying maybe it'll shake something in you." He shrugs sweetly. "I feel like it shook something in me."

A woman elbows me accidentally as she passes, sloshing my hot cider off the lip of my cup and down my hand. I hiss at the mild burn.

"Is it always like this? I don't think I realized everyone else in Park City procrastinates as much as we do." I bend, licking the sweet drink from my finger. I might be imagining it, but I swear Andrew does a double take.

"I bet most of these people don't live here and are also vacationers getting their own last-minute trees." He pushes his hands into his pockets. "Dad always complains that it's a madhouse."

"Parking must be a nightmare. Why don't we have them drop us off every year?"

Andrew gives me that look, the one that tells me it's a silly question. *We do it because that's how we've always done it*, his eyes say. *Tradition, duh.* How many things like this do we do without thinking, just because it's the way we've always done it? The same food at every meal; the same games every night, with the same teams. The same songs. I'm the worst of all of us—I'm never willing to give up a single thing.

Being hit with the realization is like having a light turned on in my brain.

Holiday music plays overhead and Andrew bops contentedly along beside me. With these new eyes, I wonder if he's been suffocating under the predictability of the holidays—if we all have.

"Do you hate the traditions?" I ask. "Snow creatures and sledding and all the games?"

He gives his answer a second of quiet consideration. "I *love* the sledding and don't hate the rest. But, yeah, sometimes I want to mix it up a little. We've been doing the same thing for our entire lives." He points as we approach a beautifully symmetrical Douglas fir. "How about that one?"

I scrunch my nose, shaking my head.

"I know Mom and Dad love hosting here," he says, moving on, "but don't you ever just want to get on a plane and do something totally wild? Go to Greece or spend New Year's in London?" Before I can answer, he points to another tree. "That one?"

"No . . ."

"No to the tree, or to doing something totally wild?"

I smile over at him. "Both? And New Year's in London. Hmm. Would we all be together in this imaginary scenario?"

His eyes sparkle, and sensation zips up my spine. I swear he's never looked at me like this, like he's seeing me for the first time. "Of course."

"Okay, then yes, that sounds amazing. Even though the cabin is my favorite place on earth, I'm starting to think that it wouldn't be so terrible to mix things up. Maybe we should do things because we love them, not because we've always done them that way." I pause, carefully wording the next question in my mind. "Andrew?"

He turns his face up to the sky, admiring a towering tree. Tiny snowflakes have started to drift down, spinning from the clouds. "Mm?"

"The cabin needs a lot of work, doesn't it?"

His smile fades and he looks back at me. "A fair bit, yeah."

"Like what?"

"Gotta refinish the floors," he says. "Paint the interior and exterior. Most of the appliances are as old as I am. New roof."

"How much is a new roof?" A ball of dread worms its way through my gut.

"The conservative estimate was twelve thousand dollars," he says. So they've looked into it. "If we go with cedar shingles like the original, we're looking at double that. Not to mention there's probably some decking up there that will need to be replaced once we start tearing everything off."

Holy crap.

I just come right out and ask it. "Your parents want to sell, don't they?"

Andrew doesn't even seem surprised by this. "I think so."

"Do you and Theo want to sell it?"

He carefully maneuvers past two kids playing tag

around a tree. "I don't, but I'm in Denver. I don't really feel like I can urge them to keep it when I'm not here to help out. Theo just bought that land down in Ogden. He'll be building soon and won't be around as much. Mom and Dad aren't as flexible and energetic as they used to be. It's a lot for them to take on by themselves."

"But why should they when we're all here?"

Andrew stops in the path and looks down at me. "You're in California, and Kyle and Aaron are in New York."

"I mean, we could come out and help throughout the year."

His hair pushes out rebelliously from under his knit cap, and when his gaze fixes on me, I'm dizzy with infatuation. "Dad is proud," he says, glancing briefly over my shoulder, I presume, to make sure that his dad is, in fact, not approaching. "He doesn't like asking for help, and he's terrible about accepting help offered. Especially from us kids."

I know this is true; I can even remember times when I was younger and Ricky would insist that Mom didn't have to cook when she was at the cabin, like he could ever stop her. But I don't just mean help from other parents. There's a beast in me that's pushing against my skin from the inside, clawing its way out. I don't want to be a child anymore.

"We aren't kids, though."

His gaze sinks lower, and I don't miss the way it pauses at my mouth. "We haven't been kids for a long time."

The effect of his rumbling words is not unlike taking a muscle relaxant. "And your parents like hosting, I know.

They love being parents, love taking care of all of us. But it's time we all stepped up."

He turns to start walking again. "You say that as if your parents don't like being parents."

Instinctively, and even though it's Andrew asking, I tread carefully here. "You know Mom is amazing, and fiercely protective. But their relationship has always been so messy, it's hard to push to the front sometimes."

"We've never talked about the fact that your parents are divorced and still come here every year."

"Mom's husband, Victor—"

"The husband who does not spend Christmas with his wife?" Andrew says, grinning slyly at me.

"That's the one. He has two daughters, and they have families of their own. They're both on the East Coast, so even though he lives for my mother, he's happy to get time with his girls over the holidays without the complication of stepfamilies. I know this sounds silly, because I'm supposed to be an adult and shouldn't need my mommy and daddy to be together at Christmas, but this is the one week of the year that we act like a family again."

"I don't think that's silly," he says. "I used to feel so bad for you."

I'm a little startled by the track change. "For me?" He nods. "Why?"

Andrew looks at me like this should be obvious.

"No, seriously," I say. "Why?"

"Because for a few years I saw how much you struggled with your parents being together at the cabin, but it was obvious they weren't *together*. You were all here physically, but there were times you looked so . . . sad," he says. "And then the year they announced their divorce, it was like you could breathe again."

I stare at him, stunned. He saw all that in me?

"I'm sorry," he says quickly, "I'm speaking out my ass, I don't—"

"Don't," I cut in. "Don't apologize. I'm just surprised, I guess. That you saw that."

"I've known you your whole life, Mae. How could I not?" He grins at me again. "And here you are this year, impulsive and taking up space and flipping all expectations. You're all take-charge and bossy."

"I'm just seeing things with fresh eyes, I guess. It's time to grow up."

Andrew bats at some fluffy snow on a branch. "Coming into this holiday like a wrecking ball."

A rebellious streak races through me. "It's more like, I see my life stretching out ahead of me and figure, why not go for what I want?"

"Jam *and* applesauce on your blintzes," he jokes. "Cocktails on the porch. Snowball fights."

The word rockets from me: "You."

His smile freezes, and then slowly slips away. "Me?" An awkward laugh escapes. "Well, you've got me." He grins and spreads his arms wide, gesturing around us to the trees and snow, the twinkling lights overhead.

"It's more than wanting your company at the tree farm, and I think you know it." My heart is racing. "But we can pretend that's what I meant, so it doesn't get weird."

Andrew stares at me, and I'm both proud and horrified to

realize I've made him speechless. "You mean . . . like . . . ?"
His brows rise meaningfully.

Adrenaline spikes my blood. "Yeah. Like that."

"I sort of assumed you and Theo—"

"No."

"But he—"

"*He* may have, but I haven't." Guilt flashes coolly
through me, and I clarify, "I've never felt that way about
him, I mean."

"Oh." Even in the low light, I can tell he's blushing hotly.
Have I ruined what was burbling between us? Maybe. But
all of this is instructive, I realize. At least the next time I
reboot, I'll know what *not* to say.

"Come on." I tug on his sleeve. "Let's find a tree."

We move forward, but the silence hangs heavily. The
crunch of snow between our boots, the audible gulp of Andrew swallowing a sip of cider. I scrape around in my brain
for a way to change the subject, but I can't find anything.

Finally he manages, "Do you, um, have any goals for the
New Year?"

God, this is painful. And all of the answers that immediately pop to mind are things I can't say—*I'd like to figure out
why I keep time traveling*—or most likely impossible: *I'd like
to kiss you on the mouth. I'd like to quit my job . . .*

I stop in the path. "Yeah. I do, actually."

On an impulse that feels like a damn revelation, I pull
out my phone and start a new email to my boss.

Neda, please consider this my 30-day notice. I
appreciate all of the opportunities you've given me,

but I am ready to explore new adventures. Happy to talk more after the holidays.

All my best, Maelyn

Before I can question myself, I hit send. Deep breath in, and another one out. Neda appreciates frank and straight-to-the-point. It's fine.

Oh my God. I really did that. Relief falls over me like a weighted blanket. "Wow, that felt good."

"What's that?" Andrew asks.

I grin over at him. "I quit my job."

"You—? *Just now?*" His eyebrows disappear beneath his wild curls. "Wow. Okay. You are figuring things out, aren't you?"

"I'm trying." I close my eyes and take another long, slow breath. "It was time. I hope it changes things."

"How could it not? That's a huge decision."

I look up at him. "It's just hard to know which choice is right until it's all over, I guess."

"Isn't that the truth?" Andrew stops in front of another tree, spreading his arms out like he might hug it. "This one."

But this tree isn't right, either. My biggest fear in the car before the accident was the prospect of things changing. But isn't that what I wanted when I threw that wish out to the universe? For *everything* to change?

"I don't like any of these," I admit.

"These are literally perfect trees," Andrew says.

"I think that's why."

Change can be good.

I push through a row toward the back, where they hide

the trees that are flat on one side, sparse in obvious places. Too short, too skinny, too crooked.

And there, at the end of the row, is a tree that is all of those things. "That one."

Andrew laughs. "Dad will have a stroke if we bring that out to the truck."

"Actually, no." I stare at it, grinning, and feel Andrew's stance match my own. "I don't think he will."

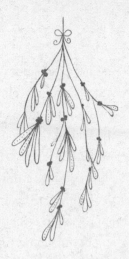

chapter fourteen

While Ricky and Dad unload the tree from the car and get it into the stand, and the twins and Lisa dive into the boxes of ornaments to find their favorite ones to hang, I linger at the back of the room, sitting in this weird new energy. Every other year—even this one—I was down there with the kids, diving into the decorations. But if change means telling Andrew how I feel and finally quitting my job, it also means loosening my stranglehold on tradition and letting Kennedy and Zachary take the lead on decorating the tree.

And since we're barreling into this grown-up thing, change also means helping more, and not leaving it to Aaron or Benny to clean up the cocktail-hour detritus strewn around the living room.

As I gather and carry dishes into the kitchen, I take the time to really look at the cabin. I notice scratches in the floors, wear on the banister from generations of hands sliding over the smooth wooden flourish at the bottom of the stairs. Paint is peeling near the crown molding, and faded on the walls near the front door and down the hallway. Without the lens of nostalgia, I see that this house is well loved, but worn. Those are just the cosmetic things, too. The cabin is old, spending a third of the year in snow and another third in stifling dry heat. It's going to take more than love and appreciation to help Ricky and Lisa keep this place.

Benny comes up behind me as I'm loading dirty dishes into the dishwasher. "Hey, Mayday."

"Hey, Benihana."

"How was the tree farm?" His smile pushes through his accent, curling around the words.

I turn to face him, leaning back against the sink. "It was awesome, actually."

Benny's intrigued. "'Awesome'? I saw that handful of sticks and figured it had to be the last tree."

"Come on," I say. "You have to admit it's hard not to root for the underdog. That poor tree was otherwise destined for the chipper. We saved it."

Benny concedes this with a little eyebrow quirk, and I look over his shoulder to make sure we're still alone. "But that wasn't entirely why the tree farm was awesome." I pause, biting the tip of my thumb. "I told Andrew about my feelings."

His eyes go wide. "You did?"

"I mean," I say, "not like, 'I want you, Andrew, and if you proposed right now I would say yes without hesitation,' but we made a joke about me going after what I want this week and I said that I wanted him."

"Wow." He steeples his hands and presses them to his lips.

"Oh, and I quit my job."

At this, Benny takes a surprised step closer. "You what?"

"Yup. I emailed Neda and gave her my thirty days'."

"Just like that? Just . . . *now*? While you were out?"

"Yes! And it's so freeing! What a revelation. I'll have to look for a new job—but so what? What's the worst that could happen?"

Benny flinches. *"You're really saying that?"*

I pull my shoulders to my ears, bracing as I look around the room to make sure the ceiling isn't sagging just above my head. "Oops. Okay, that was stupid."

"But . . . what did Andrew say?" Benny asks. "About your feelings?"

"Not much, actually." I frown. "It wasn't exactly awkward, but it wasn't like he blew out a big relieved breath and told me he's always felt the same, either."

My brain seems to be calming incrementally the longer I'm here and not bolting awake on the plane. It's a relief to let these things out in the open, but embarrassment sends a shiver through me. "Ugh. Actually, now that I think about it, it was a little awkward."

"Andrew is a laid-back dude," Benny reminds me. "Hard to rattle."

True, but . . . "He didn't say much."

"He's an American with an Aussie soul," he says, laughing. "He tends to chew on things. Doesn't overreact in the moment."

I pull out a kitchen chair and sit down at the table. Benny

does the same. "Maybe, but even if he never mentions it again, it's okay." I give him a resolved nod. "If I'm going to do this vacation over and over, I might as well just put everything out there at least once."

"You don't necessarily *know* that you're going to do this over and over," Benny reasons.

I've been thinking about this myself. "I've almost made it through two whole days."

He reaches for a high five, but I leave him hanging, before tapping a single finger to the middle of his palm.

"*Oi*," he protests.

Down the hallway, a commotion erupts when Kyle and Mom are caught under the mistletoe, which has apparently been transferred somewhere in the living room. Benny and I take a beat to grin at the sound of my mother laughing hysterically as Kyle plants one on her.

But back to business: "Tomorrow is December twenty-second," I say. "Day three."

"Isn't that good?"

"Well, I'm thinking there might be a pattern here." I tick off on my fingers: "The first time, I was sent back to the plane on the first night. The second time, I only made it to the second morning. There's a really good chance I'll make it to the third day—tomorrow—but then have to start all over again." Seriously, could anything sound more terrible? Having to live in a time loop over and over, and each time you add just *one* new day at the end?

Torture.

"I'm not sure that's the only possibility," Benny says, and takes my hands in his. "You always hold back so much.

Maybe it's not about making the right choices exactly, but making the right choices because you're finally being *you*. Maybe that's what you needed."

"Or maybe it has nothing to do with me? I don't know," I tell him honestly. "I'm just tired of being so careful all the time."

He leans back with a bright smile, pointing at me. "*Exactly*."

• • •

With these words echoing in my thoughts, I follow Benny back into the living room, where the twins are directing the tree decoration. Kyle is mixing new drinks for whoever wants them, Aaron is on the couch in a fitted track-suit, Dad is on his stomach under the tree, futzing with the stand, and Theo approaches, handing me a tumbler with a clear, sparkling liquid—very little ice—and a slice of lime. His expression is tentative and guilty, like he feels the wedge between us but obviously has no idea what's causing it.

I haven't given myself a second to mourn the change in our relationship, and how I know that even if everyone else has the luxury of ignorance, I don't. Our mistake—and Theo's reaction the next day—would have created a fracture in this weird, wonderful group. There's no question about that now.

Friends our whole lives, and Theo couldn't put on a brave face over his denied boner for a single morning? This group survived the awkwardness of my parents' divorce, so I trust that it can handle something infinitely less dramatic than that, but I never want to take these friendships for granted.

I bend, smelling the drink.

"It's just sparkling water," he says, mildly offended.

"Oh. Thanks."

"Wanna hang later?"

I take a sip. "Hang where?"

"Downstairs? Miles and I were talking about playing some games after dinner."

That sounds decidedly more wholesome than I was expecting. "Board or video?"

I can tell he's getting annoyed. "Whichever gets you to play. I've barely seen you since you got here."

Are we really only grounded in such childhood habits? In order to spend time together, do we have to find a game to play? It feels so obvious.

Before I can answer, Aaron speaks up from where he's now squeezing in between Lisa and Mom hanging ornaments. "Interesting choice here." He's definitely been working out because he winces as he tries to hang an ornament and finally just . . . weakly tosses it in the direction of his target, hoping it hooks on the landing. "Were they all out of normal trees?"

"It's the one Mae wanted," Andrew says from out of sight on the other side of the pine. "I like it."

My chest fills with warm, glowing embers.

Mom comes up behind me, putting her arms around my waist and her chin on my shoulder. "I agree with Andrew."

She hums happily, and at the sound of her voice, my

stomach drops to my feet with a daughter's instinctive uneasiness: somehow, in the past hour, I managed to keep from pondering how I'll tell my mother that I quit my job, that I did it impulsively, and that I have no idea what I'm doing next.

It doesn't matter, I remind myself. *None of this is going to stick.*

She kisses me, saying, "Love you, Noodle," against my cheek.

I'll tell her later. If and when I have to.

Despite the jokes about this wacky, knobby tree, I can tell from their expressions that everyone sort of digs it. *National Lampoon's Christmas Vacation* plays on the TV in the background, and while we watch Clark Griswold attempt to bring his mammoth tree inside, we do our best to fill this tiny one with lights, and ornaments, and the popcorn garland the twins and Mom spent the evening making. By the time we're done decorating, the room is bursting with joy. It's nearly impossible to see any bit of actual tree underneath all the everything, but it is, oddly, perfect.

However, it takes almost a half hour to get a reasonably acceptable group photo in front of it. With this many people, of course it's expected there will be a few closed eyes, or a handful of awkward expressions. If only we were that lucky. Lisa sets up a tripod but can't get the timer right. In two photos Zachary is picking his nose, in one he's trying to feed the treasure to Miso. We catch Miles midsneeze; Mom can't get her Rudolph earrings to flash in sync with the camera. Theo is looking at his phone in one, and checking to see if his zipper is down in the next. (It was.) For the next, Miso jumps in front of the camera. Then Miso jumps on Kennedy and it takes a little while to calm her down. Ricky's kissing Lisa in one and can't manage a casual smile in the others. The more we point it out, the worse it gets.

I remind myself that change is also not crying out "But—tradition!" when Theo impatiently steps in for Lisa and resets the tripod with his phone.

Good news: now we're all in frame. Bad news: Kyle's highlighter is so on point and in focus that he looks like a disco ball.

"Fuck it," he says just as the oven timer goes off for dinner. "Good enough."

• • •

After we've stuffed ourselves, we scatter around the living room, falling into a comfortable quiet.

The living room is a majestic place—I mean, it is massive—with vaulted log ceilings and old wood floors covered in wide woven rugs. Along one long wall, the fire crackles and snaps, heating the room to just below too warm. It's wood from town and nothing smells like it. I want to find a candle of this, incense, room spray. I want every living room in every house I live in for the rest of time to smell like the Hollis cabin does on December evenings.

The hearth is expansive; when we were about seven, and our chore was sweeping out the fireplace at the end of the holiday, Theo and I could almost stand up inside it. The flames actually roar to life. Even once they mellow into a rumbling, crackling simmer, the blaze still feels like a living, breathing creature in here with us.

A plate of cookies sits on the coffee table. Mom and Dad occupy opposite sides of the love seat, reading their respective books. Benny, Kyle, and Aaron are doing a puzzle on the floor with Kennedy while Zachary sits on Benny's back and pretends he's a motorcycle. Christmas music plays quietly in the background, and Lisa futzes around, adjusting the lights, poking the fire, fetching throw blankets for us. Ricky is on a call in the kitchen, and Theo slumps on the couch, scrolling through his phone.

Seeing him sparks a memory in me: this night, the first time around, I was sitting next to him and we spent the evening going down various Instagram rabbit holes together, totally oblivious to other people around us. Which was such a teenage-y thing to do, now that I think about it. Why didn't we hang with the others, and how often were we like that? Is that why Andrew thought that Theo and I . . . ?

Maybe if I had spent this evening just enjoying the ritual and the sheer bliss that comes from being in a room full of people I adore, things wouldn't have turned out the way they did.

I shuffle over to the tree, sliding beneath it and lying on my back so I can look up through the gnarled branches. It's a kaleidoscope of color and texture: the smooth light bulbs, the prickly pine needles. Ornaments of glass, and silk, and spiky metallic stars. A little

wooden drummer Theo gave Ricky nearly twenty years
ago. Laminated paper ornaments of our handprints from
preschool, handmade ceramic blobs that were supposed
to be pigs, or cows, or dogs. Nothing matches; there's no
theme. But there is so much love in this tree, so much
history.

Beside me, a shadow blocks the heat and light of the
fire, before sliding beneath the tree. I turn my head, coming
eye to twinkling eye with Andrew.

My heart trips over itself. After the tree farm, I wasn't
sure whether he'd keep his distance.

"This looks like a good idea," he says, turning his face
up to the branches overhead. His profile is illuminated
with blues and yellows, reds and greens. A few lights make
flashing patterns through the ornaments and onto his cheekbones. "Smells good, too."

"It's pretty, isn't it?" I shift a little, scooting deeper
beneath the branches. I wonder what we look like from
the outside: two sets of legs, sticking out from under the
tree like the Wicked Witch of the East trapped beneath
Dorothy's house. "A good thinking spot."

"And what were you thinking about?" he asks.

"I was thinking about how much I like this tree."

He reaches over, eyes unfocused as he moves his
thumb across my cheek. An echo of electricity lingers on
my skin once he's lifted his hand, and it takes me a second
to focus on the thumb he's showing me. "Drop of water,"
he says.

"Oh."

"Must have dripped from the tree."

I laugh. "Are you saying I have a moisture problem again?"

Andrew blinks before he bursts out laughing. "What?"

Oh, crap. That wasn't this timeline. That was before. This Andrew isn't in on the inside joke. "Pretend I didn't say that."

His eyes gleam in delight. "Did you actually just say you have a *moisture problem*?"

"No." I might die from this. "Yes." I bite my lip, trying not to laugh. "Ignore it. Let's move on."

I can tell he's a cat who'd like to play with this mouse a bit longer, but he gives me a little shrug, gamely singing, "*Okay.*" Andrew turns his attention to the branches above him, using his old-man voice. "Maisie?"

"Yes, Mandrew?"

"You know what just occurred to me?"

"What just occurred to you?"

"We brought this tree in, like, two hours ago. What if there's a squirrel still living in there?"

We stare at each other, wide-eyed, and shout in unison: "Ahhh!"

I've completely forgotten that my phone is in my pocket until it buzzes, interrupting our laughter. There is no one in the world I need to talk to right now who isn't in this room with me, so I ignore it. It immediately buzzes again.

"Your butt is vibrating," Andrew says.

"If it's my boss replying to me right now, I'm going to need something stronger than sparkling water." I pull it out and look. It isn't Neda, thankfully; it's a text from Theo.

Whatre you doing in there

No punctuation, no context. Just Theo, typing like a teenager.

Hanging with Mandrew.

Come out here and hang with me

I realize Andrew is reading over my shoulder when he lets out a little laugh through his nose. "See?"

I feel myself recoil. "See what?"

He lifts his chin, indicating my phone. "You haven't spent any time with him, and he's grumpy."

"We were just talking earlier," I counter, not quite a lie.

"Are you mad at him?" he asks.

I swallow, staring up at the lights. A scattered view blinks in and out of focus. "Not exactly."

"What does 'not exactly' mean?"

I turn my head, and Andrew blinks, brows pulled low.

"It's hard to explain," I admit. "I'm not mad at him, I'm just aware that he and I are close because we've known each other forever, but not because we're *actually* close anymore." I shrug. "Just normal drifting that happens when people grow up, I guess."

He smiles at that. "Mae . . ."

I grin back at him. "Yes?"

Andrew clears his throat, a sweetly pointed *ahem*. "About what you said earlier."

Oh.

"Yeah?" The paradox of a hammering heart and dissolving stomach makes me feel light-headed.

"I appreciate your honesty," he says.

Ugh. The worst thing he could say right now.

"You don't have to let me down easy, Andrew." I reach over and playfully smack him and the tree trembles above us.

"Andrew, Mae, what are you doing in there?" Mom calls out.

"Nothing!" we answer in unison.

"Well, don't shake the tree," she chides.

Again, we answer together: "We won't!"

He turns back to me, whispering, "Are you sure Theo doesn't think you're into him?"

"Are you saying I've given him the impression that I am?"

"No, but if I assumed . . . maybe Theo assumed, too."

Well, huh. I guess if Theo thought I was into him, it might explain why he was so cold the morning after I pushed him away.

I shake my head, and Andrew turns his face back up to the lights so it's hard to read his expression. "Is it weird that I sort of worried you'd . . ." He flounders a little. "I don't know, get together and then get hurt?"

I can't even wrap my head around this. Andrew worried that I would date Theo and get my heart broken? Am I in the Upside Down? "Um, yes, it is very weird."

Andrew gives a helpless shrug in response. "He's a player. You're good."

This actually makes me laugh. "I'm *good*?"

"I don't mean—romantically, or, like, sexually," he says,

chuckling with the slightest edge of discomfort. "Not that I would know about that. I meant your soul."

"What are you even talking about?" It's a good thing I'm lying down.

"Okay, bad word choice. I mean, you're a *good* person." He turns and looks right at me. We're so close. "You love being here, you love each of us for exactly who we are. You're, like, the most generous and least judgmental person I've ever known."

"I'm not—"

"You moved home when your parents split," he rolls on. "You loved your crappy apartment and gave it up because your family needed you. You took care of Miles, you were there for your mom."

I bite my lip, glowing from his compliments.

"Do you remember when the developers built those condos behind us?" he asks. "You were so sad because Dad liked to look at the trees while he drank his coffee in the morning, and you worried the deer wouldn't have any-place to go. Theo was just happy he'd have fewer leaves to rake up."

I laugh through the fog of feelings. This is the most ex-tensive letting-her-down-easy I could possibly imagine. It is both incredibly tender and incredibly awkward. "Well, it's a non-issue. I've never been into Theo. But I'm sorry if what I said made things weird."

He reaches up, scratches his cheek, and I'm having a hard time looking away. I never get to be this close to him. He has light stubble, but it looks soft. I can make out at least four different shades of green in his eyes.

When he licks his lips, it does something electric to my pulse.

"I guess that's what I'm saying. Had I known it was a—" He stops and seems to chew on his words. Meanwhile, my brain is a nuclear reactor, melting down. Had he known it was a *what*? "I've always really admired you," he starts again. "You're one of the few people in my life I hope I'll be close to forever, and I didn't want things to be weird after the tree farm." He glances at me, his face illuminated. "I wasn't sure if I responded the way I should have. I was really surprised when you said it."

"That's okay. I was surprised when I said it, too."

He grins. "It took a lot of bravery to tell me how you feel, though, and I just wanted you to know—" He gestures between us. "It won't change this."

I know exactly what he means—we'll be the same as we've always been—and of course I'm grateful for that.

But even though I never—not in my wildest dreams— imagined he would share my affection, when he says this I am consumed with rejection. I mean, of course the entire point of telling him how I felt was so that nothing would stay the same.

"Let's move on," I say, pushing forward.

Andrew laughs. "Okay, good idea."

"You can travel anywhere, where do you go?"

He doesn't even have to think about this conversational pivot: "Budapest. You?"

"Besides here?"

Andrew rolls his eyes. "Yes, besides here."

"Okay, fine." I mentally scroll through postcard images

of various locations, feeling vaguely uninspired by my own game. "No idea. Maybe Hawaii?"

"You have the entire world to choose from and you go to Hawaii?"

"What's wrong with Hawaii?"

He shrugs. "It just feels so easy. What about Tahiti? Mallorca?"

"Sure, they sound nice."

Andrew laughs. "Okay, it's settled. With that attitude, I'm in charge of all of our future travel."

The words settle heavily between us, and we both go still.

"I made it weird," he says finally, grinning over at me.

I burst out laughing, relieved that this time it wasn't me. "You totally did."

Our laughter dies away and silence engulfs us. I don't know how to read the mood. I told him how I felt, giving him an opening to reciprocate, but he didn't. And yet . . . there's a strange understanding blooming between us.

"Okay, I have an idea," he says. "No speaking for five minutes. Let's just look up at the tree together."

"And hope we don't get our faces eaten off."

He bursts out laughing again and then wipes a hand down his face, saying playfully, "God. Why can't you ever be serious?" He wipes at his eyes. "Okay. Five minutes."

I follow his lead and focus on the tree. "Five minutes."

As odd an idea it is, it's also brilliant. It saves me from having to think about what to say, which is good, because my mind is a mortified blank sheet of nothing.

For the first thirty seconds or so, I feel like I'm drowning in the sound of everything else in the room and the contrasting quiet between us. But then the stilted awareness dissolves, and I can focus on the lights, the dangling gold ornament just to my right, the laminated picture of Theo and Andrew as little kids hanging on the branch nearby. I can focus on his warm, easy presence next to me. Andrew's arm presses along the length of mine and we just lie like that, breathing in tandem.

His stomach growls, and it makes me giggle again, and he shushes me. I turn to look at him, and he's already looking at me, and with a knowing twinkle in his eyes, he lifts his finger to his lips and whispers, "No talking. I just want to be under the tree with you."

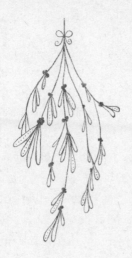

chapter fifteen

December twenty-second. Still here.

And today's theme—Sled Day—is my favorite. Unfortunately, I can imagine a million ways the universe might give me a failing grade and send me back to the start: An enormous tree branch on my head. A boulder thrown in my path. Comedic music as a backdrop while the camera captures me— the lone holiday tourist—caught at the center of an avalanche.

With trepidation, I set my feet onto the cold basement floor.

The house is quiet as I shuffle across the kitchen to stand in the window—my breath fogs up the cold glass in front of me. The gently falling flakes from last night transitioned into a full-blown storm while we slept, and the world has turned wintry white. Trees bow under the weight of fresh snow. The mountains wear sparkling, powdery caps. I'd never get tired of this view.

Lisa's cookie bars are still on the counter, so I pick up the plate and dump them straight into the trash, covering the evidence with yesterday's coffee grounds, and start a fresh pot. What do I have to lose?

On a roll now, I get breakfast started. Why wait for Mom to get up?

The smell of coffee and cooking meat is like a siren call and people slowly tumble in. Soon the TV is on in the other room, the theme music to *How the Grinch Stole Christmas!* filtering through the house.

"Thank you for getting this started, honey." Mom pulls her hair back into a bun, slips on her Mrs. Claus apron, and takes the wooden spoon from my hand, wordlessly telling me that she'll take it from here.

When I stand over the sink, I see Andrew already outside and shoveling the driveway. He's got a beanie tugged low over his hair but even from here I can see his cheeks flushed against the cold, the way his coat stretches across his back. The coat is thick, but I can easily imagine the way his muscles shift with the effort he's taking to dig the shovel beneath heavy piles of—

"Mae, honey, can you hand me the—*oh*."

I startle, turning to find my mother standing beside me. "What? What's '*oh*'?"

She struggles to look oblivious. "Nothing. Just needed"— she grabs a spatula from the drying rack—"this."

"I was just looking at the view while I clean up."

"Of course."

I turn on the water, rinse a clean dish again. "It's pretty out."

She lifts a brow and glances at the window. "It *is* pretty."

I give her a look. Indulging my mother in this kind of thing will only lead to disaster. "The *snow*."

Feet shuffle behind us, and a groggy Theo mumbles, "Did it snow?"

"It did." Mom looks at Andrew once more, and then gives me a playful smirk before walking away. When I turn back to the window, Andrew is looking up at the house, and when our eyes meet, he throws a cheeky little wave.

My face flushes and I return the wave before turning off the faucet. I have no idea if he caught me watching him, or if I just caught him watching me, but my heart is pounding. No matter what he said last night, I don't think we're going back to normal anytime soon.

• • •

I'm sure no mother alive would be surprised by how long it takes us to get out of the house. Is every family such a mess? Miles walks in on Aaron in the shower and slips on the bathmat in an attempt to flee. Kyle can't find his boots. Ricky can't find his keys. Kennedy doesn't like pants, and Theo gets sidetracked looking for WD-40 in the basement because his truck door is squeaking. When we're all *finally* ready, we pile into our small caravan of vehicles for the short drive up the mountain. Once we step out of the cars, the wind is bitingly cold; we're no longer protected by the thick trees near the cabin. In the end, Kennedy is glad she wore pants.

Bundled head to toe, we hop on the ski lift and watch as the trees and sledders on the slopes grow smaller and smaller beneath us. It snowed way more up here than in the valley, and the view is glorious. The sky is crystal blue, and the air is clear and smells like cold and pine, the storm having knocked down any lingering haze.

The wind at the top is brutal, and we all bend into it as we negotiate who is sledding with whom. Dad hovers, waiting for me to climb on board with him, but the truth is that I'm pretty sure he wants off the hook anyway.

Dad is a terrible sled partner. He can drive a car as capably as the next guy, but he's like a nervous grandmother on the sled. Reactive and anxious and jittery. More often than not we end up tumbling over sideways, which makes Dad feel justified in his trepidation. We'll spend the rest of the descent slowly scooting our way down the mountainside, with Dad's heels dug into the trail and his hand liberally working the brake, while other sledders get run after happy-screaming run down the slope.

With Kyle standing to the side, already shivering in his one thousand layers of clothing, I decide to channel Fuck-It Mae.

"Dad, do you really want to do this?" I ask.

"Of course," he says, unconvincingly.

"You don't even like sledding." I point to a teeth-chattering Kyle. "Why don't you two go hang out in the lodge?"

Kyle shuffles closer. "Did someone say 'lodge'?"

Dad frowns at me. "Don't you like sledding together, Noodle?" But it's a half-hearted guilt trip at best. The idea of being in the lodge instead—hanging with Kyle and drinking spiked cider near a roaring fire—has quickly captured him.

I lift my chin. "Go."

They don't need to be told twice: Dad and Kyle hop on the ski lift and head back down the mountain toward warmth, food, and booze.

Miles is already off, flying down the hill solo. Mom and Lisa are riding together. Aaron has Kennedy, Ricky has Zachary, and a quiet hush falls over the ten-foot radius around me, Andrew, and Theo as we do the math: there are two sleds remaining, one single-rider and one two-person.

These guys are both well over six feet tall; they couldn't share a sled even if they wanted to. At five foot five, I know I'm going to ride with one of them, and usually I'd ask Theo to go with me because I would be nonverbal with nerves if I rode that closely with Andrew.

But now, the thought of settling between his spread legs, of his arms banded around my waist and his breath in my hair doesn't make me nervous. It makes me hungry.

How does it make Andrew feel, though? Yes, he followed me under the tree last night, and yes, he seemed to like being there. But the very last thing I'd ever want to do is put him in an awkward position, now that he knows how I feel.

Before I can offer to go with Theo, Andrew steps forward, grabbing the rope for the two-person sled and giving me a little waggle of his brows. "Wanna ride with me, Maisie?"

I require no arm-twisting. "I do."

If Theo is at all annoyed, it doesn't show, because he jumps in front of a couple in their twenties, hops on his sled, and takes off down the slope with a whoop. Thank God.

Andrew drags me out of my thoughts. "Why aren't you wearing a hat?"

I reach up, touching my hair. "Shit." I left it in the car. Not only is it insanely cold out, but my coat doesn't have a hood. Once we hit full speed on the sled, my ears are going to turn into icicles.

Andrew pulls his from his head and tugs it down over mine, but I protest. "Mandrew, you don't have to give me yours."

He lifts his hood up and grins at me. "My lice will like your hair better anyway."

"Gross." I lean in to plant a thank-you kiss on his cheek, connecting with the soft, chilly stubble there.

I'm suddenly glad that Theo is already halfway down the mountain, that my mom isn't here to give me her little raised eyebrow, and that the people behind us have no idea how long I've wanted to do that.

I pull back and he grins at me, but suddenly there's an obvious awareness there, because while I hug him all the time, I don't kiss him that often. Now I don't know where to look. My gaze wants to sink to his mouth, but that would be a terrible choice because I worry it'd be stuck there, immobile. Too late. His lips are red from the wind, full like usual, totally fascinating. When I drag my attention back up to his face, Andrew's eyes seem extra bright out here, more intense than usual.

"What was that for?" he asks.

"The hat?"

"Well, for the record, I'm always here for kisses."

Pardon?

He breaks the tension and sits down, sliding to the back of the sled and patting the space between his legs. My pulse trips. "Climb aboard, Maisie." Andrew looks up at me, and my heart does an aching nosedive. "There are adventures to be had."

It was one thing to hug him, but it's an entirely different experience sliding between his strong legs, feeling one of his arms around my waist and the low vibration of his voice in my ear.

"Ready?"

No.

I nod, leaning back just a little, and Andrew releases the brake, lifts his feet to bracket my calves, and pushes off with his free hand. We work together, humping the sled forward in a way that makes me want to explode in embarrassment because it is beyond sexual, but then we are gaining speed, sliding faster and faster down the hillside.

His arm tightens around me, and without thinking I grab on to his legs, holding them tight, leaning back into him. I can feel the sturdy weight of his body behind mine, the way he grips me with his thighs. I've always known Andrew to be kind, generous, and playful. But the way he engulfs me on the sled makes me aware of his physical strength and brawn. A flash of an image tears through me: Andrew's bare legs, his stomach clenched, head thrown back in pleasure.

I nearly swallow my tongue, brought back to the present only when he calls out happily in my ear, whooping and laughing as we really start flying down the slope. There's none of the uncertainty I feel sledding with Dad, none of that unbalanced sensation that we could tip at any time. With Andrew behind me I feel safe, balanced, and centered. I want the ride to last forever.

"You good?" he shouts above the whipping wind.

"Yeah!"

A small pause, and even though we are surrounded by the screams of other sledders, the sound of wind, and the ski lift, I can almost hear his breath catch.

"I'm gonna say something," he calls above the fray.

I squint into the bright sun, and we lean to the side in unison to steer our sled around a sapling. "Okay!"

His mouth comes right up beside my ear. "After what you said last night, I thought you were going to kiss me back there. *Really* kiss me."

It's my turn to lose my breath. I can't turn around and look at him, can't read his tone.

"Like on the *mouth*?" I call out over my shoulder, but my voice disappears into the wind as we go screaming down the mountain.

Andrew leans forward, spreading his hand across my side, pulling me closer into his body. When he speaks, he sounds breathless. "Yeah, on the mouth."

I stare ahead of us, and the figures on the slope start to blur. My eyes water with the cold wind.

His voice is quieter, but everything else has fallen away somehow, and I can hear him perfectly. "You've never been for *me*, Maisie. I never knew you were an option."

"What do you mean?"

We hit a bump and veer to the left, and his fingers tighten at my waist. When we straighten out, he doesn't let go; if anything, he tightens his grip, pulling closer and wrapping more of his arm around me. His fingers curl, brushing just under my jacket.

His breath comes out warm against my neck, voice shaking: "It never occurred to me that you might be mine."

chapter sixteen

Two hours later and the impact of that first ride down the slope still hasn't dimmed; I hear it—*It never occurred to me that you might be mine*—as clearly as if Andrew's said it again right into my ear, even though he's sitting next to me at the basement card table and not holding me tight as we sprint down a mountain.

For the first hour of the sledding trip, I didn't feel even the slightest bit cold. I was a campfire inside, a roaring inferno. Eventually, though, my fingertips went numb and my butt was almost dead from the chill of the wooden sled beneath me. Now back in the cabin, we've holed ourselves up in the basement—Theo, Miles, Andrew, and me— to escape the cloying heat of the roaring fire upstairs, as well as the roaring cackles of our parents engaging in some preholiday day-drinking and catching up.

Theo shuffles a deck of cards absently while we all

decide what we're in the mood to play. Under the table, a socked foot finds mine, and the other foot comes around it, gently trapping me in a foot-hug. A careful peek belowdecks tells me it's Andrew, and I suddenly feel like I'm wearing a wool sweater in Death Valley. Clumsily, I reach down, tugging my sweater up and over my head. It gets tangled in my hair clip, and Andrew has to shift forward to help extract me.

It means that he pulls his feet away, and once I'm free, I catch him biting back a knowing smile.

"Thanks."

He holds my gaze. "You're welcome."

I take a few deep drinks of my sparkling water to cool this ridiculous fever. You'd think I'd never been touched by a man before, good God.

Looking at me from beneath his lashes, Andrew reaches up, scratching the back of his neck.

"Today was fun," Miles says, and tries to take Theo's beer, but is instantly smacked away. "I'm glad you talked Dad into just heading for the lodge. If I had to ride with Mom this year, I think I would have bailed."

"Thanks for taking one for the team and sledding with Mae," Theo says to Andrew, and then smirks at me. "Worst sled steerer ever."

I glare. "Hey."

Andrew gives a magnanimous shrug. "I'm a humanitarian."

I smack him. "*Hey*."

His eyes sparkle when they meet mine, and the smiles fade into that same buzzing awareness. I finally blink down to the table. We rode the slope about six times, and I guess I'm grateful that nothing was as loaded and heavy as that first ride down, because I probably would have had some internal combustion issue and ended up back on the plane from a heart attack. There was plenty of Andrew being Andrew: he sang terrible opera on one trip, swore he closed his eyes the whole way down on another, and said hello to every other sledder we passed on a third, but it was just normal again. Which I loved, and hated.

Turns out, where Andrew is concerned, I apparently like heavy and loaded.

"We need to call ourselves something other than 'the kids,'" I say, breaking the quiet. Theo sets down the deck of cards in the middle of the table. "'The kids' are the twins now."

"Aren't the twins 'the twins'?" Miles asks.

"We could be called the 'kid-ups,'" I suggest, laughing, and Andrew beams over at me, thrilled with this suggestion.

Andrew slides the deck of cards closer to him, tapping, shuffling. I watch his fingers, trying not to think about his hands and how big they are. He has long, graceful fingers. I don't think I've ever noticed a man's nails before unless they were dramatically unmanicured, but Andrew's are blunt, clean, not fussy. I think I'd like to see those hands roaming and greedy all over my bare skin.

Theo clears his throat and my attention flies away from Andrew's fingers, guiltily.

"Two truths and a lie," Theo says, and gives me a bewildering wink.

Andrew looks up from his shuffling and deadpans, "I don't think that's a card game."

Ignoring this, Theo lifts his chin to Miles. "You first. I'll give you a sip of my beer."

"Miles hasn't lived enough to have interesting truths or lies, and he's definitely too young for day-drinking," Andrew says.

"Actually," Miles says, "we did this game as an ice-breaker in chemistry last year. It was hard thinking of things that were appropriate for school."

I hold up my hands. "Pardon?"

Andrew laughs. "Don't break your sister, Miles."

"It's your idea," Miles says to Theo. "You go first."

I can tell with a little annoyed tilt of my thoughts that this is why Theo suggested this game to begin with: he wanted to share some scandalous stories. And really, if I think back, nearly every game Theo suggests is a ploy to subtly or not-so-subtly talk about what a wild and exciting life he leads.

"Let's see," he says, leaning back and cracking his knuckles. "Okay, one: in college, one of my fraternity brothers kept a chicken living in his room for an entire year and none of us had any idea."

Inwardly, I groan. That's right. Whereas Andrew lived in a messy but comfortable apartment off-campus at CU Boulder with some of the funniest and weirdest guys I've ever met, Theo was in a fraternity with a bunch of players and trust fund men-children. I know there are lots of great, progressive fraternities out there, but Theo's was not one of them.

"Dude, why was he hiding a chicken?" Miles's face pales. "Was he being gross with a *chicken*?"

I turn to my brother. "Miles Daniel Jones, don't *you* be gross." And then I turn to Theo. "And don't you break my brother."

"Two," Theo continues, laughing this off, "I have a tattoo of a parrot on my hip that I got when I was in Vegas with some friends."

"A *parrot*?" Andrew's expression is a hilarious mix of bewilderment and deep sibling judgment. "On your *hip*? Why have I never seen this?"

Theo smirks and rocks back in his chair.

Andrew shivers as he gets it. "On your groin is what you're saying."

"I'd like to go back to the part where he thought it would be a fun time to get a tattoo in Las Vegas," I say. "I'm really hoping that one is the lie."

"And three, I'm not ticklish," he says, and then turns his eyes to me, adding, "anywhere."

This wink is definitely lascivious. Rude.

"Um, I'm going to go with number one," Miles says, still stuck on the chicken.

"I'm glad there are some things I don't know about you." Andrew wipes a weary hand down his face. "I'm with Mae: I'm hoping number two is a lie."

"I also hope it's a lie," I say, "but my guess is that number three is the lie. No way do you not have even one tickle spot."

"Wanna check?" he asks, smirking.

"I . . ." I flounder. "No, I'm good."

"Well," Theo says, "you're right. As Ellie T. discovered my senior year in college, I'm ticklish behind my knees."

What must it be like to have had sex with so many people that you have to first name–last initial them?

"What do I get for winning?" I ask. "A chicken?"

Miles winces. "Oh, please no."

Andrew pins me with a teasing smile. "You get it to be your turn."

"I hate this sort of game," I admit.

"Imagine how I feel." Andrew, the world's worst liar, laughs, sweeping a hand over his messy curls. They pop back over his forehead in a display of careless perfection.

"Okay, one," I start, "I hated my college roommate so much that I used to use her toothbrush as a fingernail brush after volleyball practice."

"Gross," Miles mumbles.

"Two, in college I had a crush on a guy who, I eventually found out, was legally named Sir Elton Johnson because his parents were clearly insane. He went by John."

"That," Andrew says, pointing at me with an elated grin, "is the best story I've ever heard. Goddammit, please let that be true."

"And three," I say without fully considering that my brother is sitting right here, "I broke up with my last boyfriend because he tasted like ketchup."

Miles falls over as if he's been shot, convulsing on the floor.

Both Theo and Andrew narrow their eyes thoughtfully.

"No way is that true," Theo says, shaking his head. "He

always tasted like ketchup? What does that even mean? Number three is the lie."

"Agree," Miles moans from the floor. "Besides, I don't think that's possible because you've never kissed anyone before."

I practically cackle. "Whatever helps you sleep at night."

But Andrew just watches me, eyes still narrowed. "Toothbrush. That's the lie. You wouldn't ever do that, no matter how much you hate someone."

I point at him, grinning. "You're right. That was the lie."

"Wait. I hope that's not why you broke up with Austin," Miles grumbles. "I liked him."

"It's one of the reasons. And you only liked him because he let you drive his car."

I watch, surprised and mesmerized, as a pink flush works its way up Andrew's neck and across his cheeks. He looks flustered and a little annoyed. Is Andrew Hollis jealous?

• • •

Once we're done with our ridiculous game, and no one feels like actually playing cards or Clue or any one of the other fifty or so board games, the boys all file upstairs to get snacks, leaving me alone to curl up on my bottom bunk and succumb to the exhaustion of constantly whirring thoughts.

The craziness of the last few days catches up with me, and I nap like I've never slept before, so deep and heavy that it's almost like a post-Thanksgiving slumber, or a Benadryl-induced blackout.

I come out of it slowly, thickly, at a vague, papery rustle nearby. It takes a few seconds for my eyes to adapt; the sun has set outside, leaving the basement window wells black. Across the room, another page turns; the sound of paper crackles through the cool stillness.

At my sharp inhale, I hear the book close. A click of the far floor lamp, and then the space is gently illuminated.

"She lives." Andrew. Alertness comes at me like a shove.

My voice is thick and scratchy. "What time is it?"

He peeks at his watch. In his other hand, he's holding a paperback. "Six. Dinner should be ready soon."

I slept for two hours? Wow.

"Where is everyone?"

He looks toward the stairs, like he might be able to see from where he's sitting at the card table. "The twins were making more popcorn garlands with your mom. It's snowing again, so the dads are shoveling. My mom is, um"—he winces—"baking something."

I make the *eep* face, and he nods in agreement. "I think this one is some sort of coffee cake."

"I threw the cookies out." I push off the covers and sit up, running a hand over the back of my neck. It's warm under all the layers, and I feel groggy and overheated.

His eyes widen. "Rebel."

I stretch, groaning.

"You okay?"

I look up. "Just oddly exhausted." Who knew time travel was so draining? *No*. Wait. Who knew time travel was *real*?

He turns the folding chair he's on around and sits backward on it. "Maybe some ketchup would perk you up."

I point a playfully accusing finger at him. "Are you stuck on that?"

"Maybe." Quiet eats up the space between us until with a sly grin Andrew finally adds, "I'm just wondering if you meant—" He motions to his face. "Or . . ." He tilts his head to the side, winking.

Bursting out laughing, I say, "You are a pig."

His eyes go wide in playful outrage. "*I'm* the pig?"

Upstairs, I hear a lot of pots banging and boys shouting, followed by Mom yelling something. "What is even happening up there?"

"Your mom was going to start dinner soon," he says, "but Benny told Theo and Miles to do it." He sees the surprise in my expression. "Benny said something about you wanting us all to help out more."

"How nice of him to give me credit while I was taking a monster nap."

Andrew laughs, his throat moving with the sound. Slowly, quiet swallows us again as he sets the book down. I want to ask him about the way he held me on the sled. I want to ask him about the foot-hug under the table. I really want to ask him why he seems jealous of my ex.

"What're you doing down here?" I ask instead. "There are about seven hundred more comfortable places to read in this house."

"I came down to get you," he says, "but couldn't bring myself to wake you up."

"So you just hung out nearby while I slept?" I ask, grinning over at him in the dim room.

"You were cute. You kept smiling in your sleep."

"I thought you were reading." He shrugs, and I laugh. "How Edward Cullen of you."

He frowns. "Who?"

"Oh my God, Andrew, *no*. We cannot remain friends."

"I'm just kidding. I know the guy from *The Hunger Games*." He bursts out laughing when my horror deepens. "You look so insulted! Is that your test to weed out the bad ones?"

"Yes!"

Still laughing, he stands and waves me up. "It's a good thing I've always been an excellent student."

Oh.

"Come on." He takes my hand. "I told the twins we'd play Sardines before dinner." In the darkness, his eyes shine wickedly. "I'm hiding first, and I have a killer spot."

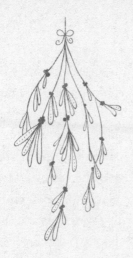

chapter seventeen

After the secluded, dark basement, it feels obscenely bright in the kitchen, like we're walking onto the set of a salacious talk show. My guilt complex is behaving as though we were naked and rolling around on the scratchy basement carpet. Everyone looks at us expectantly when we emerge from the downstairs, and I'm sure it's just my imagination but I can't help but feel that a suspicious hush has fallen over the room.

I wave, like an idiot. "Hey. Sorry I fell asleep." I point behind me, down the stairs. "After we were talking. And playing cards. You know."

Miles screws his face up. "Thanks for the update."

He tugs at the strap of a floral apron around his neck and picks up a can opener. Granted, it's a sort of fancy version of a regular can opener, but my brother turns it around in his hands like it's a complicated rocket engine part salvaged from NASA. Are we really entrusting this fetus with dinner preparation for thirteen people?

Andrew starts to explain to him how to use it, but I stop him with a hand on his arm. "No. He will learn through the suffering." I turn to give the same warning look to my mom, but she seems perfectly content at the kitchen table with a glass of wine in one hand and a paperback in the other.

Miles looks like he would very much like to give me the finger, but then his expression clears and a smirk pulls at his mouth. "Dude." He points upward. "You two are under the mistletoe."

In unison, Andrew and I turn our faces up to the doorway overhead. Miles is right. The festive sprig is now hanging from a red ribbon pinned into the doorway.

"I didn't know that was there," I burst out defensively.

"I didn't either." Andrew looks down at me, and even when his mouth isn't smiling, his eyes always are. Does the clock stop? It sure feels like it. Of all the times I've imagined luring Andrew under the mistletoe, never once did the fantasy include half of our respective families standing nearby.

"You guys could each take *one step* backward," Theo says gruffly, but it's pretty hard to take his anger seriously when he's wearing Mom's Mrs. Claus apron. "You don't actually have to kiss."

Except, I think we do. Let's not break the rule.

Andrew lets out a nervous laugh, but his eyes hook to mine. Slowly, he bends. His lips—oh my God, his perfect lips—land on mine in the purest kiss, ever, in the history of time. Andrew straightens, and I focus on keeping my spine rigid so I don't lean into him for more.

It was perfect, but it was nothing. Barely lasted as long as one of my agitated heartbeats.

A flash bursts nearby, followed by Lisa's muttered, "Damn it. I missed it."

Miles scoffs. "That wasn't a kiss."

I immediately regret all those times I told my brother he's an idiot; very clearly he is a truth seer with the emotional intelligence of Yoda.

"Dude, it's fine," Theo growls.

But we're in our own little bubble now. Andrew laughs quietly. "He's right. It wasn't really a kiss."

Andrew. Kissed me. On the mouth. I shrug with feigned indifference, keeping my voice low. "It was fine."

"I promise you," he whispers, "my goal for our first kiss was not 'fine.'"

"Okay, well," I say, heart shoving itself up into my throat. "Try again."

He quirks a brow, eyes darting down to my mouth and back up again.

"*Are you gonna kiss her?*" Zachary yells down the hall.

We turn to find at least six pairs of eyes watching us with vibrating intensity, and every cell in my body lets out an aggrieved groan. A chorus of conversation breaks out all around us.

Kyle laughs. "I think interrupting a mistletoe kiss is bad luck."

"God, they're so young," Aaron stage-whispers. "I want to be that young again. Making out under the mistletoe. Staying up until three in the morning. Tying my shoes without getting winded."

"They weren't *making out*," Dad scoffs, and then adds with less certainty, "Were they?"

Why do I like my family again? Even if Andrew was intent on doing the kiss over, the moment has been doused with several proverbial gallons of ice water.

"So," Andrew says, taking a step back and sliding his hands into his front pockets. "Sardines?"

"Sure." I muster up some enthusiasm. "Let's do it."

Sardines is Zachary's favorite game, and Kennedy's least favorite game, but she agrees to play it when he asks because, as she once said to all of us at the dinner table, "I don't like standing close to people but I don't mind standing close to any of you."

Aaron got up and pretended he had something in his eye so he could go have a happy cry without her seeing it.

Zachary is explaining to Lisa how Sardines works, in an effort to convince her that she should play. Best of luck to you, kid.

Lisa scrunches up her nose. "So, we all get in a small space together and hide?"

"One of us goes to hide," Kennedy says in her small voice, "and when someone finds them, they get into the place with them."

Zachary does a snappy karate-chop dance combo, and one of his shoes goes flying. "The last person to find the hiding space is the last winner!"

"The loser," Kennedy corrects. "Daddy and Papa call it the last winner, but really the last winner is the loser."

Zachary shrugs. "I like to win."

I can see Kennedy considering taking a swing at this

one, but she just looks back to Lisa instead. "Are you going to play? Andrew is hiding first."

Lisa is clearly pleased that her son and I have given her a chance to escape. Maybe she'll move the mistletoe again. "I think I'll see if Elise needs my help with dinner."

"Theo and Miles are cooking."

"Maybe they need help?"

"Mom." Andrew winces gently.

She laughs. "Fine. I'll go find Elise."

He turns back to the twins. "Who's ready?"

Two little hands go up in the air.

"Okay, then. Cover your eyes, count to fifty." He looks at me. "And Mae?"

"What?"

"No peeking." His eyes gleam flirtatiously, and my lady parts wave the white flag of surrender.

"I wouldn't dare." Bringing my fingers over my eyes, I start to count along with the twins to the sound of Andrew's tiptoeing retreat.

"One . . . two . . . three . . .

"Twenty-four . . . twenty-five . . . twenty-six . . .

"Forty-eight . . . forty-nine . . . fifty."

"*Ready or not, here we come,*" screams Zachary.

The kids peel off in different directions: Zachary down the hall toward the kitchen and basement, Kennedy into the dark dining room. Me, I pad upstairs. I have a pretty good hunch where Andrew's gone.

When our entire group hasn't descended on the cabin, the Hollis boys don't actually have to sleep in the basement; there are four bedrooms upstairs, plus the attic. Dad sleeps in the study, and Mom sleeps in Theo's bedroom. The room where Kyle and Aaron sleep is Andrew's.

With my heart hammering, I push open the door and am hit with the intense essence of *Andrew*. Lisa puts candles in each bedroom, but whereas she and Ricky favor lavender, and Theo gets sandalwood, the eucalyptus is specifically for her oldest son. Beneath it, there's also the clean scent of laundry, and that unmistakable feel of *him* everywhere. As soon as I walk in, the room goes tense, like the walls and furniture are sneakily pointing to the closet and hissing conspiratorially, *He's in there*.

The light is on, too, which is another clue. Kyle is a notorious energy saver, but Andrew wouldn't want the twins to have to search a dark room.

I walk over, hovering outside for a deep, steadying breath. A hundred times we've played this game and not once have we ever managed to huddle alone together, hiding.

I crack open the closet door.

Andrew cups his hands over his eyes, blinking into the bright light. "That didn't take you long."

"It wasn't exactly a stretch of the imagination." I step in beside him, and the small closet shrinks to the size of a shoebox when our situation hits me.

"Where did the twins go?" he asks.

"Downstairs. Dining room."

He doesn't say anything in response, but I feel him shift beside me. I am immediately drowning in the deep, aching tension of proximity.

"So . . . is it hard for you to give up this room over Christmas?" I finally ask.

I can barely see him because the only light we have to work with is a tiny sliver illuminating us from below, valiantly stretching up from underneath the door. But I can still see him shake his head. "I'm not here much anymore. Besides, I can sleep anywhere."

I know this to be true. When we were kids, Andrew was famous for falling asleep at the table after a big meal. "Then why go out to the Boathouse?"

"Because there's just something so infantilizing about sleeping on a bunk bed in the basement," he says. "I know it seems crazy, but I just could not do it another year."

"I see it more as a summer camp vibe, but I get that this is your red button."

"It is."

I think about the cold, dark, empty space of the Boathouse, and it makes me shiver. "Don't you get creeped out, sleeping by yourself out there?"

Andrew laughs and leans a little into me. "What's going to hurt me out there, Maisie? A ghost? The wolf-man?"

"I was thinking more like a deranged serial killer roaming the area." He laughs at this. "What scares you, then?" I ask. "Anything?"

"I fell in love with audio work by watching *Halloween* and *The Shining* and *Return of the Living Dead*," he says, and I can hear his sweetly proud smile. "I watch movies like that to unwind."

What a paradox he is, this bowl-of-sugar man who loves horror.

"What's your favorite scary movie?"

He laughs, all deep and hoarse. "That's the killer's sig-
nature line in *Scream*."

"It is?"

"Literally everyone knows that, Maisie."

I laugh now, too. "I'm telling you I can't watch anything
scary, even funny-scary." I elbow him gently in the dark.
"But really, what's your favorite?"

"For sound?" he says, and I shrug.

"Sure."

"Probably *A Quiet Place*. But my all-time favorite is
Silence of the Lambs."

Thrill glitters across my skin. "We saw that together,
remember?"

"I remember you wouldn't let me move more than a foot
away from you on the couch, and I even had to check under
your bunk in the basement later."

"Listen," I say, laughing, "I'm a wuss. I'll always take
kissing over killing."

I can sense how he leans his head back against the wall
at this, exhaling like he's got a lot on his mind. I do my best
to not imagine running my tongue over his Adam's apple.

"You okay?" I nudge his shoulder with mine.

I feel him turn to look at me. "I'm okay."

"Just okay?"

"Overthinking, probably."

A storm erupts in my blood, and I deflect nerves with
humor: "About how I'll forever think you're just a fine
kisser?" I joke.

His laugh this time is half-hearted. Even in the darkness,
there's a sizzle-snap in the air. I blink away to the shadowed

view of his jaw, but that doesn't help because he's so angular and edible. I look down at his neck, which is similarly problematic. Finally, my gaze drops to his forearms, exposed in the slice of light. He's rolled up his flannel shirt, and they're muscular, lightly dusted with hair, and even more amazing than his neck. I want to sink my teeth into them.

"This year has been so odd," he says quietly. "Theo's building a house. Mom and Dad are talking about retiring. Everyone seems to know where they're going and—" He breaks off. "I love my job, but I have this restless sense there's more out there. More life, more adventure. More than just a few dates a month."

My heart squeezes. "I know that feeling."

"I meet people," he says, "but one date bleeds into another. I haven't really *dated* someone, like, long term, in a long time." In all the time we've known each other and although I've known he's had them, Andrew has never talked about a girlfriend near me. "And then you . . ." He lets the sentence hang, and I worry if I try to speak, my voice won't work. "It threw me. Not in a bad way. Do you know what I'm trying to say?"

"Not really." I hear the way my words come out wavy.

I mean, I *think* I know where he's going with this, but I need him to articulate it carefully. He could mean a lot of things. Like, this year is different because Theo and I aren't super close. Or this year is different because I finally told Andrew how I feel about him. Or, for example, this year is different because I've traveled through time, and he has no idea.

"Remember how I said I was at a party a couple months

back," he whispers, "and a friend of a friend was reading tarot cards?"

"Yeah."

"I was teasing her about it, I guess, and she made me sit down. Put these cards in front of me and was like, 'I'll do your reading.' What do I have to lose? She doesn't know me. So I told her, 'Sure.' She looked down at the cards and said I could be happy being second at work. Told me I didn't need a big life, didn't need to set the world on fire. She's right—I don't. But then she told me I'd already met the love of my life, I just wasn't *listening*." He laughs. "And all I do is listen."

There is a swarm of dragonflies inside me, colorful and bright and taking up too much space. It's hard to breathe, because I feel this weight of all the things that he might mean by this.

"I still can't believe I didn't ever know," he says, and turns his head down. "How you felt about me."

I gnaw on my lip. "I can't figure out if you've been put off by that," I whisper. It feels like a decade passes before I decide to push the next words out: "Or turned on by it."

He shifts beside me, angling his body into mine. When I realize what's about to happen, my heart is no longer a heart, it's a gloved fist, punching the wall of my ribs again and again. Andrew lifts a hand, so unhurried, and rests it on the side of my neck.

His breath shakes when he exhales. "Turned on."

And just like that, Andrew's lips are on mine. Again, he breaks it too soon, but even in that single, perfect second, his touch was hungrier, playful. It was nothing like the public moment under the mistletoe.

And even though our lips are no longer touching, the intensity continues to ratchet higher because he stays right there, maybe only an inch from me, and he's struggling to breathe just like I am. It's dark in here, compressed and warm. A few of his shirts are on hangers—slid to the side so they bracket us—and they smell like him. Those same shirts have been on his skin when he's worked and sweated, napped and played cards with me in the basement, and now they're brushing against my back just after he kissed me.

"Is this okay?"

"It's better than fine," I whisper.

He laughs, breathlessly, and this here—breathing with him, deliciously anticipating what comes next—is easily the most erotic moment of my life.

I stretch forward just as he bends again, and his mouth is there, lips parting. When his arms come around my waist, pulling me into him, I moan and he takes the opportunity to sweep his tongue across mine.

That's it.

I get it. I will no longer snort derisively at descriptions of women in novels falling to pieces with barely a touch. I can't imagine what kinds of noises I'd make if I ever managed to get this man naked.

Heat blazes a path from my mouth down my throat, across my pounding chest, and down the center of my stomach. A million times I imagined this, but my brain is an uncreative disappointment in hindsight, because this is beyond anything I've conjured. Andrew tastes like peppermint and chocolate, smells like the smoke from the wood in the fireplace, and feels like sunshine. If you put all my favorite things in a Willy Wonka machine, I'm pretty sure Andrew Hollis is the candy that would come out. It's all I can do not to press my hips against his and push that flannel shirt off his shoulders.

"You look growly," he says on his own growl.

I've never known this side of him, but it's like being shown a glimmering, dimly lit hallway. Gemstones line the floor. Gold winks on the walls. *Let's see where this goes*, a voice says. For just a breath, I panic that this isn't the right path. That kissing Andrew in a closet isn't what I'm supposed to do.

But then he bends, nipping at my jaw, and the hesitation dissolves.

"I *feel* growly," I admit.

"Whoever thought Maelyn Jones would be totally fucking irresistible," he muses to himself, kissing down my neck.

"Not me."

His hand grips my hip and slides up over my waist, stopping painfully far from my breast. "For so long, you were just a kid," he says. "And then a couple years ago, you weren't."

I'm out of words. Instead, I just reach forward, running a finger down his neck to his collarbone.

"I'd had a sex dream about you," he says, and then breaks out laughing.

"You what!"

"In the bunk bed," he admits. "Mortifying."

"When we were all here?"

Andrew nods. "You know how when you have a dream like that, it just stays with you all morning?"

"Yeah."

"After breakfast, you and Theo were wrestling on the floor, and you were screaming laughing. Having the best time. I just had to push the thought aside—of seeing you that way. I couldn't give it any more space to breathe."

Every word he says requires me to rewrite my mental history. "If I knew that back then, I would have happily reenacted the dream."

Andrew laughs. "And now you told me you wanted me, and I remembered the tarot cards, and—I don't believe any of that, or at least I didn't think I believed it, but I just thought—'What if all this time, she's been right in front of me?' It felt so obvious. When we were on the sled?" he says. "And you smelled like caramel and sweet shampoo?"

"Yeah?" I'm in an Andrew trance.

"I almost leaned forward and kissed your neck. Just like that. Just out of the blue."

Without thinking, I make a gentle fist in the front of his shirt, pulling him closer. When he lets out a quiet grunt, his breath mixes with mine and suddenly I want to take this sunshine man and do very, very dirty things to him.

"I've had almost the identical thought," I say. "Many . . ." He stretches but then diverts away from my lips. His open mouth lands on my neck, sucking, teeth sinking gently in. I can barely think. ". . . *many* times."

Andrew's hand slides down over my ass to the back of my thigh, and he pulls my leg over his hip, leaning in. A slow grind. I feel him, the heat of his hips against my legs, the solid weight—

Bright light slices across us, and a small body bolts into the closet.

Andrew drops my leg, jerking backward. I throw my hands up like I'm under arrest. We are both breathing so hard and fast we sound like we just did closet CrossFit.

"Found you!" Zachary whisper-screams giddily.

"Oh—hey!" Andrew takes a deep, steadying breath and reaches up, adjusting the neckline of his shirt. "Took you long enough, squirt."

Even in the dim light I can see the flush on Andrew's neck, the quick flicker of his pulse beneath the skin. I wouldn't be surprised if I looked down and found that my skin was on fire.

"I thought you'd be in the Boathouse," Zachary says.

Andrew guides him to sit between us and closes the door with a gentle click. "There's nowhere to hide out in the Boathouse."

Zachary sounds dejected. "That's what Uncle Ricky said."

"Where's Kennedy?" I ask.

"Still looking." Zachary's dark eyes shine when he looks at me over his shoulder. "But don't call her a loser, okay?"

"I would never," I assure him.

Over the top of Zachary's head, Andrew and I stare at each other. I feel hot and achy all over. Unsatisfied and jittery.

"To be continued?" he whispers.

Oh, without question.

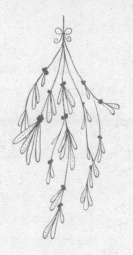

chapter eighteen

Andrew pulls out a chair for me when we get to the table, and I have to do a mental double take, trying to figure out if this is normal behavior. Have we ever reached the table in unison before, and if so, has Andrew pulled out my chair for me? A restrained laugh is still shining in his eyes and I know he wants to give me so much crap for being patently uncool right now, but does he not still feel my mouth on his? I certainly still feel the imprint of his kiss.

Benny catches my eye and slowly raises a single brow. I look away.

Objectively, dinner is terrible. The table is cluttered with plates of unidentifiable food: a mass of red and brown that I suspect is an attempt at meat sauce, a bowl of pasty white noodles all clumped together. Charred garlic bread cut into uneven chunks. Limp, suffering greens drowning under what must be a cup of ranch dressing.

The kitchen looks like a bomb went off, Miles and Theo have broken at least four dishes, and I know I'm going to have to clean the mess up later, but fuck me if it isn't the best meal I've ever had. Andrew said *to be continued*! I'd happily eat glue right now.

"Seriously," I sing, "this is *delicious*."

Andrew's elbow makes a gentle nudge to my side.

Ricky takes about a teaspoon of meat sauce and passes the platter on. "What does everyone feel like doing tonight?"

I nearly choke on a bite, and Andrew politely pats my back, answering with a casual "We could play Clue?"

"Ooooh." Mom likes this idea. "We haven't played Clue yet."

"We haven't been here that long," I remind her—and myself. Frankly, it feels like it's already been a month. I quickly do the math: seven days of original holiday, plus another six in the Land of Repeats.

The sauce makes its way around the table. Zachary mimes throwing up when it moves in front of him, and Aaron doesn't even chastise his son. Instead, he studies the sauce suspiciously before offering a vague "Probably should take a pass since I'm on a diet," and then hands it to Dad, bypassing Kyle entirely.

I'm sure he's trying to save his husband from having to eat it, but Kyle chases it with a hand. "Come on now, I have to work for these curves." Everyone laughs—because Kyle is nothing but muscle and sinew—and Aaron apologizes with a kiss.

The moment is so simple and sweet. I look away in time

to catch Mom and Dad exchanging a knowing look. Dad tucks his chin to his chest, his shoulders shaking.

"Okay." I point between them. "What's happening here?"

"When I was barely pregnant with you," Mom explains with suppressed laughter, "I asked your dad if I looked pregnant yet and he said, 'No, it just looks like you're letting yourself go a little.'"

Dad covers his eyes. "As soon as the words were out, I wanted to drag them back in."

"You'd think a man who interacts with pregnant women for a living would be smarter," Ricky teases him, and then immediately shrinks at the wry look from his wife. "Oh no."

Lisa points an accusing finger at her husband. "Do you remember when I started taking that pottery class at night, over at the U?"

Ricky slides lower in his chair, letting out a giggling and ashamed "Yes."

She turns to the rest of us. "I told him I felt so old and frumpy around all these young college girls, and he said, 'That's okay, honey, I love you anyway.'"

Everyone laughs at this, and Theo lets out a groaning "Dad, no."

Ricky turns to his son. "Are you kidding me? You got a call from a girl the other day and couldn't remember who she was."

"I didn—!" Theo starts, but Ricky holds up a hand.

"When we were here over Thanksgiving, what did you have hiding in your closet after Grandma left?"

Both Andrew and I go very, very still.

Theo closes his eyes, pretending to be embarrassed by this. "A woman."

"A woman," Ricky repeats. "Just hanging out in your closet waiting for us to finish eating." Surprised laughter breaks out at the table, but inside, I feel like I've dodged the world's largest bullet. "Theo, you are in no way prepared to give me shit about anything."

"Earmuffs," Aaron mutters to the twins, who belatedly clap their hands over their ears.

Miles is the last to get over his laughter about all of this, and Theo turns to him, teasing, "At least I've got game, bro."

To my brother's credit, he doesn't look fazed by this in the slightest. "I'm seventeen. Am I supposed to be hiding people in my closet?"

"No," Mom and Dad say in unison.

"Mae and Andrew are awfully quiet over there . . ." Lisa singsongs.

The entire room goes still, and every gaze swings our way. I look up from where I'm cutting my spaghetti into smaller clumps and realize Andrew is making nearly the same *Who, me?* expression to my right.

"I'm sorry, what?" Andrew says through a bite of salad.

"Oh, we're just talking about how above reproach you two are," Dad says, and Mom looks undeniably proud.

"These two certainly aren't sneaking around, hiding booty calls in their bedrooms," Ricky chides Theo.

While I struggle to swallow down a bite of gluey noodles, Andrew nonchalantly spears a piece of lettuce, saying, "That is technically correct."

"Mae would have to date for that to happen," Miles says, and I glare at him.

"Your sister is not interested in 'booty calls,'" Dad says, bringing a forkful of spaghetti to his mouth before reconsidering.

My brother drops his fork in disgust. "Can everyone stop saying 'booty call'?"

I feel Andrew's foot come over mine under the table and am suddenly very, very interested in the composition of the meat sauce, blurting, "This is so unique, Theo, how did you make it?"

Flattered, he waxes happily about frying the meat, dumping in canned tomatoes, finding some dried herbs in the pantry. The conversation moves on, and I'm able to mostly tune it out . . . which is good because it's taking nearly all of my energy to not be completely focused on Andrew's every movement next to me. I would not be good for any conversation right now.

I think he's intentionally brushing elbows with me, but it's hard to know, because he's left-handed and I'm right-handed. But then I'm thinking about hands, and fingers, and the way he gripped my leg, pulling it over his hip before rocking against me.

I'm thinking about those hands sliding under my shirt, up over my ribs. I'm thinking about those fingers pulling the button on my jeans free, teasingly tugging down my zipper. I'm thinking about that mouth moving breathlessly down my body, over my—

"Mae?" Mom's voice rises over the noise.

"Mm?" I look up, realizing again that everyone is watching me. Apparently, I've missed a direct question.

Her brows furrow. "Are you okay, honey?"

With horror, I realize my entire face and neck are flushed. "Yeah, sorry, was just chowing on my dinner."

Theo leans on his elbows. "I called Professor Plum, and you didn't even blink."

"Oh." I wave my fork. "I'll be whoever's left."

I can feel the ripples of shock make their way around the table. I am laid-back about few things, it's true, and none of those things are Professor Plum. Like any self-respecting woman of twenty-six, I take my Clue very seriously.

And yet.

"What's the big deal, guys?" I ask. "Sometimes a little change is good."

● ● ●

I'll have you know that Colonel Mustard won Clue tonight, and Professor Plum is already off to bed, pouting that not only did I take the good luck juju with me to a new character, but Professor Plum himself was the murderer, in the conservatory, with the rope. I don't think Theo enjoys my victory dance, but Andrew sure seems to.

He and I pack up the game pieces in the living room while everyone else wanders off to their corners—bedrooms for the grown-ups, basement for the kid-ups, and then it's just us, standing together with the fire crackling down to embers and the sexual tension roaring, wondering what comes next.

At least, that's what I'm wondering. I'm not remotely tired and therefore I'm not remotely interested in going down to the basement. I definitely have some more making out in me tonight.

With a tiny tilt of his head, Andrew leads me to the kitchen—where I think we both plan to escape outside and to the Boathouse, but instead we find that there is still a sink full of dishes to do.

"Oh, right." Dreams of imminently ripping the flannel shirt from his upper body die a sad, quiet death. "I said we'd do these."

Andrew rolls up his sleeves and gives me a playfully annoyed look. "'Let's help out more,' she said. 'We need to be grown-ups,' she said."

Laughing, I put my mostly full glass of cider near him on the counter and turn to collect stray dishes from the table. "Sorry."

"You really are a terrible drinker," he observes, dumping the contents of the glass down the sink and slotting it into the dishwasher.

"I know." I watch him close the dishwasher and then wash his hands at the sink. "But so are you."

Andrew grins over his shoulder at me. "I make impulsive decisions when I'm drunk. Like, I'm probably only ever one to two drinks away from getting a bad music quote tattoo."

This makes me laugh and I clap a hand over my mouth to keep the sound from echoing past where we stand in the quiet kitchen. The last thing I want is Miles or Theo coming back upstairs to join us. "You mean you wouldn't get a parrot?"

A full-body shiver worms through him, and he plugs one

side of the sink to fill it with soapy, warm water. "The thing I can't get past is why a *parrot*?"

I shrug, biting my lips. "Why not a parrot?"

"A cool parrot on your arm or back? *Maybe*." He points finger guns down at his crotch. "But a parrot—here? Right next to your dick? Why?"

I'd respond, but this has fried the part of my brain that makes words. As soon as Andrew looks up at me, he can see it all over my face. "Did I fluster the lady?"

"A bit." I reach for a dish towel, intent on drying the dishes I assume he's going to start washing, but he takes two steps closer, cupping my face.

"You're making this expression like you're not sure this is really happening."

"That is a frighteningly accurate assessment."

He rests his lips on mine, smiling.

"We have dishes to do," I mumble against his mouth.

"We'll do them in the morning," he mumbles back.

"We aren't going to want to do them in the morning."

Nipping at my bottom lip, he growls and turns away. "Fine. Be logical."

He moves over to Ricky's old cassette-playing radio on the counter and snaps a tape into place, hitting play with a clunky click. Sam Cooke filters from the small speakers, quiet enough that I'm pretty sure it doesn't make its way down- or upstairs, and even if it does, it's Sam Cooke, not Ozzy Osbourne; we're probably safe to assume we'll be left alone.

Don't know much about history . . .

Andrew sings quietly, washing the dishes, and the first

couple of times he hands me something to dry he gives me a flirty smile, but then we get into a quiet rhythm after a few minutes; we settle into the best combination of lifelong friends and new lovers.

He rinses his favorite unicorn mug and hands it to me to dry. "You want to hear a story about this?" I ask.

"Hell yes I do."

"When I painted it, I wrote 'Mae plus Andrew' in white and then painted over the whole thing in pink."

He gapes at me, taking it back and immediately flipping it over. "You did not."

"I did."

He holds it to the light, squinting. "Oh my God, there it is!"

We lean together and he points, outlining the letters with his index finger. He's right. The raised shapes of the letters in thick paint are barely visible.

"I knew it was my favorite mug for a good reason."

I laugh. "So dorky."

"Uh, no, Mae, it's awesome." He leans over, kissing my cheek. "So I guess you weren't kidding," he says, "about your crush."

"Of course I wasn't kidding." When I turn to look at him, he leans in again, brushing his mouth over mine.

And if this one could be with you . . .

We fall back into a rhythm with the dishes, and I don't realize we've shifted so that we're touching until his arm slides down mine as he reaches into the sink to wash the final platter, but we make eye contact afterward. I'm infatuated with him beyond distraction. This is everything I've always wanted: to be here, exactly like this with him—and maybe we aren't "together" in a defined sense of the word, but we're already undeniably *more*.

A second thought sinks into me like a weight dropping in a warm lake: *I am happy. I have never been this happy in my entire life.* Maybe Benny was right and I'm finally being me.

I lean over and kiss his neck. "Let that dish dry in the rack, I'm going to put away the spices and stuff."

I grab the jars of oregano, parsley, and some mix called Pasta Sprinkle and tuck a few unused cans of tomatoes under my arms, ducking into the walk-in pantry. Behind me, the water shuts off, and I turn just as Andrew comes in after me, wiping his hands on a dish towel.

"What are you doing?"

"Being sneaky." When he closes the door behind him, his smile is swallowed by the shadows and still somehow the brightest thing in this small space.

"Do the Hollis men have some sort of closet fetish I should know about?"

"Isn't this what the holidays are all about?" he asks. "Kisses under the mistletoe? Making out in a pantry?"

"Nosy relatives."

His mouth is only inches away when he laughs and slides his lips over mine. Like a dry-erase board swept with a cloth, I am wiped free of any other thought. There's just the feel of his kiss and his arms coming around my waist, my own hands sliding up his chest and around his neck.

I want to ask him, the words are at the tip of my tongue—*Does this kiss feel like the best kiss ever?*—because to me it does. And it isn't just because it's Andrew, it feels clearly like the perfect kind of melting together; his mouth just seems to fit against mine. We kiss the same.

He moves from my mouth to my jaw, and lower, pressing these perfect sucking kisses to the sensitive skin just over my pulse, moaning against me. The sound puts me in a rocket ship and launches me to Jupiter. In a flash, I imagine the sight of his head between my legs.

The idea of watching him do that makes me both shy and ravenous; my libido has turned into a fanged monster. Andrew doesn't seem fazed in the slightest by how I pull him closer and kiss him deeper, by my sounds and the intensity of my grip. Here in the dark pantry, I can pretend we're alone, that there aren't eleven other people in this house. I send my hands up under his shirt, seeking the soft, warm skin there, skating over his ribs with my fingertips.

"You feeling me up?"

He's teasing, but the way his words have gone all raspy tells me he approves. "Yes. You're yummy under here."

"My turn." His fingers play with the hem of my T-shirt and then his hand is on my stomach, my ribs, and his kisses don't slow or lessen. I want to eat this sensation, to swallow it down and gorge myself on it.

"Do you think everyone would freak out if they knew what was happening in here?" he asks.

"Not everyone," I say, "but certainly some of the more influential ones . . ."

His thumb sweeps under my bra, back and forth. "I think they'd be happy for us."

The thought of this existing out there for everyone to

see makes it both wonderfully and terribly real. Keeping it a secret from our families feels like keeping it a secret in general, and I can pretend that the universe isn't watching, either. Yes, I'm happy, and I find myself believing that is the goal here, but what I don't know is why, or how to hold on to it. Nobody can be happy all the time. What happens when I'm not?

His thumb slides beneath the underwire, pushing the fabric up over the curve of my breast. "This okay?"

I don't care how desperate I sound when I tell him yes. I want his entire body touching me right there, each electron of his energy focusing on my skin.

His palm comes over my breast beneath my shirt, and we both let out these ridiculous moans in unison into each other's mouth, and then pull away, bending in silent laughter. We are the same kind of idiot.

With an unfocused glaze in his eyes, he feels the shape of me, teasing, gently pinching.

"You're perfect," he tells me. "You're so soft."

I send a thousand thank-yous to the sky because, pressed against me, Andrew feels anything *but* soft.

This is the best kiss, my brain screams again when he puts his mouth over mine again, sweetly distracted by his hand.

A harsh white light lances across my field of vision and instinct whips us both away so that we're facing the shelves. Andrew's front is pressed all along my back, and my heart launches itself into my windpipe.

Holy crap, we need to find another place to make out; closets are not working well for us.

"Uh, up there!" I shout to cover, praying Benny was the one who opened the pantry door.

"Why was the door closed? Why are you in here?"

Oh God. My brother.

I grapple to pull my bra back down. "I was grabbing, um—"

"This." Andrew stretches behind me, reaching over my shoulder for something on the top shelf. I have no idea what he's getting, and frankly, who cares. His hips press against my backside and I feel him. I mean—*wow*. He is very, very hard. My brain melts.

Miles must be focused on what Andrew's reaching for, and thank God because I am entirely focused on the feeling of Andrew pressed against my butt. *I did that.*

I want that.

He pulls the object down and hands it to Miles, somehow managing to turn me in the process so I'm facing Miles and still standing in front of Andrew. *Covering* him. I remember he's wearing sweatpants, and from the feel of things down there, his status would be difficult to hide.

Miles studies the object in his hands. "You were getting this . . . ceramic sombrero?"

At my brother's words, I actually look at what Andrew's handed him. The chips-and-salsa dish is ancient. It is absolutely covered in dust. I haven't seen this thing in at least a decade.

"Yeah, Mae was feeling snacky."

Andrew gently pinches my waist when I don't immediately play along. "I was!"

"You can't eat some chips and salsa from a regular bowl?"

Miles, just let this go!

"I was feeling festive?" I try.

He blinks, and grimaces. "You're all *red*."

"I am?"

"She is?" Andrew asks with restrained laughter as he turns back to the shelves. "I'll grab the chips, Maisie."

We're so busted. Oh God, poor Miles. First the ketchup-mouthed boyfriend, and now this.

When I emerge from the pantry, Miles pulls me to the side. "Were you two kissing in there?"

"Of course not!" Seriously, this is mortifying. Why won't my brother just read the room and leave? "We were doing dishes, and I got the munchies. Just—go back to bed."

With a final skeptical glance into the pantry, Miles grabs a cup of water and shuffles back down to the basement.

Once I'm sure he's gone, I look over to Andrew, who's adjusting his sweats and grinning at me. "Well, that was awkward."

"The most awkward that has ever existed."

There's something in his expression: like a curtain has been drawn open, revealing the next phase of our night of adventures.

"Oh." I point at him and grin. "I sense a transition."

He leans in conspiratorially. "I was thinking—"

"A very dangerous thing to do."

"—that instead of hanging out in the kitchen and getting busted by our siblings, perhaps the lady would like to return with me to the Boathouse for a nightcap."

"By 'nightcap,'" I whisper back, "do you mean kissing with shirts off?"

He nods with playful gravitas. "Correct. And in the interest of transparency, I should tell you I don't actually have any interesting nightcap options out there."

I pretend to think this over, but inside I am doing a thousand backflips. "I want to go out there, on one condition."

Immediately his expression shifts. "We don't have to do anything you don—"

"You walk me back here afterward," I interrupt, voice low. "There's no way we would survive our mothers' inquisition if I got busted sleeping out there, but I don't want to walk back alone."

A knowing gleam sparkles in his eyes. "*Silence of the Lambs* flashbacks?"

"One hundred percent."

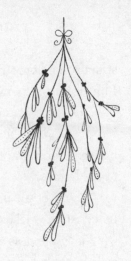

chapter nineteen

Outside, the sky is full, a deep ocean blue overrun with tiny, glimmering silver fish. The air is so sharp it takes a few breaths for my body to adapt, to clear out the dry indoor air. Two steps off the back porch, and Andrew's hand comes over mine, fingers threading between as if he's done it a thousand times.

"We never get skies like this at home," I say.

"I forget how much I love it up here until I'm outside at night, and then it's like whoa, yeah, it would be hard to give this up."

A tiny strangled noise escapes me, and I turn it into a cough. "Maybe try to convince your parents to keep it?"

His quiet pause tells me that he probably won't do that. "I just want them to do what works for them, you know?"

I reach up, running my free hand through my hair. The

strands that come away are wound around and around, and I finger-flutter them away.

"You have so much hair," he says quietly. "It's so pretty."

"It's a pain. You should see my brushes." The deep brown is all Mom, but its sheer density is from Dad's side of the family.

"Think of all the birds' nests you've helped build out here," Andrew jokes.

I laugh, but as we move forward through the darkness, over snow that is illuminated blue and so cold we can walk across it without sinking in, a fear hits me like a brick of ice.

"I just want to say," I begin, "before we get to the Boathouse, that if this ever feels weird or wrong, please just don't stop talking to me. I promise I'll be okay if you decide this isn't what you want to do, but I wouldn't be okay if you ignored me."

"Do you really think I would do that?"

In truth, no. I can't imagine it. "You're right."

"And why are you assuming I'm the one who'll change his mind?"

"I'm just trying to protect us and our families. It feels so good, but I know it's a huge deal."

He bends when I say this, brushing his mouth over mine. It feels like the next sentence in the conversation, the unspoken *Trust me, okay?*

We're at the Boathouse now, and he turns, reaching forward and pushing the squeaky door open to reveal the dark hollow space. I'm not really sure why, but seeing the Boathouse tonight with Andrew, under these circumstances, makes the cold blackness tantalizing rather than eerie and uninviting. Yes, it's freezing in here, but I know in that far corner there is a pile of sleeping bags, and in a few minutes, I will be cuddled inside them with Andrew pressed all alongside me.

What if we have sex?

The word—*sex*—flashes into my head, buzzing fluorescent and neon. Only a matter of hours ago, I discovered what it felt like to kiss him. But here we are, no longer children, friends our entire lives. If the intensity between us is anything like it was in the closet and pantry, and with over a decade of pent-up lust trapped beneath my skin, I don't know how we'll keep from ripping all of our clothes off as soon as we lock the door.

The door seals shut, and Andrew reaches past me, turning the dead bolt. The click echoes once, contrasting with the staccato of my heartbeat.

"Come on." He leads me to the back of the room and turns on the little lamp in the corner, illuminating a cone of space with a soft yellow glow. "Ta-da."

When he steps back, I see he's arranged the pile of sleeping bags on the floor, and it takes me only a few seconds to realize it's because the cot is really only wide enough for one body. But by zipping the flannel-carcass sleeping bags together, he's made a cozy little bed for two. There are pillows propped against the wall to lean against, if we want. He's even brought a couple of bottles of my favorite sparkling water out here from the kitchen.

I must have hearts in my eyes when I look at him. When did he even do this?

"You said you didn't have beverages."

"I said I don't have any nightcaps," he says, grinning, "but I do know what you like."

I'm trying to keep my brain from doing it, but a tiny flash works through, of the handful of guys in my past who would be hard pressed to remember how much ice I like in my drink or name one of my favorite anythings, let alone procure it for me.

Without any careful calculation—only gratitude and want—I move right up against him. My arms go around his neck and there's no hesitation on his end, either; my God, it's like an explosion in reverse, a melting. His arms pull me in, and his mouth comes over mine with a laugh-moan of happy relief. This feeling is sunshine. There's no pause like there was in the closet, no careful consideration of who might find us. Here, there's only the heat of his smiling mouth, the tiny relieved exhale.

Andrew turns us, pressing me against the wall. Playful and sweet and light Andrew is washed away in the shadow of the man in front of me who smiles still, but it's dark and exciting. His hands grip my hips, pulling me flush to him, letting me feel that he's still just as hungry for this as I am.

We move to the floor. My shirt is slid up and over my head. I finally get to push that soft flannel off his shoulders and run my hands down his arms, feeling the smooth definition there, the bunching of tension in his back as he hovers over me, pressing just where I want him.

The neon sign is back. *Sex. Sex. Sex.*

We've been in the Boathouse for maybe four minutes, and we're half-undressed. It's not that I'm surprised, but . . . I don't want to be stupid.

"Andrew," I mumble against his mouth.

He pulls back, and even in the dim light I can see the worry on his face. "What?"

Do I say it? Or do we figure it out as we go? But honestly, that's never a good idea. The heat of the moment is a real thing, and we are right in the middle of it. "This is awkward, okay, but I don't have . . ."

He waits for me to finish the sentence, but suddenly it feels too presumptuous. Too fast. We just have our shirts off, Mae, settle down. "Never mind."

"Don't have what?" he presses. He shifts forward slightly, leaning into that distracting heat between my legs.

"Um. Not that we are going to. I mean, of course we probably aren't. But if one thing leads to another, and—"

There's a smile in his voice. "Maelyn Jones, are you thinking about birth control?"

I don't think I could be more mortified.

"Like I said," I say immediately, "I'm not saying we're going to go there, we just got *here*, but I like to be—"

"Safe." He drops the teasing voice and squeezes my hip with a gentle hand. "I've got it taken care of. Don't worry."

Andrew bends and it's sweeter now, less frantic, like we've let out some of the pressure by just saying the possibility out loud.

The air in the Boathouse seems colder than the air outside, but in the zipped-together sleeping bags it is toasty warm. Andrew wrestles briefly with my bra, which I find both reassuring and endearing, and then it's gone, tossed somewhere over near his cot. His mouth is a trail of heat down my neck, over my chest, tiny bites and kisses.

It's like wanting to hit the brakes and the gas all at

once; I want to go faster, feel him moving in me, but want to savor every second of this because it's so many of my life-long fantasies come to life and he's perfect, like he read the Guidebook on Mae's Body and is determined not to miss a bullet point. I'd had no clue that Andrew felt anything but big brotherly feelings toward me until today, but, with my very simple invitation to explore an *us*, he's on board. Totally. It's almost as though he's been waiting, too. He's had fantasies of his own that he's finally able to bring to life. Which is completely surreal.

He disappears beneath the top of the sleeping bag, and with a combination of kisses, dexterous fingers, and determined hands, he manages to unbutton my jeans and get them down my legs and shoved to the bottom of the sleeping bag.

I can't see him, can only feel his mouth on my knee, my thigh, the smallest press of his mouth between my legs and, good God I might die, I don't think I have ever wanted something more in my life, like I would sacrifice anything just to feel the direct, heated press of his kiss there—

Andrew scrambles up my body, crawling in a panicked flurry, and takes a deep gulping breath of air once he manages to emerge from the sleeping bag. "Holy shit." He sucks in another breath. "I have never been that close to death."

It's a combination of shocked laughter and mortified cry that escapes me.

Obviously everything down there is terrible and horrifying? Why has no one ever told me the truth?

I clap my hands over my face. ". . . Are you okay?"

"I'm great. I wanted to—but I couldn't hold my breath—"

He gasps, inhaling again deeply. "It is so hot in that flannel sleeping bag, there's, like, *no air*."

I burst out laughing, dropping my hands. "I was making a mental deal to sacrifice all of our loved ones if it'd keep you going, but it isn't worth your death by suffocation."

He bends, leaning his forehead on my bare shoulder. "I accuse Mae, in the sleeping bag, with her vagina."

I completely lose it when he says this, and he's shaking with laughter, too. Honestly, laughing with Andrew while I'm naked might be the best feeling I've ever had. He slides to the side in the giant double sleeping bags, propping his head on his hand. With the fingers of his other hand, he draws little circles on my stomach, my chest, my neck.

I like looking at him in this light; with the way it's angled across the room, it makes him a perfect combination of angular and soft. Sharp jawline and cheekbones, the gentle bow of his lips, his impossibly long eyelashes.

"Has anyone ever told you that you have the most beautiful eyes?" he asks. "You've got this doe-eyed, innocent Gidget thing going on."

I laugh. "That's an awfully old-man thing to say, Mandrew."

"No, listen," he insists, pushing up and hovering over me. "I used to watch reruns of *Gidget* when I was home sick, and I'm not kidding, I think Sally Field was my first crush."

"Is that weird?" I ask. "I can't decide."

"Not weird." He bends, kissing my jaw. "She's a babe. Even in her seventies, she could get it."

"Did you know Tom Cruise is almost sixty?" I ask.

He looks mildly concerned. "Do you have a thing for Tom Cruise?"

I scrunch my nose. "Definitely not. I just think it's funny that he looks eternally forty."

He hums thoughtfully. "Did you know Christopher Walken is almost eighty?"

I laugh. "Why do we even know these things?"

"We're the good kind of weird?" His mouth moves up my neck.

"But is it bad-weird," I say, "that I'm naked and we're talking about Christopher Walken?"

"It is good-*good* that you are naked. And frankly," he says, "I'm happy to share this moment with Christopher Walken."

I'm overcome with a fondness so consuming that I cup Andrew's face and pull him to me. It isn't just about how good this feels or how flat-out gorgeous he is, it's about how easy and natural it is to be with him, to talk between kisses, to be totally unselfconsciously naked, to laugh about Andrew's near-death experience between my legs.

The kiss starts sweet and calm, but when he grazes his teeth across my lip, I make a noise that seems to uncork something inside him, and he's over me again, elbows planted beside my head, kissing me so good I'm dizzy with how much I want him.

My fingers toy with the waistband of his sweats, and skim just beneath and then—why not—I push them down his hips, and his warm skin slides over mine. I think for one second that it's moving too fast, but I sense the same aware-ness in him because he shifts back and away.

I've never been in sync with someone like this. It feels like hours pass while we're kissing and touching, talking and breaking into spontaneous, loud bursts of laughter. The sex is right there, but so is the blackness of night, reminding us that no one is in a hurry and we have plenty of time for fun. Even the fumbling condom unwrapping leaves us in hysterics. He's still laughing into a kiss when he moves over me, and into me, and then I get to see the quiet, focused side of Andrew, the one who makes it his life's work to listen, because he works so carefully to respond to every single sound I make.

When we finally pull our clothes back on and he walks me across the moonlit expanse of snow, there are two things I want with equal intensity: I want to turn around and go back to being naked in the sleeping bag, and I want him to follow me into the kitchen, sit down at the table, and talk to me for hours.

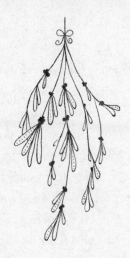

chapter twenty

At five thirty in the morning, two and a half hours after Andrew walked me back to the house, I give up on sleep and shuffle upstairs to the kitchen. I am a sewer creature emerging into daylight; a woman who very definitely needs eight full hours of sleep. Today should be interesting.

Ricky stumbles in about the same time I do, and we both freeze at the sight of his son at the end of the table, bent over a bowl of cereal. My heart falls into my stomach, and I watch in horror as Andrew lifts an arm and casually wipes away a drip of milk from his chin.

He hasn't heard us approach, I know, but the view of him bowed over the table, the silence that seems to stretch like a canyon across the otherwise warm, inviting space . . . it's so similar to that horrible morning with Theo that I am instantly queasy with dread.

Is this the catch? The surprise ending? *Gotcha! You've*

made the same mistake with Andrew. Did you really think the point of all this was for you to be happy?

A sound creaks out of me, something between an inhale and a groan, and Andrew's eyes shoot up, and then back over his shoulder to his dad, before returning to me.

His sleepy gaze immediately shifts into twinkling happiness. "Well, good morning, fellow early risers."

He's looking at me like I'm exactly who he wanted to find this morning, but my doubt takes a beat to wear off and the feeling keeps me from moving deeper into the room.

Ricky looks at me, then the coffeepot, and then me again meaningfully before he eventually gives up and walks over to it himself. "What're you doing up so early, Drew?"

"Couldn't sleep." Behind his father's back, Andrew winks mischievously at me, and my insides all turn into a heated tangle. An echo of his groan, a flash of his throat arched back in pleasure snaps my thoughts clean of anything else.

"Too cold out there in the Boathouse?" Ricky turns to smile at me, too, like he's really got Andrew where he wants him now.

"Actually, I was toasty as a bear in a den," Andrew says, poking at his cereal. "Just stayed up too late and then couldn't shut off my brain."

"Something worrying you? Work stuff?" Ricky pulls down three mugs as the coffee starts to slowly dribble into the carafe.

"Work was the last thing on my mind, actually." Andrew gives his dad an easy shrug and takes another bite of cereal. "Just wide awake and buzzing."

I look down at the linoleum, faking a yawn to smother my delirious grin.

"Well, you'll be tired after today," Ricky says, sitting at the table, "that's for sure."

Today: December 23. Scavenger Hunt Day. We pair up in teams pulled out of a hat and disperse around Park City to collect photo evidence of a long list of random things Ricky and Lisa dream up for us—a silver ornament, a giant candy cane, a dog wearing a sweater, things like that. Occasionally video evidence is needed, like last year when we had to get video of a group of people doing the cancan. Permission is required, and asking strangers to do weird things can be mortifying, but mostly it's a blast.

The hunt also gives us the chance to do any last-minute Christmas shopping we might need—Theo and Miles never have their shopping done beforehand—and is usually a much-needed break from the confines of the cabin. Mom, Kyle, and Aaron usually stay back to start cooking tomorrow's feast. They prepare the same, beloved menu every Christmas Eve: ham, scalloped potatoes, roasted vegetables, macaroni and cheese, homemade bread, and about ten different pies we all look forward to every year.

The rest of us are unleashed and turn ruthlessly competitive. One year, Dad even bought a woman a new shirt so no one else would have the chance to cross off the "someone wearing a Broncos jersey" item on their list.

My feet finally unlocked, I walk across to the table, pull out a seat, and sit shoulder to shoulder with Ricky.

"What about you, Mae?" he says, nudging me. "You sleep okay?"

I should probably lie, but I'm too tired to be coy. "Not really."

Andrew puts on a mask of dramatic concern. "Oh no. You too?"

Ricky bolts up as soon as the coffeemaker beeps that it's done brewing, and I use the opportunity to give Andrew a warning expression that I can't seem to hold; it immediately cracks into a smile that feels like sunlight on my face. In my head, Julie Andrews sings and spins on an Austrian mountainside. Confetti bursts from a glittery cannon. A flock of birds take glorious flight from the top of an enormous tree. I am silvery, glimmering happiness.

Ricky slides a mug in front of me and lets out a tiny sound from the back of his throat. "You don't *look* tired, Maelyn."

"You actually look a little flushed." Andrew innocently slides another bite of cereal into his mouth, chews thoughtfully, and swallows, adding, "If you need a nap in the Boathouse later, it's quiet and really warm in the sleeping bags."

Well, now I'm sure my cheeks are hot and my eyes are gleaming. I lean over my mug, inhaling the warm, nutty scent. "I think I'm good."

"In any case, we'll get you to bed extra super early tonight," Andrew says, and catches my eye over the lip of his own mug. "Scout's honor."

• • •

A half hour later, he catches me in the hallway with my shower bag, preparing to climb the long staircase to the upstairs bathroom with the best water pressure. Andrew tugs me into the dark, secluded dining room and hides us behind one of the thick velvet curtains, burying his face in my neck.

"Hi." He pulls in a deep inhale. "Don't shower yet." His mouth opens, teeth press into the sensitive juncture of neck and shoulder. "You smell like the Boathouse."

"Your flirting was very subtle back there," I tease.

Laughing silently, he pulls me right up tight against him, a stand-up cuddle. "Kiss me."

So I do.

"You want to know why I couldn't sleep?" he asks.

I laugh. "Why?"

"Because I kept thinking about all your little sounds last night."

"My sounds."

His mouth comes up my neck. "Yeah. Right in my ear." His voice goes quiet. "'*Don't stop. Please, don't stop.*'"

I honestly have few recollections of anything that concrete—just blurry flashes of him moving over me, of this spiraling, back-bending pleasure, and of his own breathy, gravelly noises when he came. "I don't think I realized I was saying anything coherent."

"Not all of it was coherent." He laughs. It turns into a groan. "How are we going to hide this? I'm sure I won't be able to keep it off my face. Maybe we shouldn't try to keep it quiet."

Is he serious? He can't really think we'll announce this today, after one day of togetherness? Does he not know our families at all?

But I don't actually want to think about any of them right now. I wind my arms around his shoulders, and he starts to feel me up. "You know, it might look suspicious from the outside when the curtain starts to wiggle."

He pulls back in feigned shock. "What are you thinking we're going to do in here?" Even so, his palm comes over my breast.

I still feel the rhythmic echo of last night all over. In a twist I can only blame on my semi-uptight upbringing, guilt casts a shadow over my elation. Mom has left a lot of her own mother's prudishness behind, but her biggest conservative holdover is her preference that sex not happen casually. She knows I'm not a virgin, but I'm also sure she wouldn't love to know I was having sex with Andrew in his parents' cabin. I don't regret it, but I don't want to flaunt it, either.

Andrew sees the shadow fall over my thoughts; his hand slides back down to my waist.

"What's wrong?"

It's also more than just the reality that I had sex with Andrew so quickly—which, frankly, is shocking enough. But in the past several hours, I've let myself forget that I'm actually on a wild, cosmic trip, that I might be living on a timer. I've been in this exact day and hour before and I don't know what might propel me backward all over again. Do I feel more firmly rooted here than I did last time, when the branch fell on my head? Maybe? I made it through day three without returning to the plane, but I also didn't make any new declarations or have any heavy realizations yesterday. I was just . . . happy.

And being happy was the only thing I asked for.

So what happens when I'm *not* happy? What happens

when this vacation is over, and Andrew heads back to Denver, and I return to Berkeley, and I'm devastated to be away from him, and jobless and broke? What if I can't keep up this trajectory? Will I fail this particular test? Will I find myself back at the beginning of the game, tasked with reliving all these moments again and finding a way to keep the balloon in the air eternally?

"Nothing's wrong," I say, and hope I wasn't quiet too long. "Just processing it all."

"Oh, shit." His face falls. "We're moving too fast." He runs a hand down his face. "We should have taken it slower last night. It was so good, though, and I was just—"

"It wasn't only you. It was fast," I admit, and his admission that it was good makes me hot all over again. "But it wasn't too fast. I'd wanted to do that with you since I knew what sex was."

A wicked smile pulls up one half of his mouth.

Sobering, I add, "I mean, it's only too fast if . . ." I swallow. "If it's just an over-the-holidays thing."

He pulls back and looks genuinely hurt. "Is that a serious concern?"

"I don't actually know, because you're more private than Theo is about these things. But I'm definitely not like that."

He toys with the strap of my tank top. "I would never do that with you, Mae. That's not what this is."

"This is complicated by a lot of things, but let's start with the fact that our parents are best friends and we live hundreds of miles apart." I chew my lip. "Sorry. I don't mean to get all intense."

"Are you kidding?" He bends at the knee so we're eye to

eye. "The only way to do this is to be open about it. Even if you feel like we didn't move too fast last night, we definitely went from zero to sixty. Talk to me."

I guess there's no point delaying this conversation. "I know you want to tell everyone about us, but are you sure about that?" I slide my hand under the hem of his T-shirt, seeking warmth. He swallows a groan, and distracts me momentarily with a deep, searching kiss that makes an ache drop from my pounding heart into my navel. "I don't want everyone to get overly invested before we even know what this is."

From Andrew's nod, I know I don't have to explain myself. I grew up with a prime example of a relationship that didn't work. Even the simplest of breakups can get messy, and I don't want anyone here to feel forced to choose sides if this doesn't work out perfectly right out of the gate.

Resting his lips just at the corner of my mouth, he says, "Then why don't we just keep following this for a bit before we say anything to anyone? I'm so happy right now I feel hammered. But I'll try to play it cool."

The problem is, I don't know how to do that, either. I've essentially handed my heart over to the person who's had it on reserve for half my life, and I'm terrified that he doesn't realize what he's holding.

Footsteps come to a stop just a few feet away from where we're hiding in the curtains, and Andrew goes still, eyes wide. My lungs turn to concrete.

"Hello, whoever is there," Andrew says, wincing. "Was just, uh, checking this window lock." As he reaches past me to rattle the lock, we stare wide-eyed at each other, probably both praying that it's Kennedy or Zachary and we can pretend to be playing Sardines again.

But then a throat clears, and I have to admit neither of the twins would clear their throat and sound like a grown man.

"I know a good locksmith."

Benny.

Andrew throws back the curtain, blowing out an enormous breath. "Oh, thank fuck."

Benny laughs. "Should I even ask? What were you two doing in the curtain?"

I put a hopeful shine on my words: "Fixing locks?"

But Benny's not having it. "Is that what the kids are calling it these days?"

"Making out," Andrew says with a shrug. "But you are sworn to secrecy."

"I feel like I'm carrying a lot of secrets lately." Benny eyes me sideways.

Andrew notices and looks back and forth between the two of us. "What's going on?"

I shrug like, Benny *said it, not me.*

"Mae's going through some stuff."

"Good or bad?" Andrew asks, turning to me, immediately concerned that I'm hiding something from him.

"Oh . . . I'd wager good," Benny says, raising his eyebrows meaningfully at me.

Over Andrew's shoulder, I give Benny the thumbs-up. Behind Andrew's back, Benny does a dorky little dance of celebration. He stops abruptly when Andrew turns back to him. "But I *was* coming to warn you guys that Miles is look-ing for Mae."

"And you knew to find us in the curtains?" I ask him.

Benny turns to leave and grins at us over his shoulder. "It was pretty easy to follow the giggles."

• • •

I find my brother on the porch, sitting on the swing, scrolling through his phone. He looks up when he hears my foot-steps and drops it into his jacket pocket, tucking his hands between his knees. "Hey."

"Hey."

It's freezing out here, and fresh out of the shower, I feel like I've just stepped into a walk-in freezer. Teeth chatter-ing, I cup one hand around my warm mug of coffee and use the other to zip my parka up to my chin.

"Benny said you were looking for me."

Miles pauses, blushing, and in an instant I know what this is about. Why didn't I see this coming?

I sit down next to him on the swing, bumping his shoul-der with mine. "What's up?"

"I was right last night, wasn't I?" he asks, and then looks at me. My brother got our mother's enormous eyes and he knows how to use them. He can make them round with in-nocence or narrow them in mischief. Right now, he winces a little, looking mortified to be asking me this but also, I know, hoping I won't lie to him.

"Right about what?" I ask, wanting to be sure.

"That you and Andrew are hooking up."

"Yes," I say simply.

"Does Theo know?"

A defensive wave sweeps briefly over me. "No. And please don't tell him. If we decide this is going anywhere, we'll tell everyone ourselves."

Miles nods at this and turns his eyes out to the snow-covered front yard. "Are you sure you know what you're doing here?"

"Not really."

"Because you know Mom will have no chill about this."

The thing about moving home is that I went from independent adult back into kid mode. Mom still does most of the cooking because she loves it. She does most of my laundry because she uses the activity to unwind while she's thinking about how to fix one of her paintings. Of course, I love these perks but they mean I can't complain that she also never thinks twice before giving me her two cents on every aspect of my life.

"Trust me," I say, "that is reason number one why I'm not saying anything yet."

Miles takes a deep breath and lets it out slowly. "I think Theo is in love with you."

"What? No, he isn't," I say.

"How do you know?"

I laugh dryly. "Theo is used to everyone wanting him. I don't. He's the kind of guy who wants what he can't have."

I watch Miles absorb this information, and then he seems to understand, nodding slowly. "Okay. I just—I don't want him to be upset."

Kissing my brother's temple, I tell him, "You're a good boy."

He pretends to be grossed out by this, pushing me away, but turns back before leaving. "Hang out with him today."

"Why?"

"Because I think he misses you."

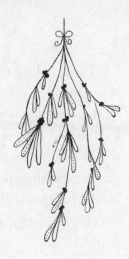

chapter twenty-one

I suppose it's fate, then, that Miles and Theo broke the bowl we always use to hold the scraps of paper for picking teams. Ricky grabs his cowboy hat instead and this time, when Theo's name is pulled out, mine is the one that immediately follows. Andrew throws me a little *womp-womp* face, but I've got no doubt that he and Miles are going to crush the scavenger hunt; their team has the killer combination of Miles's doe eyes and Andrew's ability to charm a stranger into doing anything.

Which is good, because this year's list is heavy on the video evidence, including:

- *A stranger singing "Jingle Bells"*
- *A dog doing a trick*
- *Someone reciting their Christmas list*
- *A teammate performing an act of kindness*

Theo comes over to me, holding the list and smiling shyly, and it's disarming. How can this self-conscious turtle be the same guy who licked my face and refused to talk to me the next morning? It's impossible to reconcile. We used to text about everything—homework and school, his soccer practice and my art projects. He'd complain about the snow and I'd send him a photo of my mom's garden, still in bloom. We haven't done that for a really long time. I wonder if he misses it.

I really don't want Miles to be right about this.

"Guess you're stuck with me," he says.

I smack his arm, laughing. Too high, Mae. Too fake. And Theo knows me too well for it to go over his head: he pulls back in mild suspicion. But he's also not the kind of person to ask about it in front of everyone—or ask about feelings in general—so we're left standing in awkward silence as the rest of the teams are formed.

And then we're off—piling into Ricky's van. Up front, Andrew puts on Nat King Cole's Christmas album, and we all sing along badly, perusing our lists, making fun of Ricky driving like a grandpa, and already excitedly talking about how amazing dinner will be later.

We barrel into town, finding a parking spot in a small lot and tumbling out of the van and into our teams. With instructions to meet back at the van in two hours, Ricky releases us, reminding us to be polite, get permission before taking pictures of people, and "If you want to just give up now, that's fine. Kennedy and I are going to win anyway."

Theo turns his back to the rest of the group, and we form a two-person huddle. The feeling of being this close to him shouldn't be weird—I know him just as well as anyone else in my life—but I can't shake the heavy awareness. It isn't just about hooking up with him in a past reality, or the fact that I'm now hooking up with his brother. It's the layers of things that Theo doesn't know, and the truth that I feel like I got to know him even better—and not for the best—the first time I lived this week.

He holds the list, scanning it with a finger. "We should start with the quick stuff. The candy cane prop," he says, reading further. "A picture of us both wearing Santa hats. A picture of a moose on something." He looks up at me. "These should be pretty easy."

Especially since I know where to find most of these things, I don't bother to add.

"Lead the way." I smile up at him, but it's forced. Everything feels forced between us. I hate it.

He turns, heading left from the van onto Main Street, and I look behind us to where Andrew and Miles are headed in the same direction, but crossing the street to give us some space. When our eyes meet, Andrew winks. It's soothing, like water to a parched mouth, and the perfect reminder that even if we have to navigate this carefully, we get to navigate it together.

We kissed.

We had sex.

Things are really, *really* good.

I jog to catch up with Theo, linking my arm with his, feeling freshly buoyant.

"There she is," he says, and grins down at me.

Before Park City became known as a popular skiing

destination and home to the Sundance Film Festival, it was a mining town. Now nestled between two giant resorts, the small valley was discovered when soldiers stationed in nearby Salt Lake City set out through the mountains to find silver. When the railroad came through and word spread, it was flooded with prospectors in search of their fortunes.

Main Street still bears some resemblance to that old mining town, with old-timey storefronts and historic buildings, but instead of saloons and general stores the street is filled with trendy boutiques and restaurants, museums, and even a distillery. Park City is also money. With more tourists than residents in the area, the Hollises' property is probably worth a fortune. No wonder they decide to sell.

Theo and I rack up a few easy photos for the hunt—a moose on a sweatshirt, a picture of a cowboy, a dreidel, a snowflake on an ornament. A photo of an object with the words *Ho, Ho, Ho.* We stop a couple on their way down the street and ask if they'd be willing to sing "Jingle Bells" for us. It takes a moment of awkward convincing, but thankfully they are game because I've already spotted Andrew and Miles getting video of at least four different people out on the street, and ahead of us, Ricky and Kennedy seem to be flying through their list. The benefit of having an adorable and precocious five-year-old as your partner.

It's not even that I care about winning, but this activity is doing an amazing job of taking my mind off the increasingly shrill voice in my head telling me that everything is on the verge of falling apart.

I can't quite put my finger on why that feeling is rising, but it is; that twinge of panic is growing. Yes, everything is different and for the better. But I've never trusted my own decisions, and when you get everything you've ever wanted, you don't know exactly how to manage it. I wanted Andrew, but it isn't as simple as kissing him and being happy. If there were only some indication, some wink from the stars that I've got it all sorted, I could maybe breathe. Right now, I just want to get through December 26—past the point where I've ever been before—before I can relax and know that everything is settled. That I'm here to stay.

With a few items checked off our list, Theo stops in front of one of the small shops. "I need to grab a couple of things for my parents." I follow his attention to a window display filled with fancy cooking gadgets, spice mixes, and kitchen knickknacks.

Honestly, a kitchenware store seems like the last place he should be shopping for Lisa, but just down the block, I see Andrew duck inside a storefront. Without Miles—who's probably doing some of his own late shopping. My heart grows three times in size. "I'll just be down there." I point. "I have some shopping to do, too. Meet me there in twenty?"

If Theo saw his brother go in, he doesn't let any reaction show. With a little lift of his chin, he urges me to go, and it's all I can do not to sprint to Andrew.

• • •

The window is lit up with an old feather Christmas tree and an assortment of antique toys. I step inside to a blast of warm air and holiday music, and make my way through aisles of retro electronics and worn furniture, stacks of old records and used kitchenware, searching for Andrew.

I find him in the back of the shop, turning an old record over in his hands to read the song list on the back.

"Hey, you."

He turns, and when he grins, the world around us briefly glimmers golden.

"Hey." Glancing around us first, he leans in and gives me a quick kiss. "How's it going with Theo?"

"It's fine," I say, picking up a record out of the box he's perusing. "A little tense. Not sure why."

"Probably because you're sleeping with his brother and he has no idea."

I glow inside at the casual mention that we're *sleeping together*, but guilt shadows the edges. "I feel like I'm lying to him." And then I remember: "Oh. And Miles knows."

"Knows we . . . ?" Andrew looks mildly horrified and makes a vague sexual gesture.

Laughing, I say, "I don't think he knows more than that we were kissing in the pantry." Off Andrew's look, I add, "Oh, come on. He's seventeen, not seven. And he asked me point blank."

Andrew gives a regretful wince. "Poor Miles."

"He promised he wouldn't say anything, but I feel like it's just a matter of time before everyone figures it out."

"Especially when I come visit you in Berkeley in a week because I can't stay away from you."

I beam up at him. "You what?"

"Maybe?" he says, grinning winningly. "Would that be weird?"

I bite my lip, shaking my head. "I feel like everything is about to change."

"Yeah?"

"Miles is leaving for college in a few months. I'm going to have to find a new job." I smile up at him. "Me and you."

"We could brainstorm the job thing together," he says. "What are you thinking?"

I shrug, gnawing my lip. "Something artistic. I could freelance graphic design until I figure something out."

"I could see if there's anything we need at work," he says. "Website stuff?" He shrugs, and it's clear he has no idea how any of that works, but it's endearing anyway. "I can ask."

"That would be amazing." I smile up at him. "I know I should be more nervous about not being employed, but . . ."

But it's hard to worry when he's right here. Every time I start to panic—about the time jumps, about my job, about telling my parents any of this—looking at him immediately calms me down. That has to mean something.

Almost as if he knows what I'm thinking, Andrew looks at me, eyes searching. He steps away from the records and turns, cupping the back of my head and pulling me into a kiss. My thoughts go from *Oh, this is happening,* to *Oh, I need this man's hands on me immediately.*

He tilts his head, his tongue brushes mine, and he lets out a quiet, vibrating sound. Everything about the way I hear it and feel it and taste it reminds me how it felt to be totally immersed in him last night. I stretch, wanting to press as tight to him as I can, even though in the back of my mind, I'm scrambling to hold on to the filmy awareness that we're in public and our families could be anywhere. His hands slide down my waist to my hips, and he pulls them flush to his before he seems to remember where we are, too, and shifts his hands away.

With his thumb brushing the underside of my jaw, he presses one final kiss to my lips and then pulls back, grinning. "Well, that got dirty fast."

I swallow, feeling warm and definitely unsteady. "You almost just got laid in a souvenir shop."

Andrew's eyes flare and then he takes a deep breath, getting some physical distance. "Don't tempt me." He goes back to looking through the records. "I need a second to, uh . . ." He exhales slowly.

"Didn't realize talking about our brothers would get you so worked up, Mandrew."

He laughs. "I assure you, sweetheart, it's your proximity."

I absorb this and it feels like taking a hit of a drug. "Everything is so much better this time."

Andrew pauses. "What's that?"

Oh, shit. I open my mouth to cover, but his attention is snagged over my shoulder.

"Oh my God. Maisie, look."

Relieved, I follow his gaze. There, on a turquoise velvet couch with a FOR SALE sign on it, is a pillow with a needlepoint of Christopher Walken wearing a Santa hat and words below him reading *Walken in a Winter Wonderland.*

Bursting out laughing, I say, "Well, *that's* a coincidence."

Andrew looks delighted. "We might need to get this and keep it in the Boathouse. I have very fond memories of discussing Christopher Walken in there."

"You do?" I ask, hugging him from behind and pressing my lips between his shoulder blades. "Elaborate, please."

"You see, it was just before I had sex in there last night," he whispers over his shoulder in teasing confidence, "with a woman who I've known forever and who used to wear my brother's Batman underwear as a pirate hat."

I stretch to playfully bite his shoulder. "Look at that giant bag of peppermint Hershey's Kisses. That is my dream right there. I could live off that for a month."

He follows my attention to the five-pound bag on display and gives a dramatic shudder. "You're kidding."

"They're my favorite! I can only find them this time of year, and I eat so many I get a stomachache."

Andrew turns in my arms, frowning down at me. "Are you a white chocolate evangelist?"

"One hundred percent!" I laugh-yell. "Oh my God, are we having our first fight?"

"I will die on the White Chocolate Is Not Chocolate hill."

"It may not be chocolate, but it is delicious."

"Wrong, Maisie," he says in Mandrew voice. "It tastes like fake mint and ass."

"Like fake mint and ass?" I reply in outraged Maisie voice. "You're the one who steals the crappy, plasticky chocolate from the Advent calendar."

"Well . . . it's hard to argue with that." He starts to bend to meet my kiss, but we both go still at the sound of Theo's voice behind me.

"Whoa, whoa. What exactly am I seeing right now?"

• • •

It is as quiet as midnight when I turn around. Theo stares at me, and then at his brother, before he laughs dryly and stares at the floor. "Didn't see that coming."

"Hey, Theo." I don't know what else to say.

Andrew has turned behind me but hasn't moved away. In fact, he snakes an arm around my waist, pulling my back to his front. "Theo. Hey."

"*Hey.*" Theo gestures between us. "So—is this a thing?"

"Yeah. It is." Andrew lets that sink in before adding, "You okay, man?"

Theo studies us for several painful beats. "Not sure what to say." He looks at my hands over where Andrew's fingers rest gently on my stomach. "You've clearly kept it from everyone."

"It's new," I say.

"How new?"

"Couple days. Or maybe years," Andrew jokes, smiling down at me. "It's hard to say."

I want to be charmed, but that may be the worst thing Andrew could have said right now.

Theo looks directly at me. "Mae, do you have a second to talk?"

In all practicality, I've already lived this day once before. I might have all the time in the world. Even if there are seven million things I would rather be doing. "Sure?"

I look over my shoulder at Andrew, and he releases me, giving me a small nod. Theo is already halfway to the door, and I have no choice but to follow, leaving Andrew behind.

My mind is vibrating with nerves; it feels like I have no more words in my head. The night with Theo feels like a hundred years ago, but I worry it will forever color how I see him. And I can't even tell him about it.

Out on the street, Theo keeps walking—passing a diner, a small art gallery, a few other stores until we reach a quieter stretch of Main Street. He turns to face me, leaning against the front of a closed-up shop with sandstone bricks, wood trim, windows papered over. He tilts his head back, staring skyward.

"I don't even know how to start," he says. "I'm still trying to figure out how to react."

"I'm sorry you found out like that."

He laughs, running a hand through his hair and looking past me down the street. It's so cold, but I'm not sure if the color that blooms in his cheeks is from the way the temperature seems to be dropping by the second or from anger. A car drives by. A couple with happy smiles and shopping bags approaches on the sidewalk, and Theo and I step out of the way to let them pass.

Finally, he says, "I feel so stupid."

I'm already shaking my head. "No, don't. It surprised me, too."

"We were tight, Mae," he says. "You and me. We were always closer than you and Andrew."

"When we were kids, yeah," I agree carefully. Another car passes, and another close behind it honking loudly at some pedestrians who unexpectedly step into the street. "But as friends. Theo, we were only friends."

"Have you always liked him that way?"

I nod.

"How long?"

Forever? I want to say. "A long time."

I can tell this surprises him, and color makes its way down his neck. "Did he know?"

"Before this week?" I ask. "No."

"Why didn't you tell me?"

"I didn't tell anyone."

"Except Benny," he guesses.

"Benny knows everything."

He takes a few slow breaths. "I just—" He laughs again. "I don't know how to say this so I guess I'll just come out with it: I feel like you led me on."

What the hell? My heart has spent a lot of time racing lately, but not like this. Not out of anger and indignation. "How did I lead you on? By being your friend—"

My words are cut off when, not ten feet away, a brilliant explosion of sound, shimmering in its proximity and volume, cuts through the icy air. We both startle violently; a car has run the stop sign and hit another at full speed. It is a blast of metal crunching and glass cracking, of tires screaming on asphalt. Theo dives on me, covering me as something is propelled toward us, shattering the window just behind where my head was only a second ago.

We sit up, dazed. My ears are ringing, and after a hiccupping inhale, adrenaline dumps into my bloodstream. My entire body starts to shake.

"Are you okay?" Theo asks, and his voice sounds like it's coming through a hollow metal tube.

Numbly, I nod. "Are you?"

"Yeah."

We stare out at the accident, at steam rising from both

cars. My attention catches on a patch of green—a mangled wreath and red velvet ribbon tied to the hood of the larger car.

In the commotion, people pour out of storefronts, crowding around the crash, making sure everyone is okay. What was once a mass of chatting, dawdling, laughing late-shoppers is now a street full of onlookers standing with their hands over their mouths as the drivers emerge, stumbling, from the surprising ruins of their cars.

Theo helps me to my feet, but even once I'm standing— legs shaking beneath me—I can't move from where I'm rooted. That debris was meant for me, I know it. I've done something wrong, taken a bad turn somewhere, and I have no idea what it was, or what's coming for me next.

But it was a warning.

My time here, in this version of reality, is running out.

chapter twenty-two

I step away from the broken glass and shards of metal that litter the sidewalk nearby, Theo moving behind me. Once the onlookers' attention moves from the accident in the street to the aftermath all around us, a fair amount of concern is thrown our way, as the two bodies in the immediate vicinity of the crash.

With the scavenger hunt now completely forgotten, our families frantically run over as soon as they spot us in the middle of the chaos. For a few minutes following the relief that no one was gravely injured, Theo and I are drowning in the adrenaline of what everyone saw, what happened, and how close it was. Andrew hugs me, checks that I'm okay, and presses breathless lips to my hair until the others crowd in for their turn. But smack in the center of my stomach is a leaden ball of dread.

I search for him again, seeking his arms and steadying

gaze, but it's already locked in silent communication with his brother. Very quietly, Andrew says, "I don't understand why you're mad."

"Don't lie, Drew. You get it." Theo digs his hands into his pockets and looks around self-consciously as the rest of the group falls into a hush, realizing there's another conversation happening.

Ricky steps closer, putting a hand on each of their shoulders. "Hey. Guys. What's happening here?"

Theo shrugs out of Ricky's grip. "Stay out of it, Dad."

Ricky frowns. "What am I missing?"

I want to disappear. My eyes shoot skyward. *Kidding!*

Theo lifts his chin to Andrew. "Go ahead. You tell him."

Andrew shakes his head. "Not right now. Not the time."

"Tell me what?" Ricky asks.

Andrew looks at me then, his expression searching for permission, and I feel the way awareness spreads in a silent wave around the circle. Maybe it's how Miles looks down at the ground, or Benny steps closer to me, shoulder to shoulder in solidarity, but anyone with even a modicum of emotional intelligence must know what's being left unsaid.

Well, I guess except Ricky. "Seriously. What's going on?"

"Maybe we can do this when we get home," Benny says quietly.

I look gratefully at Benny—the last thing I want is a scene, and I'd prefer to tell my mom myself—but Theo exhales sharply: "Mae and Andrew are hooking up."

What reaction he was expecting, I have no idea. But the group falls deadly silent before swinging their collective attention to me and Andrew.

"What is considered 'hooking up' these days?" Lisa asks quietly, and my stomach drops in mortification.

"Wait," Ricky says. "Sorry, I feel like I missed something."

"Whatever." Theo turns to walk down the sidewalk. "Doesn't matter."

"Theo." I chase after him, jogging to keep up with his long strides, and reach out to grab the sleeve of his jacket, but he tugs free. "Wait."

I hop over a patch of ice and slow to a bewildered stop in front of a small ice cream shop that's closed for the season. Is he seriously just running away?

"Theo!" I shout, but he keeps going. I take another step and then freeze at the sound of a metallic groan, followed immediately by a cacophonous crash just behind me.

Turning, heart hammering inside my chest, I see that the metal frame beneath the shop's awning has crumpled, plummeting to the sidewalk not a foot away from where I stand. The innocent patch of ice I stepped around is now buried beneath it.

I turn my face up to the sky. "What?" I throw my arms out. "What am I supposed to do? Am I not supposed to follow Theo? Am I supposed to just stand near Andrew? What! Just tell me!"

Benny comes over, a gentle hand on my shoulder. "Mae. Honey. Calm down, it was just an accident."

"It *wasn't*, though." Hysteria has taken over my brain, my blood, my pulse. It pours through me, silvery and hot, obliterating anything rational or measured. "The car crash? *This?*" I motion wildly at the twisted mess of fabric and metal. "*Clearly* it was my fault."

Dad steps forward, gently murmuring, "Mae," with Andrew right at his side. "Honey, what's wrong?" He looks to Benny. "What is she talking about?"

Andrew comes close, putting his hands on my shoulders. "Maisie. What's going on?"

I look past him to Benny. "I can't act like this isn't happening anymore. It's exhausting. I don't know how to keep the act up."

Benny gives me a helpless look.

I turn to Andrew, and then my dad and my brother. I scan my eyes across the group. "I'm stuck in some sort of time loop, and I don't know how to get out of it. I mean," I say, "a few days ago, I wanted out of it so bad. But now I don't want to mess it up."

Andrew takes my hand. "What are you talking about?"

"I don't know how to explain it."

Benny clears his throat. "We think Mae is in a *Groundhog Day*–type scenario. She's been to the cabin a few times, and each time she gets injured and then wakes up back on the plane on December twentieth."

Andrew lets out a little incredulous laugh. Everyone looks around at each other like, *Are we all hearing the same thing?*

"I'm trying to keep track of everything," I admit, "and I realize this sounds crazy, but I'm scared something terrible is going to happen, so can everyone just take a few steps away from me?"

No one moves.

"Please," I plead, and pull my hand out of Andrew's grip. "Back up."

My composure feels like a string being slowly dragged

along the serrated edge of a blade. I turn to my brother, who is watching with wide, worried eyes. "Miles. Punch me."

He lets out a disbelieving laugh. "What?"

"In the face. Hard."

A few voices murmur my name in pity, but I'm not having it. "*Punch* me. I want to go back to the plane."

"Mae, I'm not going to—"

"*Punch me!*"

He takes a step behind Benny, looking to our dad for help, and then I realize that Ricky has picked up Kennedy, that Lisa is holding Zachary, and that everyone—even Andrew—is looking at me like they're afraid of me.

I turn and run away down the street. I don't know where I'm going. I'm praying with everything I have that all of this ends and I wake up in seat 19B. *Take me away from this nightmare.*

The only voice I hear behind me is Benny's gentle "Let her go, Dan. She needs to be alone."

●　　●　　●

Two hours later, Benny walks into the small diner where I've been sitting. He does a brief scan of the interior, spots me, exhales in relief, and makes his way over.

I'm sipping my fourth cup of coffee, hands vibrating as I shred a napkin into smaller and smaller pieces. Pretty soon they'll be microscopic, a smattering of dust on the Formica tabletop. A tinsel-covered Christmas tree stands in the corner, glittery paper snowflakes flutter overhead, and a small rock fireplace burns nearby. None of it helps. None of it makes me feel anything.

"Hey, Mayonnaise," he murmurs, kissing the top of my head.

When I don't reply with a silly name, he pulls out the chair opposite me and sits down. "You're not answering your phone," he says. I can see the worry in the tiny lines around his eyes, the downturn of his mouth.

"I turned it off." The bell rings over the door as a couple of teenagers come inside. "Is Theo okay?"

"Everyone's fine. We're all worried."

"I sound insane," I say. "There's no way to explain this to them. I've been sitting here for two hours, and Andrew hasn't tried to come find me. I'm going to be terrified of something horrible happening to me every second for the rest of this trip—maybe every second for the rest of my life—and everyone must think that I'm losing my grip."

He winces sympathetically. "If it makes you feel better, they all wanted to come find you. You didn't scare Andrew away, I just told him to give you some space."

The opening notes to "All I Want for Christmas Is You" play through the diner speakers. I cast my eyes toward the ceiling. "Did you know they've played this song every twenty-two minutes?"

He doesn't give any outward response to this, just lets me silently work through my thoughts. Groaning, I bend to rest my forehead on my arms. "Benny, I realized something while I was sitting here."

His hand comes over my arm. "What's that?"

"I asked the universe to show me what would make me happy."

"I thought we already knew that." He sounds confused.

"No," I say, pushing myself back up to face him. "I mean, I asked it to *show* me. I didn't say, 'Give me what will make me happy,' or 'Let me be happy forever.' I said, 'Show me what will make me happy.' So, it showed me, but clearly I don't know how to handle it, or what to do, and I can't keep pretending everything is normal."

Benny shakes his head, brows low. "Mae, this doesn't have to be so complicated. Just go tell Andrew what you told me. Explain to him what's going on with you. Andrew is smart. Of any of us, he'll be open to the idea that the world isn't always what we think it is."

"Well, that's the problem." I feel a hundred years old. "How do I explain it? How do I show him?"

"The same way you did with me."

I shake my head. "But the first time it happened, and I talked to you, it was the beginning of the holiday. Things were still happening the way I remembered. I could point things out in advance, because they hadn't changed." I shred my napkin a little more. "But now *everything* has changed. I don't even know what's going to happen next. I don't know how to prove to him that I'm not making this up."

"What about what you said about Ricky and Lisa selling the cabin?"

"He already knows about that. And I've been talking about it, asking about it. It isn't that big a leap for me to guess that they were going to tell us eventually."

"Come on, Noodle. Let's head back."

Pulling my coffee closer, I hug it like it's my last true friend. "I needed to make some changes anyway. This table is my home now. Forward my mail."

Laughing, Benny reaches into his back pocket, fishing out his wallet. "You'll feel better after you talk to Andrew."

"Are they all waiting at the van?"

He shakes his head and pulls a clean hundred-dollar bill out, dropping it on the table. "They all headed back a while ago." He stands. "We can take a cab."

I stare at the bill on the table. "Holy Benjamin Franklin. My coffee was, like, four dollars."

"I don't have anything smaller on me."

"Let me just pay with my debit card." I start to stand, but he puts a hand on my arm.

"Mae. I got it. It's almost Christmas, and this nice little restaurant has kept you safe from cars and awnings and all other dangerous flying objects." He shrugs. "You ever hear of Spotify?"

"Uh, yeah?"

He grins. "I got in early."

"How early?"

"Early." He lifts his chin to the door. "Let's go."

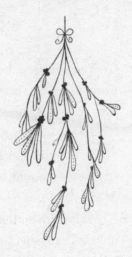

chapter twenty-three

I spend the drive home thinking of every time loop movie I've ever seen, and then berating myself because I've barely seen any. No wonder I'm screwing this up. The taxi drops us off, and I don't go into the main house. Instead I ask Benny to let everyone know I'm fine but need a little space, and make my way through the snow to the back, in search of the one person who—I hope—can make me feel better.

I hear Andrew strumming his guitar from outside, and reach up, knocking tentatively. "It's me."

He gives an immediate "Come in."

The sun wanes, dropping behind the mountain, casting the Boathouse in an eerie twilight shadow when I step inside.

"Hey. I've been hoping you'd come soon."

Relief blooms in me. "Hey."

He sets his guitar down near the cot and walks over.

Cupping my face, he leans in and kisses me so intensely the world around us goes milky. "You had a rough afternoon," he says once he's pulled away.

"Yeah, I was hoping to explain a little about—"

"You were almost killed twice in five minutes," he says. "Any of us would have been freaked, too. I was worried, Mae."

I kiss him for that; even though he doesn't know or probably believe what's really happening to me, he isn't leaving me hanging in this emotional skydive.

He reaches up, pushing my coat from my shoulders in a way that reads hungry and ready. It is exactly the distraction I need. We move through the room, leaving a path of discarded clothing: boots, socks, shirts, pants, bra . . . shivering, we dive into the sleeping bags together.

He's already hard, and comes over me with a groan of relief, his face pressed into my neck. "I'm so glad you're okay. This has been the longest day of my entire life."

Andrew reaches down and unzips the two bags, opening one side so that he can toss it open like a blanket. I catch a glint in his eye when he looks up at me briefly, but it's dark so it takes me a few seconds to realize what's happening.

He kisses down my neck, across my chest—lingering— down over my stomach and hips, and then his kiss is there, vibrating with the sound he makes. I throw an arm across my eyes, wanting to block out everything except the way he wraps his arms around my hips, the way his fingers dig into my delicate skin.

I'm never good at shutting off my own brain, and the past few days—today especially—I've been a mess of nerves and confusion. Even right now, when it's nearly impossible to let any other thought in but how good it feels, I've still got that tenderness at the edge—the fear that somehow this is all going to go away and I'll wake up on the plane with these deep, real emotions that only I remember.

Falling apart with a cry, I reach for him, urging him up and over me. He rips the condom wrapper open with his teeth, impatient hands shaking, and only seconds later we're moving together and he's pressing a groan into my neck. I wonder if, now that I've managed to restart time, I can figure out how to *stop it*, because I never want this night to end. I want it to go on and on forever. I want him to never get enough of me. But then Andrew is moving faster, and his breath goes jagged, and the muscles of his shoulders bunch tightly under my hands. He says my name on an exhale and shakes over me.

Going still, he breathes in uneven bursts against my neck. "I've loved you my whole life, but this new thing . . ." He sucks in a deep breath. "It's amazing and scary."

When he says this, it feels like having a drink on an empty stomach: a shot of heat straight down the middle of my body, followed by the sensation of being immediately tipsy.

And then a ringing screams in my head. I can't have heard him right.

I start to panic.

Catching his breath, Andrew pulls back and looks down at me. I can't see his expression very well; it's dark and my vision is blurry, but I feel the weight of his gaze. "You okay?"

I nod.

He lets out a little laugh and rolls beside me. "Shit. Sorry. It was too much. I ruined the moment."

"No, you didn't." The problem isn't what he said—I wanted him to say that, of course I did—it's that I'm suddenly unable to imagine a situation where I can keep him, where *this* won't all go away in the next second, or the one after that, or later tonight, or first thing tomorrow. I have no control over anything anymore, and it feels how I imagine jumping from a plane without a parachute might feel.

"It's not okay," he says, pushing up onto his elbow to hover over me. "I can tell it upset you."

"It didn't upset me. I want to hear you say that."

He laughs again, for real this time. "Clearly. You've suddenly turned into Robot Mae."

"Are you kidding?" I ask, trying to keep my voice level. "I've wanted you my entire life. There is literally nothing I want to hear more than that you feel the same way. I promise." I take a deep, shaking breath. "But I really need to tell you something hard, and I'm not sure where to start."

He pauses, and I feel the realization as it passes over him. "Do you have a boyfriend back in California?"

"What? Of course I don't."

He deflates in relief. His mouth comes over mine in the dark, and I chase it, pushing up and over him, suddenly wanting to wash away my anguish with the feeling I love most in the world right now, which is having Andrew all to myself.

"Hey, hey." His hands come to my shoulders, and he coaxes me back and away. He's nothing but a series of angles and shadows in the darkness. "Is this about the *Groundhog Day* dream Benny was talking about?"

"Do you remember when I got here," I say, "and I ran

into the house like a crazy person? I told Kennedy not to trip over Miso, I told Dad not to eat the cookie. I went through the thing about Theo's hair being fine, about your dad and the gin. All of that?"

He nods slowly. "Yeah. I remember your arrival being sort of . . . wild." He quickly adds, "But funny. I liked it."

"But specifically," I say, "do you remember me saying those things? And the weird hunches you asked me about?"

Andrew shifts my weight on top of him. "Yeah."

"I had all those weird hunches because, by that point, I'd already been through it three times before."

He lets out a long, slow breath. "Sorry. I don't—"

"I knew your mom would have made those terrible bars," I say, "because Dad broke his tooth every other time I'd lived it."

Andrew lets out another incredulous laugh. "No way."

"I knew Kennedy would skin her knee. I knew you'd sleep in the Boathouse. I knew where to find the sleeping bags."

"Well, okay," he says, trying to work this out. "Why did you get sent back in time, then?"

Relief that he's listening and not immediately running away courses warm through me. "I made a wish."

Andrew laughs, a bright, happy burst of sound that immediately dies when he realizes I'm completely serious. "A wish."

There's no way around this. Taking a deep breath, I say, "The first time around—okay. Things were different with me and Theo."

"Different how?" Andrew asks quietly.

"The first time I lived this holiday," I say, "on the last night, we were in the basement playing board games—Christmas night? We drank too much eggnog. You left to go to bed, and we came back upstairs—Theo and me—and we ended up making out in the mudroom."

Even in the darkness, Andrew visibly pales.

"It was awful," I rush to add, "and we both went to bed, and then the next morning, he got up early and didn't even acknowledge me." I pause, that's not right. "Actually, he said, 'It was nothing, Mae. I should have known you'd make a huge deal out of it.' It was our last day here, and it was completely miserable."

Andrew still doesn't say anything, so I continue. "It was so awkward. You came out and teased me because you'd seen us—"

"Are you sure you didn't dream this?" he asks.

"I'm sure. Your parents told us that they were selling the cabin, and then my family left for the airport. I was freaking out and made a wish to find out what would make me happy." I swallow. "We got in a car accident. I woke up on the plane headed back here. And the same thing happened two more times—once, I fell down the stairs, and once a tree branch fell on me."

He shakes his head as if he can somehow dislodge what I've just said. "You made out with Theo three times?"

"No—God—just the once. Each time I was sent back, I would try to figure out what was happening. I assumed it was like a puzzle, you know? I would think I had it figured out, and would decide some course of action, and then boom, gone. I kept getting sent back because I wasn't doing something right." I wait for him to respond, but he's gone still and quiet beneath me. "But once I was like, 'Screw it,' and just went for what I wanted, everything fell into place."

Still nothing. No reaction from Andrew.

"I was melting down on the street in town," I say, "because you're what I want, and I have this feeling that we won't be able to keep what we have. That it will all disappear. And then everything started to go wrong."

"So that's why you asked Miles to punch you?" he asks, confused.

"Yes!"

His silence stretches, and my thoughts turn foggy with worry that this is all sounding manic and impossible. "I knew we'd build the snow monkey. I knew Miso would destroy your sweater—"

"Miso hasn't destroyed my sweater."

"Well," I falter, "no, not yet, but—"

"Mae." Andrew lets out a long, tired breath, and in the darkness, I see him lift his hands to his face. "Can you just—" He pauses, and then shifts farther away from me. A chill runs down my bare arms, and I suddenly feel too naked. I reach for the sleeping bag, trying to move closer to him, but he holds me away. "Please. Don't—I just need to . . ."

"I know it sounds insane," I say, genuinely worried that I've scared him. I put my hand on his shoulder, but it feels cold. "I *know* it does. But I think I got to do this over and over again so that I could do things right. I really do. For you, and the cabin. And my *life*."

"I thought you weren't into Theo."

My stomach drops. "I'm not. I wasn't. Ever."

"But you're saying," he says slowly, "in some version of the past, you made out with him?"

"For like a *minute*."

He rubs his hands over his face. "I'm not even sure if this happened, but you certainly seem to think it did."

"I know it sounds impossible, I get that, but it did. I was feeling sad and desperate. It wasn't great, he was really cold afterward, and I immediately regretted it. I don't—"

"Sad and desperate over what?"

"You, partly. And just the state of my life."

"So you made a wish for the universe to show you what would make you happy and—" He shakes his head. "I'm the result of that? I'm the prize at the end of the game?"

"I mean," I start, stumbling, "Yes—I mean no, but—"

"Why not just tell me how you felt? That seems, I don't know, *a million times easier*?"

"Because I was scared. Because I've known you my whole life and didn't want to ruin it. Because I assumed you weren't interested in me. But being sent back to the plane over and over made me realize I didn't care if I failed. I had to try."

"So which Mae is real? The one who goes for what she wants, or the one who makes out with my brother when she's afraid of facing her real feelings and then wishes it away?"

"This one. The one right here, telling you that I want this to happen with you."

"I need—" he starts, and slides his hands down his face. When he looks up at me, even in the low light I can tell that the glow in his eyes is flattened, like a candle has been blown out. "I need you to give me some space."

His words leave a ringing silence in the cold, cavernous room. My stomach dissolves away, painfully acidic. "Andrew. It wasn't—"

"Mae," he says very calmly, "don't. Don't make it sound like it isn't a big deal. You made out with Theo because you'd decided—without ever even talking to me—that you and I weren't going to happen. Whether you're remembering something from a dream, or you hit your head or—I don't know—you're somehow repeating time, don't make it seem like it's not totally strange that you think you and Theo actually—" He stops abruptly, unable to finish the sentence. "And then instead of dealing with your life the way it is, you—make a wish?" Frustrated, Andrew rakes a hand through his hair. "God. I can't even process this—whatever this is."

"Andrew," I start, and there's a waver in my voice that I have to work to swallow down. "It's not like there wasn't a weird sense of fate for you here, too. You told me about the tarot cards."

"Oh, come on, Mae, of course we know that's bullshit."

A tiny fire ignites. "What's happening to me isn't *bullshit*—whether you believe me or not."

"Yeah, well, I don't think destiny includes kissing one brother and then the other."

"How many ways can I say that was a mistake?"

He bends, scrubbing his face with a hand. "I think you have more feelings for Theo than you're admitting."

His vulnerability here makes me ache. "Andrew, I know

you're having a hard time believing this, and I realize that what I'm telling you doesn't help my case here, but no. There's nothing there for me. I think I got another chance to make it right. And maybe also to save the cabin."

He laughs, but it isn't an Andrew laugh I've ever heard before. It's a hollow husk of a laugh. "You need to get over your savior thing with the cabin."

Ouch. I try to string together a few words in response, but my brain has gone blank with hurt.

"This is so weird," he says, mostly to himself, and then he pushes out of the sleeping bag and walks back along our trail of clothes, picking them up as he goes. Gently, he places mine in a pile in front of me, and starts pulling on his boxers, his pants, his shirt, sweater, socks.

"I don't want to talk about this anymore," he says quietly. "You should probably head back up to the house."

And . . . that's it.

I get dressed in mortified silence. I want Andrew to watch like he did last night, with his hands tucked behind his head and a sleepy, satisfied smile on his face. But he turns his back to me, bent over his phone. When I move wordlessly to the door, he follows, walking me back to the house. I'm not surprised, though I'm heartbroken. Andrew knows I'm afraid of the dark and even when he's mad at me—even when I'm pretty sure we just ended things—he's still the best man I've ever known.

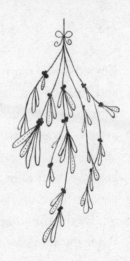

chapter twenty-four

Another sleepless night.

I vacillate wildly, staring up at Theo's bunk in the darkness with an odd mixture of mortification and anger. My gut says I shouldn't have told Andrew what happened with Theo, but my gut has always been an idiot. This is the kind of thing I'd have to share with him eventually, right? Isn't that what people do when they care about each other? They share their flaws and mistakes just as readily as they share their strengths?

But how did I expect him to react? Did I expect him to laugh it off? To believe me blindly and chalk it up to a giant cosmic mistake? I close my eyes . . . I sort of hoped he would. I wanted Andrew to find it as ridiculous as I do now. At the very least I wanted him to commiserate. At this point I can't even fathom what led me to hope for that.

Theo didn't come downstairs until late. I listened as he

slipped down the stairs in the dark, shucked off his jeans, and climbed into the top bunk. It took me five minutes to gather up the courage to say his name, but he was already asleep. Or at least he pretended to be. Not that I can say anything, really, considering I slipped into the house myself last night and went straight to bed to avoid having to talk to anyone.

By the time I've replayed everything for the hundredth time, my thoughts have reached a fever pitch. I suspect Andrew isn't faring any better out in the Boathouse.

Nauseated, I throw the covers back, grab my phone, and head upstairs. It's one thirty in the morning.

The kitchen floor is ice beneath my bare feet. The hallway seems almost sinister in the blackness. I'm drawn by the quiet crackle of the remaining embers in the fireplace in the living room. They struggle to sustain themselves, flickering and glowing beneath a mountain of sooty black wood. I can't build a fresh fire without risking waking the eternal light sleeper Ricky, and not even a chat with Benny would help me right now. I grab a collection of throw blankets from the couches and chairs and build a makeshift bed in front of the hearth.

Tomorrow is Christmas Eve and I've barely thought about it. Because a few of us spend Christmas morning at church, tomorrow we'll eat a huge meal and open our gifts, and what is usually my favorite day all year is going to be awkward as hell. Andrew is mad at me. Theo is mad at Andrew *and* me. No doubt everyone knows about Andrew and me, but it will be immediately apparent that something has gone terribly awry.

Universe, I wonder, *how am I any better off than I was the day we drove away from the cabin?*

So even though I think scotch tastes like fiery butthole, I pour some into a tumbler and toast it to the dying embers before tilting it to my lips and downing it in one go.

I need sleep, and more than that, I need to escape my own head.

• • •

I'm awake with a sore back and droopy heart just when the sun starts to peek over the lip of the mountain. With a blanket wrapped around my shoulders, I shuffle into the kitchen, brew a pot of coffee, and sit and wait for the inevitable: an awkward morning with the father of two people I've kissed.

Ricky shuffles in. "Maelyn," he says quietly. "You and me are two peas in a pod."

But then he doesn't finish.

He pours coffee, sits with a groan, and closes his eyes for a few deep breaths. "You okay, hon?"

"Not really."

He nods, taking a sip. "You and Andrew okay?"

"Not really."

He nods again, studies the tabletop. "You and Theo okay?" When I don't respond, he says, "Let me guess. 'Not really.'"

I lean my head on my folded arms and whimper. "I messed everything up. Today is going to be so weird."

"You didn't mess everything up." He sets his mug down. "And even if you did, you're in the middle of a group of people who were experts at messing things up long before you came around."

I look up at him. "What are you talking about? You and Lisa have been together forever. Mom and Dad were married for twenty-four years."

"Sure, that's how it looks to you kids." He catches himself. "Guess you aren't really kids anymore, are you?"

This makes me laugh, just a little. "No."

He sniffs, scratching his jaw. "Well, the good has stretched out a long way past the bad, but everyone makes mistakes in their twenties. Hell, even in their thirties." He pauses and meets my eyes across the table. "And maybe their forties and fifties, too."

"I'll be honest, the idea of you ever being emotionally messy is . . . like, it does not compute."

Ricky laughs at this. "You know your mom and Lisa were roommates. Your dad, Benny, Aaron, and I all lived on the same floor our freshman year, in the dorm. We were immediately close, spent all our free time together," he says, and I knew that part already, but what he says next blows my mind: "Lisa and Benny were an item for a few weeks before she and I started dating. If I remember right, I think she and I started up before they really ended things."

I pull my eyebrows back onto my forehead. "I'm sorry, what?"

He nods. "You think *that* wasn't messy?"

There is so much here that requires mental realignment, the only thing I can think to say is "Benny had a *girlfriend?* And she was Lisa?"

Ricky laughs. "He did."

"But—you guys are still so close."

He stares at me in tender wonder. "Of course we are, honey. That was thirty-plus years ago. When the friendship is worth it, people work through things. Like with your parents. We've survived that because of how much we truly value each other's friendships."

"So what happened?" I ask. "Back in college?"

He sips his coffee as he thinks. "The specifics are pretty fuzzy, but if I remember right, Benny was more upset that we weren't honest about it than anything else. It was a month or two, maybe, of him hanging out with some other friends, but he came back around. We were meant to be family."

The timing is perfect—or maybe it's terrible. The back door creaks open, boots stomp in the mudroom, and then Andrew steps into the kitchen.

"Mornin', Drew." Ricky brings his mug to his lips and winks at me. I'd smile back, but keeping my face from crumpling is currently requiring all my focus.

Andrew pours a cup of coffee and looks like he's going to turn back and return to the Boathouse. But his father stops him.

"Come sit with us."

I close my eyes and try to pretend I'm invisible.

Andrew looks over his shoulder, giving a warning "Dad."

"Well, at least say 'Good morning.'"

"Good morning." With a flicker of pain in his eyes that I know is a conflicted blend of guilt and anger, Andrew ducks back outside.

Ricky rumbles a sigh into his coffee. "It'll be okay. Things always look worse from the inside."

• • •

No matter how much I want Ricky to be right—that I haven't ruined everything, that it will all be okay—I can't see how we get there from here. Theo absorbs himself in video game talk with Miles over breakfast so he doesn't have to speak to me. Mom tries to catch my eye whenever she passes me a plate, which means she's constantly trying to hand me food and unfortunately, there's no room inside my stomach with this ball of regret in the way. I can only wonder what Dad or Benny said to her because strangely, she doesn't push. When Andrew finally comes in—long after breakfast—it isn't just awkward as hell, it's painful. He passes straight through the kitchen, mutters something to Lisa in the hallway, walks out of the house, and climbs into his 4Runner.

For several loaded seconds, those of us in the kitchen—Mom, Aaron, Kyle, Benny, Dad, and me—fall into a perceptive hush. The only sound is Andrew's truck roaring to life and pulling out down the gravel driveway. Once he's clearly gone, we return to whatever we were doing before—namely ignoring the giant elephant in the room—but the mood has definitely dropped.

It's discordant for the vibe to be so dark. Normally we're all crammed in the kitchen together. Music is blasting, we're dancing and tasting as we cook, telling stories, teasing each other. Not this time; it's lifeless in here. Not even Aaron's fitted metallic joggers and giant Gucci belt bag are absurd enough to lift the mood.

The only sound is the wet, squishy squelch of Mom stirring her homemade macaroni and cheese. All I can think is how much it sounds like the zombies eating on *The Walking Dead*. I can't even laugh at this. It's like a laugh has dried up in my chest, turned dusty.

No one says anything to me directly, but the weight of the silence seems to drift steadily my way, landing squarely on my shoulders.

Ricky walks in from outside, where he'd been shoveling the back walkway. "Heard the 4Runner start up. Where'd Drew go?"

We all make vague sounds, and he walks into the living room to ask Lisa. In the kitchen, we fall silent again, leaning slightly to eavesdrop on her answer.

"I don't know," her voice filters down the hall. "Just said he wanted to get out of the house for a bit."

The volume of everyone's silent question *What the hell is going on?* turns shrill. I collect a few dirty dishes to be washed and move to the sink.

Benny follows. "Hey, you."

Turning on the faucet to warm water, I mutter, "I am the human equivalent of a fart that clears a room."

Unfortunately, I've said it loud enough for others to hear, and Benny unsuccessfully fights a laugh. With relieved exhales, they all take the burst of levity to come over to me, hug me, assure me in overlapping voices that everything is going to be okay, that they're sure I did nothing wrong. I know they don't know the specifics of what's going on, but it doesn't matter to them. They love me, they love Andrew. Whatever is happening is a blip, just like Ricky said.

To them, it's something we'll get past, and come out the other side stronger for it.

I guess I'll have to figure out what that looks like for me, getting over the feelings that have lived inside me every day for more than half my life.

Mom's voice rises above the others and I know that my respite is over, which is fine. I probably deserve whatever she's going to say. "Mae." I feel her turning me, finding my hand, and pulling me out of the fray. "Come here, honey."

She leads me out of the kitchen and down the hall. Once we're alone, she runs her hands through my hair, gazing back and forth between my eyes. Shame washes over me, hot, like warm water on a burn.

"Do you want to talk about it?" she asks.

"Not really." I close my eyes, swallowing back nausea. "I'm sorry. I don't even know what to say other than I messed up."

"What on earth are you sorry about?" she asks, cupping my chin so I'll look at her again. "You're twenty-six. This is when you're supposed to do crazy things and mess up a little."

I'm surprised she's not more upset. Mom doesn't shy away from big feelings; unlike Dad, she lets it all out as soon as it courses through her. Dad is a thinker; he bottles everything up until—out of nowhere—it comes out in a pressurized stream. Only twice in my life have I heard him raise his voice. But I expect it from Mom. I expected her to really let me have it.

"That's it?" I ask.

She laughs. "I mean, if you really want me to, I can probably work up to something, but it's Christmas. Consider it my gift to you."

"Well, in that case," I say, wincing, "I should also let you know that I quit my job. *Now* you can let me have it."

Fire flashes in her eyes for the duration of her long, controlled inhale and then, with a weary laugh, she pulls me toward her. "Come here." She kisses my temple. "You look like you want to crawl out of your own skin."

"I do." I want to crawl out of my skin and then dive into the snow outside.

"Listen up," she says, "because I'm going to tell you a secret not everyone knows: Everything is going to be okay. I mean it. I realize everyone around you being messy might make you feel like you can't ever be, but that isn't true. It's okay to be messy sometimes, honey."

When I wrap my arms around her waist and tuck my head under her chin, I feel rooted here for the first time in more days than I can count.

● ● ●

Andrew isn't around for the rest of the afternoon when we're ready to start sorting and opening presents, so we bake. A *lot*. Peppermint meltaways, Mexican wedding cakes, gingerbread, Santa's Whiskers—the same cookies we've made every year I can remember. With a plate stacked for Santa and the sky growing dark, we start setting the table.

The candlesticks we use belonged to Aaron's mom and serve as a reminder of how this whole thing started. I set the flowers in the center and the wine bottles are evenly spaced along the length of the table. The twins decorate those—and Miso, and each other—with a bag of bows they find in the living room.

Andrew slides unobtrusively into the kitchen just as the rest of the dishes are being brought out, and he chooses a seat as far away from me as he possibly could, in the distant corner, where Aaron usually sits.

I'm sure the food is delicious—it's my favorite meal all year and smells like heaven—but I can't taste a thing. I chew absently, and swallow, trying to look like I'm following the flow of conversation. I feel like I have a frozen block of ice in my stomach. Andrew won't even look at me, and I'm so miserable, I'm not sure how I'm still here, at the dining room table, and not back in seat 19B. Maybe I haven't finished thoroughly ruining everything yet, and the universe is waiting for me to really go all in. I pick up my wineglass, full almost to the brim. I'm sure I won't disappoint.

"We thought we'd wait to open presents until you got home," Ricky tells Andrew.

Andrew chews and swallows a bite quickly, guilt coloring his cheeks. "Thank you. Sorry. You didn't have to do that."

"Of course, baby," Lisa says. "We wanted to be all together."

The twins have been so patient all day, and with the prospect of gift opening finally spoken, it's like a switch has been flipped. Kennedy and Zachary explode in excitement and noise. I remember that feeling, remember wanting to rush through the meal so that we could tear into our gifts, and then afterward always being so grateful that we paced ourselves, otherwise the day would go by too fast. But this time, I want to skip it all and head to the basement. I want to climb into bed and succumb to blackness. It's dramatic, but I wonder how terrible it would be to disappear once everyone is asleep and simply fly home to Berkeley early and have a quiet Christmas Day alone tomorrow. Maybe my scarf will get caught in the escalator at the airport, and I'll wind up back at the start again. And would that be so bad? Honestly it doesn't sound any worse than what's happening now.

After cleaning up, we slowly make our way into the living room. All around me, my loved ones chatter happily about their excitement for their Secret Santa recipient to open their gift. Mom brings in an enormous platter of cookies, and Ricky follows with a pitcher of milk and some glasses stacked on a tray. Cocktails are poured, music is put on, the fire roars. It is everything I love in life, but I can't enjoy it. What a good life lesson: be careful what you wish for. I wanted to undo the damage done with Theo, but that was intro level life-ruining. What happened with Andrew feels like getting a PhD in idiocy.

• • •

Across the room, Andrew sits in a chair, staring quietly into the fire, so different from his usual chatty self. I wonder where he was all day, what he was doing. How he can look so sad after the end of a two-day-old relationship. I'm mourning something I wanted for half my life. What's his excuse?

Maybe he's deciding how to tell everyone that he won't be back next year—if we ever actually get around to next year—which, frankly, is exactly what I deserve.

When I turn back to the room, I see Kyle wearing a Santa hat, which means it's his turn to choose the first gift to be opened. Although we each draw a name, the idea that each person will get only one gift from one other person is sort of a joke. The pile under the tree is mammoth. Gifts from parents to children, from children to parents, little things that we see throughout the year and have to buy for each other. Kyle gets random things with tacos on them. Aaron loves cool socks. Dad gets a lot of joke gifts—Whoopee Cushions, gum disguised as Juicy Fruit that tastes like skunk, handshake buzzers. He loves to play pranks on his office staff, and somewhere along the line we all agreed to be in on it. The pile of gifts under the tree is a hilarious display of adoration, capitalism at work, and our complete inability to moderate ourselves in any way.

When Kyle brings me a small box, and I look at the tag and see Andrew's name in the *From* line, I feel like I've swallowed a basketball. This didn't happen the first time around. I know enough has changed in this version of reality that it might not mean something. It could be something benign he bought on a random trip to the 7-Eleven. It could be a box of Snickers—my favorite candy bar—or a can of Clamato, a literal gag gift.

But the tiny groan he lets out—like he forgot it was there and wants to somehow take it back, undo it—tells me this isn't a joke gift. It's tender.

Under the press of attention from everyone in the room, I remove the light green striped ribbon and peel away the thick red paper. The box has the name of the store we were in together, and my stomach drops. Inside is a T-shirt with a picture of Christopher Walken that reads I'M WALKEN ON SUNSHINE.

Ouch. He must have found this in the little boutique yesterday after I ran off.

The present is so perfect that it almost pulls a sound of pain from me, but I look up, arranging my features into a smile. Odds are good that I'll never manage the emotional fortitude I'd need to pull this shirt over my head. More likely I'll just sleep with it nearby. That is, until I'm eighty and it's dissolved into a pile of threads from my heartbroken stroking, and then I'll have to cuddle with one of my seven hundred cats instead.

"Thanks, Andrew."

"No worries."

"It's perfect."

He flexes his jaw, nodding at the fire. "Yup."

Benny frowns quietly at his shoes. Mom and Dad exchange worried glances. Ricky and Lisa, too.

But it's my turn to pick the next gift. I stand, walking on unsteady legs to the tree, and grab the first box there. It's for Kennedy, thankfully, and her happiness is a brief distraction.

Presents are opened. Hugs are given. All around me, the room is full of bright voices, excitement, and color. I do my best to be present; to smile when it seems appropriate and respond when someone asks me a question. I *ooh* and *ahh* in the right places—at least I think I do. My parents got me a new Apple Watch. Miles got me a giant Snickers bar. My true Secret Santa was Aaron, who got me tickets to see the Lumineers in February. For a few minutes my excitement, as I go through this all again, is genuine.

But then Mom gets up to refill her tea, and I hear the kitchen door open, and the scattery click-click of dog paws on linoleum, and then Mom's distressed gasp. "Oh. Oh no. Oh, Miso." She calls out, "Andrew?"

I don't know if he means to do it, but Andrew's eyes fly to mine. I think we both know what's coming, but when Mom comes into the living room with the ruined remnants of Andrew's ugly Christmas sweater, for just a second I think I've been saved.

He'll believe me.

But that's the problem. I can see in his eyes that he does believe everything I told him, and it's somehow worse.

Andrew stands, taking the sweater from Mom's hands, and leaves the room.

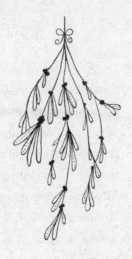

chapter twenty-five

St. Mary's Catholic Church in Park City is an intensely stunning old stone-and-wood building set in the middle of a snow-covered field. In the summer, it is surrounded by towering trees of fluffy green, but this time of year, the branches are bare and decorated with the crystalline splendor of winter.

We go to the early Christmas Mass service—Mom, Miles, Lisa, and I—in part so that we don't lose much time with the rest of the group, but also to avoid the chaos of younger kids later in the morning.

Although I love our church back home, the fact that I come to St. Mary's only once or twice a year gives it this deeply nostalgic place in my life. Inside, it is beautiful simplicity: softly arched ceilings, crisscrossed pale wood beams, unassuming stone walls. Smooth wooden pews and tall windows that keep the space bright and clear.

And then, unfortunately, there's the altar—the one thing that demonstrates that I am a terrible Catholic and probably going straight to hell no matter how I spend my Sundays. With arched stone framing an equally arched window, it looks so much like a vagina from where we sit to the side that neither Miles nor I can ever look at it without breaking into suppressed laughter.

Today, though, I stare directly at it for a full five minutes before realizing I am looking into the dark depths of the building's vaginal canal. What's wrong with me?

I blink away, focusing down on my hands in my lap. I'm warmly bracketed by my mother on my left and Lisa on my right. Their arms are pressed along mine; such a simple point of contact but so oddly grounding. My two mothers— one by birth and upbringing, one that Mom chose as her closest friend. You'd think things would be weird with Lisa today, after my emotional fiasco with both of her sons over the last couple of days, but it's not.

Probably because she's known me longer than anyone aside from my parents. She pulled me aside on the walk to the car this morning and said, "I want you to know that no matter what, I am always—*always*—here for you." It wasn't a long exchange, just a hug and a sad, understanding smile, but it was exactly what I needed to hear to let the air out of that stress steam-pipe. Disappointing the adults in my life is kryptonite to my peace of mind.

Of all of us here, Mom is the most devout, but we each have our own relationship with church. Mine has generally skewed more toward sentimental comfort: I love the songs, the community, the breathtaking beauty of church architecture (minus the vagina). I love the consistency of the rituals. Mom never demanded that we believe everything she believes—after all, Dad has a firm disinterest in all things religion—or do everything the church wants us to do, which is good, because I found that I was never able to accept the Bible as nonfiction. Mom only asks that we come and listen respectfully, and that we work to be good and kind, and live generous lives.

But this is *now*, and my first time inside a church after having real and irrefutable proof that there is another power, bigger than me, at work in this world. I'm still not sure what exactly that power is, but I guess I have to acknowledge there is way more out there than what I understand. I believe now that the universe delivers random acts of kindness, and it's on us to decide what to do with them.

It's on me to figure out how to move on from this past week and find happiness—whether that's with Andrew, or on some other path in my life.

As the priest delivers his tranquil homily about the Gospel of Luke, I close my eyes and try to blur out all sound and images. I try to be present in this quiet moment, to soak up the warmth of my mom at my side and the solid shape of the pew at my back. I'm trying as hard as I can to not silently wish for more—for Andrew's forgiveness, or for a job I look forward to doing each day. I've spent years not trusting my ability to make decisions and quietly letting life just happen to me. It can't be a coincidence that the moment I stopped being passive and followed my instincts, everything seemed to fall into place. I know what makes me happy—trusting myself. What a gift, right? I found happiness.

Now I just have to figure out if there's any way I can get it back.

Mom leans over and stretches to reach my ear. "Are you okay?"

My mother never speaks during service—especially not Christmas Mass—unless it's to hiss at us to be quiet. But she would rather cut off her own arm than let her kids struggle through something alone.

"Just thinking," I whisper back. "I want you to be proud of me. I want to be proud of myself."

"I am always proud of you." She wraps her hand around mine. "I trust you. The only person whose expectations you have to live up to is yourself." She lifts my hand to her mouth and kisses it. "I want you to find what makes you happy."

She sits back up, staring straight ahead, oblivious to the way her words just delivered a glowing ember into my heart. This is real. I have so many things to work on, but it's like my boulder moment all over again, like watching a puzzle slot into place.

The only person whose expectations you have to live up to is yourself.

When I thought it didn't matter and no one would remember, I finally started living authentically. I quit my job. I was honest about my feelings. I went after what I wanted without fear.

My feet feel the floor; my back feels the pew.

I am aware of the fresh, clear air inside, of the hum and vibration of hundreds of bodies all around me. With Mom echoing my wish back to me, I have an idea.

• • •

Miles shoulders up to me as we crunch our way back up the driveway toward the cabin. "You good?"

It's the first time we've talked, really, since that morning on the porch, and there's no doubt in my mind that my seventeen-year-old brother is super confused about what the hell has happened to his boring, levelheaded sister.

"I'm okay." I blow out a controlled breath. "Had a weird week."

"Sounds like it."

I stop a few feet from the base of the porch steps, looking up at the cabin. With a conspiratorial little nod to me, Mom follows Lisa up the steps, stomping her boots on the porch and disappearing into the warm indoors. But even though I know that part of my fix-it plan for the day is set in motion, dismay slides coolly from my throat into my gut. Today is our last full day here.

Miles drags his shiny shoes across the wet path to the house. Mom won't be happy about the slush and salt that's soaking into the hems of his best church pants, but I'm not ready to go in yet, either. If my brother wants to dawdle, so be it.

"Theo said he wishes he didn't lose it with you the other day," he says.

Oh.

His words pull my attention away from the cabin and back to him. Miles is already taller than Dad. It's so easy to see him as an eternal kid, but in only a few months he's going to leave home for college. He'll launch, and he will be just fine.

I squint from the sun reflecting off the snow-covered yard. "Theo said that?"

He nods. "Last night. Sort of out of the blue. What happened between you guys?"

"That's between me and Theo."

He blinks past me, shifting on his feet.

"What else is bugging you, cutie?" I ask.

"Is it true Ricky and Lisa are selling the cabin?"

I chew on this, unsure how much to say before they can tell us all themselves. "I think so. That's the rumor, at least. Who'd you hear it from?"

"Dad said something." He stares up at the cabin, frowning. "Sucks. I wish Mom or Dad would buy it."

There's a creak in my mind, the slow opening of a treasure chest. I kiss my brother again and jog up the stairs, chasing after my second good idea in a single morning.

• • •

"Benito Mussolini," I say, sweeping into the blessedly quiet living room. "Fancy meeting you here."

The Christmas tree glimmers like a display of jewels in the corner; the fireplace cracks and pops nearby. Upstairs I can hear the twins racing around, probably still in their pajamas and high on all of the sugar they found in their stockings.

"Well." Benny looks up from his book and tucks his thumb in to hold his spot. "What an unexpectedly chipper greeting."

"I am in an unexpectedly chipper mood. It is Christmas, after all." I point to the hallway. "Come talk to me?"

He stands, following me, and we make our way upstairs, and then upstairs again into the attic. I don't see Theo anywhere along the way, and Andrew is probably out in the Boathouse with his guitar and regret. But it's for the best: I can't have this conversation if he's around.

It's cold up here relative to the crackling heat of the living room, and Benny pulls a blanket from the bed for me to wrap around my shoulders, and then grabs his green cashmere sweater. This is a Peak Benny moment—having enough money to buy cashmere but using it to buy a sweater that looks identical to the one he's always worn.

Sitting in a rickety chair near the window, he motions for me to take a seat in the sturdier option—a wooden stool—and pushes his hair out of his face. "How're you doing, Noodle?"

"In the grand scheme of life, I am great. Unemployed but healthy, and have a pretty amazing community, if you do say so yourself." I pause, watching a bird land on a branch outside the small attic window. "But in the realm of romantic love, I am—how do I say it? Quite shitty."

He laughs despite the dark truth of this. "Was it good while it lasted?"

"The blip of my romantic life with Andrew Polley Hollis? Yes, Benny, it was truly blissful."

Benny's smile tilts down at the edges and before I realize it, it's turned into a full-blown frown. For years he's listened to me pine hopelessly over Andrew. The summer before ninth grade, Benny caught me writing our names together on a receipt from Park City Mountain, and I was so embarrassed, I attempted to burn the evidence in one of Lisa's scented candles. I ended up setting a pillowcase on fire. Benny sat with me through four hours of the online fire safety class my parents made me do so I didn't have to be alone all day.

When I was nineteen, Benny was the first to run into the room after I'd gouged my forehead because I was supposed to be unloading the dishwasher, but instead was watching Andrew strum his guitar at the kitchen table. I stood up without looking, cracking my head on an open cabinet door. There are probably a hundred stories like this, and Benny has witnessed nearly all of them.

"I'm sad for you," he says now.

"I'm sad for me, too," I say, but swallow past the lump of genuine grief in my throat, "but I guess there's a good lesson here: You can't erase mistakes. You just have to figure out how to fix them."

"Is that what we're doing up here?"

"Actually," I say, sliding my hands between my knees, "yes. But I'm not here to brainstorm the Andrew problem."

His brows furrow, and he reaches into his bag for his one-hitter. "What's up?"

"You said something in the diner about Spotify."

He nods, flicking his lighter. The spark leaves a firework of light on my retinas that's slow to fade. He inhales deeply and exhales to the side so it doesn't cloud between us, before sitting back. "I did say something about that, didn't I?"

"I realize this is incredibly intrusive, but it was a surprise to hear that you can pay a hundred dollars for my coffee when you don't have smaller bills."

"Yeah," he says, nodding with his attention fixed to something just past my shoulder, "it's been a surprise. A nice one."

"When did—?" I start, and then try again, fumbling. "I mean, we had no idea."

"Well, to be fair, I wasn't being secretive; we don't usually sully the holiday with talk of coin," he says, grinning at me. "But truth be told, I only recently sold a chunk of my shares. You know me." He gestures to his ripped jeans. "I don't care about stuff so much. I'd rather use it up and wear it out. I've really had no idea what to do with all this money. Got a guy advising me now. He's good. Smart. Trustworthy, I think."

"Well," I say, and my stomach gets all twisty and nervous even approaching this, "I'm worried about being a terrible friend cliché by doing this, but I was wondering if I could talk to you about helping me do something."

Benny gives a hint of a smile. "I think I know where this is going."

I blink. "Where is this going?"

He lifts his chin. "Go ahead."

My shoulders are slowly hunching higher and higher on my neck in preemptive regret, but I wince it out: "I was thinking maybe you could cosign a loan for me to buy the cabin?" His expression shifts. I've clearly surprised him, so I rush to add, "I can probably cover the down payment—I've saved. And once I have a new job, I can pay the mortgage. I live at home, I don't have any expenses really. I'm sure I'll find a job relatively quickly, and it would just be co-signature, I swear."

He's still frowning, and I am mortified but push on. "You could live here rent free and just do your Benny thing. Play your guitar. Putz around. I'd pay the mortgage and as I save, maybe I can pay for larger things, too. It would be an investment. I also realize this is dependent on what they're asking—okay, it's dependent on a lot of things . . ." I pause to finally take a breath. "I just don't want us to lose this place."

"I don't want us to lose it, either." He studies me for a few quiet seconds. "It matters to you that you own it?"

I shake my head. "I mean, I know that owning a home—especially an old one, and *especially* in another state—isn't easy. But if you lived here, maybe it would be easier? I don't know. I realize this sounds crazy, and to be honest the details only occurred to me about a half hour ago. It's not so much about me owning it as it is about all of us having this place to come together. I do ultimately think this is one of the things I was sent back to fix."

He nods like he understands. "I see."

"Think about it," I say, quickly adding, "Or don't. I mean, I have no idea if I've insulted you, or—"

"You haven't in the slightest."

"—or whether this is even something people do?" I grimace apologetically. "I feel really naive all of a sudden."

"I'm sorry," he says with a smile, and then leans forward, taking my hands. "You haven't insulted me, and you don't sound naive at all, honey. I wasn't trying to let you flounder; I was trying to figure out your motivations and whether I would be taking something away from you that I hadn't considered."

"Taking—?" I shake my head. "I don't understand."

"Taking your opportunity to own this place. I've already made an offer to Ricky and Lisa."

My mouth opens, but nothing comes out except for a wheezy zombie creak. Finally, "An offer on the cabin?"

He squeezes my hands. "The first time you lived through this week, you didn't know until the last day that Ricky and Lisa were selling it. And I mean, who knows? Maybe I would have stepped in later and made an offer, but I know myself. I'm hesitant to make commitments to big things. Maybe I would have just been sad like the rest of us, and briefly considered buying it, but by the time I got back to Portland I bet I'd have talked myself out of it. But you told me the very first day. So," he says, and smiles again, "I was here all week, thinking about how much I love this place and trying to imagine never being here with all of you again. Knowing what was coming made it easier for me to get used to the idea of taking that leap. And it also let me pry a little with Ricky." His smile turns wolfish. "Subtly, of course. Just a question here or there."

"I'm sorry." I hold my hands out, unwilling to unleash the euphoria. "What are you saying?"

"I'm saying that I'm buying the cabin."

I bolt out of my seat, tackling him in a hug. His chair cracks and breaks; we fall in a dusty tumble to the wood floor.

"I take it that's okay with you?" Benny laughs beneath me.

. . .

I'm confident that my next conversation cannot top the perfection of how things just went with Benny, but I'm relieved that when Theo sees me come down into the basement, he doesn't stand up to immediately leave.

In fact, he smiles.

He sits up at the small card table, wearing a Captain America Christmas sweater that looks at least one size too small and cupping his hands around a mug of coffee. "I was looking for you earlier."

"That would make one of you," I say, laughing as I sit down. "Most people in this house seem to turn the other way when I walk in."

"Aw, it isn't that bad, is it?"

I shake my head. "I'm just kidding. Everyone has been amazingly patient with my mental calamity, as expected."

"Except me."

I laugh at this, unexpectedly loud. "Except you."

"Look," he says. "I was a jerk yesterday. I'm sorry. You know me—sometimes I just need a day to cool my head."

I don't think I realized how upset I've been about the fissure in our relationship until he says that, and I feel the tears rising like a wave in my throat. Of course I know that about him. I've always known that he is slow to anger and even slower to defuse. So why didn't I ever give him the benefit of the doubt the first time around? In hindsight, he just needed to be left alone the morning after we kissed, to be allowed to dig out from his own mortification. All this time I've been upset with him for simply being exactly the person I always knew he was.

But before I can swallow them down, the tears are pouring over. He immediately jumps up and rushes around the table, kneeling to hug me. I'm sure he's bewildered by my reaction, but he has no way of knowing how badly I needed to hear this apology—for something this version of Theo didn't even do. It's like being angry at someone after they behaved badly in a dream; it isn't Theo's fault that I needed days of emotional space from him.

His question is a low rumble against my shoulder. "Are you going to tell me what's going on?"

Even the idea of going through it all again feels, mentally, like running into a brick wall. I also know that it won't help matters: If Theo was struggling with the idea of me with Andrew, the last thing he needs to hear is what happened in some alternate version of reality. Telling him won't make me feel better, won't help Theo feel better, and it won't help anything between me and Andrew.

"Do you mind if we skip the whole download?" I say. "I'm realizing that, in this particular situation, I should probably just move forward."

He pulls back and lifts his chin, studying me sweetly. "Okay. I'll let it go. But if you change your mind, you know I'm always here to give you bad advice."

I laugh. "Thanks."

After a long beat of contemplative silence, he asks, "So you were really into my brother all this time?"

I nod. "Since you and I were thirteen."

He whistles, low and sympathetic. "That's a long time, Mae. Holy shit."

"Is it weird to admit to you that I don't know what it would feel like to not be infatuated with Andrew?"

"It's not weird at all," he says. "I mean, it's cool you're talking about it with me, you know?"

"Yeah."

"Did I mess things up with you two?"

This makes me laugh. "Fear not. I did that entirely on my own."

"Do you think you can fix it?"

I chew my lip. "I'm going to give it a try."

Theo rises from his knees to sit in the chair beside mine. "I don't really know what happened with you two, but Andrew is super private. So the fact that he was immediately so up front about what was going on was pretty crazy." He runs his thumbnail along a scratch in the table. "I think that's what I was probably reacting to yesterday. The familiarity. It made me think you guys had been a thing for a long time."

I let out a dry laugh. "Nope."

"He was acting *settled*, you know? So, take that for what it's worth, but I think if you really have feelings for him, it's worth fighting a little longer before you give up."

I look at the time on my phone and realize that if I'm going to grand-gesture this thing, I'd better get started.

"It would be easier to cut off my own arm than get over your brother, so I'm not giving up." I stand, and then bend to kiss his cheek. "I've got some plans up my sleeve. Wish me luck."

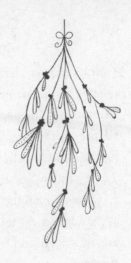

chapter twenty-six

In the first version of this holiday, Andrew wasn't out in the Boathouse alone at all on Christmas Day. Around this time—almost five in the evening—he was in the kitchen with Zachary and Kennedy, hanging metallic garlands and tissue paper holly, singing Christmas carols in Muppet voice, and making the twins giggle hysterically.

But this time, the kitchen is quiet. Presents are unwrapped and the discarded paper has been stuffed into the recycling bin. There's no garland on display, no tiny scissors on the table or paper scraps littering the floor. We'll eat leftovers in about an hour, but for now everyone is using the downtime to nap, read, or sip a cocktail by the fireplace, savoring the last of our time together. Except for me: in Benny's attic, I get to work.

And then, with my heart in my throat, I take the package Mom helped me complete, and tromp through the fresh snow out to Andrew's little Fortress of Solitude.

He doesn't answer when I knock, so I stand uselessly outside for about two minutes—debating with myself what to do, panicking because he's ignoring me, letting my hysteria rise to a boiling point—before figuring out that maybe I just need to knock louder.

"Come in," he calls this time. "It's open."

I push open the door and step inside.

Andrew's duffel bag is packed, and the sleeping bags are rolled up and leaning against the far wall. He sits on the bare cot, one leg bent and tucked beneath the other, strumming his guitar.

I'd planned to start with my little prepared speech, but the view of his packed bag throws me. I'm not sure he was even planning to say goodbye. "You're driving back to Denver tonight?"

"I am, yeah." He looks up and tries to smile. Even with all the strain between us he doesn't have it in him to be unkind. "After dinner."

I flounder, unable to think of a suitable follow-up. "Did you hear about Benny and the cabin?" I inwardly wince, remembering what he said about my savior complex with this place.

"Dad mentioned it to me late last night." His voice is uncharacteristically quiet. "Good news."

"Yeah." I'm sinking in quicksand; I have no idea where to go from here.

"I brought you a present," I say, and he frowns in surprise, watching me cross the room.

"Mae, you don't have to give me anything."

"It's not a Christmas gift," I explain, and decide to push

onward into my prepared speech. "Look, Andrew, I know you're mad at m—"

"I'm not mad at you," he says gently. "I'm mad at myself." He shakes his head, strumming absently as he thinks. "I don't usually dive into things so immediately, and I've just confirmed for myself why."

I can't help asking, "Why?"

He looks at me, eyes pained like he knows what he's going to say is going to hurt. "Because I can spend my whole life getting to know someone and still be wrong about her."

Wow. That one hits like a punch. But he's wrong: we've spent our lives getting to know each other, sure, but I was more myself with him than I'd ever been before.

"You weren't wrong about me." I take another step into the room but stop with about ten feet between us. "I mean, maybe we hit a speed bump right out of the gate, but you weren't wrong about me. And it was good, Andrew. If it hadn't been so good, you wouldn't be so upset right now."

He holds my gaze for another long moment, and then blinks down, returning to his quiet strumming.

"A few years ago," I say, "I asked my mom what it was like when she first met my dad, and she basically said that they met in their dorm, and started dating, and from that point on, just fell into this routine of being together."

He doesn't reply, but he's listening, I know. Even though he's playing his guitar, he's completely here with me.

"I asked her, 'You just knew?' and instead of explaining how it felt like fate or anything remotely romantic, she said, 'I guess? He was nice and was the first person who encouraged me to paint.' I know they're divorced and it's probably different to look back on it now, but she was talking to *me*—the product of this marriage—and there was no mention of falling in love or how she couldn't imagine herself with anyone else. They just *happened*."

I wait for him to react to this, but he doesn't. In the silence, the words to the song he's absently playing hit me like a warm burst of air.

Don't know much about history . . .

And if this one could be with you . . .

His movements are so absentminded, I can't tell if he registers what he's playing.

"I mean, obviously," I continue, "that was incredibly unsatisfying." A pause. "As much as none of us want to imagine our parents actually hooking up, we want to think there was at least some fire or passion or *some*thing fated."

"Yeah." He clears his throat and fidgets with the tuning pegs some more.

"I know this—*us*—has gone up in flames," I say, "but even so, I can't help but feel like there was a good story there. I've wanted this for so long, and you had no idea, and then when you found out, it was like . . . it clicked something on in you." I pause, searching for the right words. "What happened between us was really romantic."

He falters, but after a beat, he adjusts his fingers on the frets and continues.

"And it wasn't just romantic in theory; it was romantic in reality. Every second with you was perfect." I shift on my feet. "Picking out our tree, snowflakes in your hair, sledding, the closet—our night here. I got those moments because of a wish I made. A wish! Who actually believes wishes come true? The world is a totally different place than I ever thought it was—I mean, there's actual *magic* happening—but that's not even the hardest thing for me to believe. The most unbelievable part of all of this is that I got to be with *you*. My dream person."

Andrew tilts his head back to lean against the wall, eyes closed, and sets his guitar on the cot beside him. He looks tired, and takes a long, deep breath. I can tell he's not tuning me out. He's also not just passively hearing me, he's absorbing every word. It gives me the confidence to push on.

"And even though I wished for it, I *worked* for it, too. I could have never said a word to you about what was happening to me, or how I'd messed up with Theo." I hold my chin up. "But I'm proud of myself for telling you. Do I wish I'd explained it better? Sure. But I told you the truth because I wanted to start whatever we have by being honest.

"I was honest about my feelings," I say. "I was honest about my mistakes. I was honest in my best and worst moments this week." I take a steadying breath because I'm starting to get choked up. "And if there's one thing that we did perfectly, it was talking and being transparent and honest with each other right from the start. Right away, we *talked*. I can't think of anyone else in the world I've ever felt that comfortable with."

This gets to him, I can tell. His jaw clenches; his Adam's apple bobs as he swallows.

"There's something so intimate about sharing things out loud you could never say to another person," I say. "Letting someone really see you—minus the filters. So, I'm sorry that this whole situation is such a bummer, and I'm sorry if the intensity of my feelings for you made you move faster than maybe you would have otherwise. But I've loved you since I knew what love was, and I can't undo that. I would never wish to take that away. Loving you is all the proof I needed that love can last decades. Maybe even a lifetime, who knows." Clearing my throat, I add without thinking, "But let's hope I get over you, because otherwise that would suck for both of us *and* your future wife."

I laugh out an awkward *ha-ha*, but the room goes deathly silent . . . until I very audibly swallow. I want to be eaten by the floor.

But I can't stop now. With a rush of bravery, I walk the rest of the way across the room to hand him the gift wrapped in heavy, glossed green paper with a matte red bow. After I finished making it, Mom wrapped it for me, handing it to me with tears in her eyes and a single kiss to the palm of my hand.

"I wanted to give you this," I say. "It's called *Happiness*."

Finally, he tilts his head back down and opens his eyes, but he doesn't look at me. He warily studies the wrapped package in my hands. "What is it?"

"Just open it."

At the confused flicker of his eyes to mine, I add, "It's a Maelyn Jones original. In an Elise Jones–painted frame. We did it today."

Tentatively—reverently—he takes it. With fingertips that have touched nearly every inch of my skin, he easily pulls free the silken bow. The rip of the thick paper tears through the room. The gift hasn't been put in a box, it's wrapped as-is: a framed drawing, charcoal on paper.

I wonder briefly where Mom found the simple wooden

frame to decorate lovingly with brilliantly painted quaking aspen—whether Lisa pulled something old and unsentimental out to make room, or whether Benny helped Mom dig through the attic—but I don't really have time to dwell on the question, because Andrew sucks in a breath and then becomes an inflatable doll with all of the air sucked out. He's sweetly deflated.

In my sketch, the figure is easily in his eighties, but clearly Andrew. I worked to capture the warm kindness of his eyes, the wild disobedience of his hair, the playful curve of his mouth. And the woman at his side is very clearly me. I tried to age-soften my cheekbones, to capture the round swell of my bottom lip and the wide depth of my smiling eyes.

We're sitting on the porch swing of the cabin, side by side, fingers interlaced. My left hand rests on my lap and is decorated with a simple wedding band. Andrew has clearly said something that made me laugh; my mouth is open, head tilted back in glee, and his eyes shine with a delighted, cocky pride. We aren't hamming it up for anyone; don't even seem aware there might be someone nearby, capturing this moment.

Who knows what we've been through in the past sixty years, but we're still undeniably happy.

"Mandrew and Maisie," I tell him quietly, voice thick. "I didn't have time to do a full painting, but I think I like it like this. This way, it's only a sketch, just a possibility. Even if it never turns into more, you are the only one who makes me that happy, and I am so grateful for it."

Leaning forward, I quickly kiss his forehead, and turn to leave before I burst into tears.

I save that for the moment I step outside, alone, into the snow.

• • •

I don't feel like going back to the cabin. Indoors sounds oddly claustrophobic right now. I've had so many big revelations over the past few days that it almost seems like I need some quiet time to digest them, let everything consolidate so I can figure out where to go from here.

The driveway leading away from the cabin is about a quarter mile long and is freshly plowed. My boots crunch over the thin, packed snow, but it's an unseasonably warm afternoon and I can hear ice melting from tree branches in a lively cacophony of drips and splatters. Out at the main road and suddenly unsheltered from the wind, I zip up my coat and veer left, walking another quarter mile or so to a street that is nearly as familiar as my street back home.

Andrew, Theo, and I used to take this walk all the time when our parents wanted us out of the house. We'd pick up sticks and use them as swords, walking sticks, or magic wands. We'd take turns pointing out which of the cabins we would each buy when we were older and what we would do each day of the week once we were permanent neighbors. We'd cut into the trees and search unsuccessfully for bear dens or hunters' traps. Over the years some of the houses have sold and been remodeled or even completely renovated. But the small street lacks some of the ostentatious sheen of other parts of ritzy Park City; even the renovated houses kept the sheltered woodland vibe. In the middle of summer, if you squint down the street you can still see the winter wonderland ready to emerge.

Smoke puffs up from chimneys and an overlapping medley of holiday music filters out to the road. At my favorite home on this street—an ivy-covered stone building that feels like a gnome's house in the woods—I stop, looking up to the wide bay window facing the street from inside. Two shadowed bodies move around in the front room, near the brightly lit Christmas tree. Another is busy in the kitchen. Even out here I smell roasting turkey and the buttery salt of pies cooling, mingled with the sharp clean scent of cold pine trees. If I'd thought to bring my sketchbook with me, I would draw this scene, right here.

If I'm so happy here in the snow, I think, why don't I live somewhere it snows? It's a sudden mental realignment, the realization that I don't need to stay in California, and I don't have to try to shoehorn my life into the current template. I can move. I can dig around in the tunnels of my thoughts to imagine my dream job. I can figure out who the hell Maelyn Jones really is. I took my shot with Andrew, and it's out of my hands now, but it doesn't mean I have to let the other threads of bravery fall away.

• • •

My mood, bright from epiphany, dips as soon as I walk back inside the cabin and realize Andrew's is not one of the bodies in the living room.

"Hey, guys," I say.

The boisterous chatter comes to an abrupt stop at my entrance. Miles bolts upright. "Hi, Mae."

Everyone stares at me expectantly. I was not anticipating my return to be so carefully clocked. "Hi . . ."

Zachary rolls over facedown onto the rug, giggling.

"What's up? Do I have a bird's nest on my head?"

Aaron runs his fingers through his black-hole hair, saying, "No. You don't," like I might have been asking seriously.

Finally, Lisa asks, "Did you come in through the mudroom?"

I shake my head. "The front door. Why?"

They continue to stare at me like they're waiting for me to say something else.

"Okay. Um . . . is Andrew still out in the Boathouse?"

"He's—" Kennedy begins at the same time Ricky blurts, "Was it cold outside?"

Blinking in confusion, I give him a drawn out "Yes?"

I look down at my new watch and realize I was gone for nearly two hours and didn't look to see if Andrew's car was still in the driveway. I'd ask if he's here, but I'm not sure I want to know.

I turn awkwardly in place, unsure what to do with myself. "Well, you're all acting like weirdos, so I'll be down in the basement for a bit. Let me know when I can help with dinner."

"You should go upstairs," Zachary sings into the floor.

"I should?"

Every head in the room bobs in agreement.

I stare at them quizzically for a beat before saying, "Okaaaay. I'll do that." At least it gives me an excuse to escape. I shuffle down the hall, rounding the banister to begin climbing the stairs, but my foot lands on something and it crunches beneath the sole of my sock. I lift my foot, pick the item off the bottom, and study the silver object.

It's a flattened peppermint kiss. I'm lost in bewilderment for a breath, but then my eyes focus back on the floor, and I realize there's another one only a foot away in either direction: one leading upstairs, and one leading back to the kitchen, where I would normally come in from a walk.

Hope glimmers silvery at the edges of my thoughts. I jog up the stairs and follow the trail of candy down the hall and around the corner. It leads directly to Andrew's bedroom, and stops just outside his closet.

My heart is an absolute maniac in my rib cage as I pull open the door, and Andrew squints into the light.

"That was a monster walk, Maisie. I've been waiting to hide for like a half hour."

I'm nearly too stunned to speak, but apparently not too stunned to burst into tears. "Andrew?"

From the base of the stairs comes a burst of applause and cheers.

"I told you to go upstairs!" Zachary shouts before it sounds like someone claps a hand over his mouth and carries him out of yelling range.

With a raspy laugh, Andrew pulls me forward into the closet.

I wonder if I'm shouting, but my heartbeat is so loud in my ears it's thunderous. "What's going on?"

His voice is gentle, and the tiniest bit suggestive: "What does it look like?"

It looks like he's sweetly lured me here, like he's staring at my mouth, like he's about to kiss me. But given my fragile, blown-sugar emotional state, it would probably be a very bad idea to assume anything right now.

"Well." I bite my lip and look around the small, dim space. Stating the facts seems like a safe place to start. "It looks like you left a trail of my favorite candy so I'd find you in this closet."

He gives me a bright flash of teeth when he smiles. I feel his hand as it carefully comes over my waist and slides down to my hip, fingers pressing, coaxing me closer. "Any idea why?"

I'm on the verge of replying that, to be safe, he'd better say it, but the words feel tired and dusty in my throat. What comes out surprises me: "You wanted to get me alone in the spot where we first kissed so you could admit that I was right all along."

Andrew bends and presses his lips to mine once, gently. "You were right all along, Maisie."

I know he's talking about us, and what I said in the Boathouse, but the smell of peppermint lingers on his breath. "I know I was: peppermint kisses are delicious."

He laughs, exhaling a warm puff of air across my neck. "Did you know that they are in fact called 'Hershey's Kisses Candy Cane Mint Candies,' and they're 'white creme and the refreshing crunch of peppermint'?" He kisses my throat. "Which means, of course, they aren't technically white chocolate. I don't have to shame you for loving them anymore."

"Wow, *thank you*."

His smile straightens. "You bolted out of the Boathouse so fast, I didn't get a chance to say anything."

"I felt like you needed space."

"I wish I could come up with the words faster," he admits. "I'm just not built that way."

"But if you came up with words faster," I say, "then you wouldn't be able to grand-gesture in your favorite kind of space: a closet."

"With your favorite thing: terrible candy."

"Don't be coy, Andrew Polley Hollis, you know you're my favorite thing."

His playful smile dissolves and his expression goes slack in relief as we drop the game. Andrew cups my face and plants a lingering kiss on my mouth. It deepens, and he pulls me closer, exhaling a quiet moan when his tongue touches mine. "Can I say it now?" he asks, pulling back a few inches.

"Say what?"

"That I love you?"

My ears pop subtly, like a door has closed, sealing out the wind. Andrew's attention fixes on my cheek-splitting smile. "I love you, too."

He twirls a strand of my hair around his finger. "And you don't have to be back in California tomorrow?"

"I do not. I'm on a collision course with adventure and ready for anything."

"This is good news."

"Yeah, no kidding. The last thing I want to do is get on a plane."

He laughs. "I just so happen to have a truck, and Denver is only eight hours away. Maybe we could take a little road trip."

I stretch to meet him just as he bends to kiss me, and the relief is so powerful it feels like a rave in my bloodstream. Step one in taking charge of my adult life: I'm sleeping in the Boathouse with Andrew tonight. And every night, if I have my way. Electricity? Running water? Over-rated.

He hums in happiness, slowly pulling away after a string of kisses that feel like sugared raindrops. It takes him a beat to open his eyes, and I swear, with that small sign that he's in deep, too, I fall in love with him all over again.

"Guess I'm glad we got our first fight out of the way."

I pull back in alarm. "That was our first *fight*?"

He looks similarly taken aback. "Did you think it was the *end*?"

"Uh, yeah? You basically said you didn't know me at all." I laugh incredulously, watching his eyes fill with a smile that slowly breaks and takes over his entire face. "What? Why are you laughing at me?"

"Because you're right, I guess, but you gave up pretty easily after thirteen years."

I shove him playfully, but he can't go very far. "What was I supposed to think?"

"You've known me for twenty-six years! One day is a drop in the bucket."

"We were only together for thirty-six hours! A day is, like, two-thirds of our romance."

He laughs delightedly at this, and then the moment stills, and Andrew watches me with amused fondness. I start to fidget, defensiveness crawling up my neck.

"My parents don't fight," I remind him. "They nag, and

are passive-aggressive, and after the one big fight they had, Dad moved out."

"Okay, well, you're going to learn how to manage conflict because smart people like us in relationships don't agree with each other all the time. It's science."

"Is that what this is?" I ask, grinning. "A relationship?"

He is a meltingly sweet combination of amused and nervous. "I hope so?"

"Thirteen-to-twenty-six-year-old Mae is doing the Running Man in here right now." I tap my temple.

His answering laugh slowly straightens. "So . . . are we . . . ?"

"That depends." Pushing the words out feels like swallowing glass because it's the real moment of truth. "Do you believe me?"

"About the wish?"

It's been at once the most clarifying and bewildering experience of my lifetime, and as much as I love him, I'm not sure how I'd move forward with Andrew if he thought it was all a dream. "Yeah."

"Of course I believe you."

The tension in my shoulders crumples like wax paper. "And . . . you're okay with . . . all of it?"

"Let me ask you this," Andrew counters. "In this version of your Christmas, did your dad break a tooth on a cookie bar?"

"He sure did not."

"And did Kennedy skin her knee?"

I see where he's going with this, and grin. "Nope."

"See? You knew about the sleeping bags in storage. You

reassured Dad about the gin. You somehow got Benny to buy the cabin. And if I'd listened to you about Miso, I would still have my favorite terrible holiday sweater, wouldn't I?"

"That'll teach you to listen to your time-traveling . . ." My smile breaks, and I flounder as the rest of my sentence hangs like a ribbon in the wind.

Andrew's eyes narrow with a knowing smirk. "My time-traveling what?"

And here, for just a breath, my confidence falters. With my hope buoyant enough to lift the cabin off its foundation, wouldn't it just be perfect if the universe pulled the chair out from under me one last time?

But this time, I'm not going anywhere. "Your time-traveling girlfriend."

Andrew's smile lights up the inside of the closet. "Finally, Maisie. I thought you'd never ask."

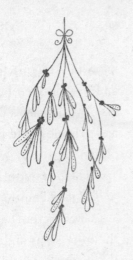

epilogue

"Oi," Benny calls from the porch. "I could spot you a mile away."

I don't have to ask which of us he's talking to. It definitely isn't me, in a muted heather-gray tank top and faded cutoffs.

"Oh, yeah?" Andrew runs his hands down his obnoxious sweater. "Are you saying I wear it well?"

"You're not sweltering?" Benny asks, and it's so hot out, I swear I can see his voice cut through the wavy air.

Andrew shakes his head. "Perfectly comfortable."

I glance at my boyfriend and witness the fine droplets of sweat pebbling on his brow in the ninety-degree heat. He's still an adorable liar. I wouldn't even hold his hand on our walk down the driveway, it's too clammy. We all know he'll sacrifice great personal comfort to make a point, and he's decided his "thing" at the cabin is festive sweaters. Any holiday is worthy. His cornflower-blue, cherry-red, and pristine-white number is a loving ode to our founding fathers, I guess. I give him until lunch before he rips it off.

"Happy Fourth!" he calls out.

"Happy Fourth. Get up here." Benny waves us on.

Gravel crunches under my sneakers as I jog toward the front steps and my favorite uncle. Our car is down on the main road, parked out of the way of the construction vehicles currently cluttering the driveway to the cabin—or The Hollow, as Benny has named it. I can already see the work that's been put in; it's astounding. The porch is new. The entire cabin has been repainted; it's the same shade of brown with green shutters, but it's impressive what a power wash and fresh coat of paint can do to a place. All of the windows have been replaced, the eaves rebuilt. New roof, new landscaping, and a screened-in side porch are underway on the western side of the house, facing the mountain. I'm dying to see what it looks like inside.

Benny's hug engulfs me, and I surprise myself by immediately tearing up. He smells like his regular herby shampoo, but he also smells like pine and aspen, like soil and wood varnish. His rumbling laugh vibrates through me and the feeling of being back here with Andrew, for the first time since the holidays, is a lot like climbing into a bubble bath overlooking the ocean at sunset. It is heaven.

Benny pulls back, holding me at arm's length to inspect me. "Looking good, Noodle."

I'm sure he's right—happiness does put a glow in our

complexion and a bounce in our step—but Benny's one to talk. He's tanned, and his hair is sun-bleached and dusty from what I can only assume is constant work on this house. His smile crinkles in a new way at the corners of his eyes, and I can see in an instant that he isn't just content here, he's out-of-his-mind happy.

Andrew gets his hug next, a back-slapping man-clasp, and when my eyes get their fill of the new porch, and their small talk and greetings make me impatient, bouncing on my feet, Benny finally leads us inside.

I am awestruck. The banister is the same as the one we grew up with, but refurbished, gleaming honeyed brown in the afternoon sun streaming in the front door. The stairs have been refinished, as have all of the floors downstairs. Benny has kept much of the old furniture, but polished, treated, and cleaned it all so that it is both bright and cozy inside. With the fresh coat of indoor paint, the space seems so much lighter.

"I can't believe you've done all this in six months," Andrew says, turning in a slow circle. "It hasn't looked this good since . . . well, probably before I was born, actually."

"Just wait." Benny leads us to the kitchen, where new flooring shines bright in the afternoon sunshine and stainless steel appliances have replaced all of the originals. The fridge is a behemoth with so much technology on the doors I suspect it could do Miles's calculus homework. Mom, Aaron, and Kyle are going to start their own cooking show in here when they see it. A new wood-slab kitchen table sits in the middle of the broad space, with seating for sixteen.

Benny has turned the never-used dining room into a sitting room with impressive built-in bookshelves stuffed with books. The basement has been finished and fresh drywall has segmented it into four separate rooms: a broad family room at the bottom of the stairs, where Benny tells us he'll put a pool table, Ping-Pong table, and pinball machine, and three bedrooms opening off the main room, with a shared bathroom toward the back of the house.

"No more bunk beds," Andrew says with glee.

"Donated them to a family down the road, that stone house on Mountain Crest." Benny reaches for a stray screwdriver on the shelf. "Both of their daughters are having twins. How wild is that?"

Andrew catches my wide-eyed gaze; his is sparkling. He knows, as I do, exactly which house Benny is talking about. He knows I walked down along that road and to that house while he was out getting candy to profess his love for me in a closet. The universe sure works in mysterious ways.

Benny scans the room, nodding to himself. "Now we've got plenty of room for everyone, and some to grow."

The bedrooms upstairs are largely the same, except for the attic, which is being renovated into Benny's master bedroom. It isn't done—it's still a cluttered construction zone—but I can see the bones of it in the mess. The stained-glass window is still there. The sharply sloping ceilings won't change. In fact, it looks much like it always has, just better.

A voice calls for Benny from downstairs, leaving Andrew and me to wander alone. The furniture in his old room is all here, and eucalyptus lingers in the bedding, the walls, the clothing in the dresser. I run a finger along the nightstand just as a pair of arms wraps around my waist from behind, pulling me—giggling—into the closet. The door seals behind us, and Andrew turns into Mr. Grabby Hands, half tickling, half groping.

"I truly believe you have some sort of closet kink."

He hums into my neck. "To think of all the years we wasted not doing this."

I squeal, playfully batting him away, and he reaches for me, pulling me into a hug.

"Come here," Mandrew says, and buries his face in my neck. He groans his *you feel good* groan, asking, "How does it feel to be back?"

"Amazing." I wrap my arms around his shoulders, digging my fingers into his hair. "And weird. But good weird."

"Christopher Walken weird."

"Exactly." I pull back, kissing his chin. "Where do you want to sleep this weekend?"

"Probably in here," he guesses, shrugging. "The beds downstairs are all singles, and the Boathouse will be too hot."

Honestly, I'm not sure how it'll feel to go out there. Nostalgic, of course, but maybe also bittersweet? I know Benny has big plans for it, but as far as I know, work on it hasn't started yet. I'd be fine sleeping out there the way it was, for old times' sake, but it's un-air-conditioned. Andrew's right, in the peak of summer it's unlikely to be very comfortable.

"Have you ever had a girl sleep with you in here?"

"Once," Andrew says, stepping back and cupping my face, smooshing my cheeks. "Liz." One of Andrew's longer-term girlfriends from several years ago. We met her and her new husband for drinks a couple of months back and she was a riot. "But we didn't fool around."

I laugh at this nonsense. I can't imagine being in a bed with Andrew Hollis and not getting him naked. "You liar."

"No, I'm being serious," he says. "Mom and Dad were, like, five feet away. I was way too self-conscious to get the job done."

"Well, your parents won't be here this time," I remind him. "And Benny's things were in one of the finished rooms downstairs so . . . game on."

Andrew growls, pressing his face to my neck again.

This weekend is just us and Benny; everyone else had conflicts. Mom and Dad are getting Miles moved into UCLA, where he's already started soccer practice. Kyle has chorus-line rehearsals for what everyone is hoping will be the new Broadway sensation. Theo is in the midst of building his own house near Ogden Canyon, an hour and a half away, and Ricky and Lisa decided to take a summer cruise from Seattle to Alaska. But Andrew and I could easily make the drive from our place in Denver. We both have the long weekend off and have been dying to see what Benny's done with the place.

There's a soft knock, and Andrew and I share a *we're busted* grimace before he opens the door, letting in a bright slice of light and a view of Benny's amused face.

Benny laughs. "I figured you two would be in here."

"Because, Bentley," I whisper, "this closet is our *sacred space*."

"I promise not to change it." He lifts his chin. "Come on. I want to show you something."

We follow him downstairs, and I try to puzzle out what's next. I already feel overwhelmed with the perfect blend of new and old that he's managed. What haven't we seen? The backyard? A cool feature of the new front porch? Andrew shrugs when I give him a questioning look, wiping his palms on the front of his thighs. He looks flushed, and I wonder if there's a part of him that struggles to see how much this house has changed. For the better, but still.

We turn at the bottom of the stairs, heading down the hall to the kitchen, through the mudroom, and out the back door.

The backyard hasn't changed, but I pull up short anyway. Andrew keeps walking, but I can't follow him, can't make my feet work because the structure I'm seeing only barely resembles the Boathouse that I grew up with. What's in front of me is a beautiful, rustic retreat. It is a little log cabin, with a giant window still facing the mountain. It has a chimney, it has steps, it has a tiny porch with two bright yellow Adirondack chairs and a small table.

I don't realize I'm crying until Andrew turns back and reaches for my hand, laughing at me with love in his smile, wiping my face with his free hand. "Come on."

He's shaking.

"Did you know?" I ask him.

He doesn't answer, only tugs me forward and inside. It's still one room—well, except for the new bathroom—but there's a four-poster bed in the back corner, a love seat and comfy chair toward the front, framed around a coffee table atop a gorgeous rug. The fireplace is obviously not in use, but the new A/C unit whirs valiantly, keeping the air inside breezy and comfortable.

My eye is drawn to all of the framed photos decorating the walls; there are at least twenty of them, some small, others at least eight-by-ten, and we're all together in various combinations: Me and Dad on a sled. Andrew, Ricky, Theo, and Lisa on the porch of the main cabin. Benny and Mom holding cocktails and toasting the photographer. Miles and the twins playing checkers on the floor in the living room. Kyle holding five-year-old me upside down near a snowman. Aaron and Mom wearing aprons and cooking. Benny with teenage me, Theo, and Andrew in the summer, hiking Iron Canyon Trail.

"These are unreal." I turn to see how Andrew is absorbing all of this, but he's not standing to my right anymore, he's—

He's kneeling.

Do I have the slowest brain in all of the universe? Maybe. But it's a full five seconds or so before I can put letters together into a word, and the word is only: "Oh."

"Maisie," he says, and opens his palm to reveal a gold ring with a perfect oval sapphire. He stares at me for several silent seconds, overcome.

"We've had our share of adventure these past six months," he continues, voice hoarse. "Your move to Denver, your new job, our new apartment. There's nothing I love more than making dinner with you, talking about our day, dreaming up what we're going to do next." He swallows, eyes focused on my face. "I haven't spent a night without you since we were here last. I don't know how we managed that, except that we've made this relationship our priority. You are my priority, Mae. I am so in love with you. It feels impossible to imagine belonging to anyone else. Please," he says, quieter now, "will you marry me?"

●   ●   ●

Only a fool would do anything other than shout *YES* and— once it's been confirmed that Benny has left us to ourselves out here—pounce on this man. Andrew spends approximately ten seconds half-heartedly trying to convince me that we should go tell Benny the good news before he gives up and lets me push him toward the bed and rip his horrible sweater from his body.

I'll never get tired of the smooth heat of his torso, the way his hands roam hungrily over me like he wants to touch everything at once, the way he digs his fingers into my hair when I kiss down his body. His abdomen tenses beneath my hand, hips arching, and then pulls me up and under him, taking his time, pressing his sharp exhales and playfully dirty words into my ear.

We've gotten good at this—we practice diligently—but I'm still surprised at the depth of emotion that rocks me whenever I sense that he's close, when I feel him start to grow tense and a little wild. He teases me about the way I watch him, but I think he secretly loves it because I swear watching his eyes drift closed right at the second he falls is the hottest thing that I've ever witnessed.

I don't let him get up, not yet. I hold my arm out in front of us and we stare up at the ring on my finger, laughing at how foreign the words *husband* and *wife* sound in our voices.

Where are we going to do it? I wonder. Andrew looks at me like I'm thick. Here, of course.

We populate the small wedding party with our chosen family. We decide Tahiti is a good honeymoon spot. Dog before kids.

Sweet kisses turn slow, and then deeper, and then I'm over him and he's watching with adoring focus, playing with the ends of my hair, skipping fingertips over my curves, guiding my hips until he's sweaty and urgent beneath me.

I collapse on the bed beside him. The sheets are soft, smooth cotton, cool against my back, and Andrew coughs out a sharp, satisfied laugh. "How do you expect me to walk after that?"

"I hope Benny meant for us to sleep out here," I say, slowly catching my breath.

• • •

But we'll need water and food, and we've still got several hours before sleep.

He looks at me and laughs. "Do you want to pull a brush through your hair?"

A glance in the bathroom mirror tells me my hair is a wild tangle, my lips are swollen and kiss-bruised. My smile is love-drunk and lopsided. I do the best I can with my fingers to fix the hair situation before giving up.

"My stuff is in the car," I say. "Benny doesn't care what my hair looks like."

It's only when we walk into the kitchen to the cacophonous "SURPRISE!" yelled by seven excited voices that I get why Andrew wanted us to go inside and tell

Benny, why he suggested I brush my hair, and why he's beet red and doubled over in laughter now. Ricky and Lisa are not on a cruise. Theo is not down in Ogden working on his new house, and although Kyle is still in Manhattan, Aaron and the twins are not. I'm not sure when they got here, or how long they've been waiting for us to come back inside so they can congratulate us on our engagement.

"Were you *wrestling?*" Zachary asks in a lisp, now missing his two front teeth, and Aaron struggles valiantly to not burst out laughing.

"Yes," Andrew answers earnestly. "And look! Mae won a ring."

I am engulfed by hugs from my future in-laws(!) and Aaron and the twins. Benny takes the opportunity to laugh at the telling disaster of my hair before pulling me in for a tight squeeze. Although this is the best surprise ever, it feels oddly quiet without my parents and Miles.

Slipping my phone from where I left it on the kitchen counter, I take a picture of my left hand, texting it to my mom:

> I bet you knew he was going to do this, but look!

I stare at the phone, waiting for the indication that she's read the text, but my message sends slowly, the bar inching across the top.

"I hear you're loving your new gig," Aaron says, pulling my attention up.

"I am!" I tell him, grinning. I am now the lead graphic designer for Sled Dog Brewing, an up-and-coming micro-brewery only a half mile from Red Rocks and the hottest biergarten in town. I have a team of two who run the website and social media, and I design all of the gear—T-shirts, pint glasses, hats, beanies, and all kinds of fun merchandise. The owner has been so impressed with my work he's asked me to redesign all of their labels, which means my artwork may someday be in refrigerated cases all over the country. So far, Sled Dog has been the most fun and rewarding job I've ever had.

"I got a bottle of that imperial stout," he says.

"How'd you manage that?" The imperial stout just won an international gold medal; it's nearly impossible to find it locally, let alone in New York.

"One of the dads at school is a distributor. He hooked me up."

"I love you." Stretching, I kiss Aaron's cheek. Even across the country in Manhattan, he's staying connected to what we're doing out west. I follow the kiss with a hand ruffling his newly natural salt-and-pepper hair. "And I love this, too."

"Yeah." He smiles at me. "Shortest midlife crisis on record."

"Hopefully Lisa got some documentation of the dye job."

"Or at least half of the dye job," he jokes.

Lisa protests, laughing, "Hey."

I don't even notice Andrew had slipped outside to the car and come back in with my bag until he hands it to me. "I hate to ruin the surprise, but you might want this."

"The surprise?"

He winces. "Your parents' flight was delayed. They're almost here."

"Really?" I squeal, and quickly pull my brush out, tying my hair into a bun on top of my head.

Just in time, because my mom is already singing my name before she's even reached the porch. "Mae! Where's my girl?"

Behind her, Dad is carrying his bag and hers, and grinning ear to ear.

Andrew comes up behind me as Mom jogs up the steps, and she throws her arms around both of us. "I knew it!" she sings. "I knew, I knew, I knew!"

"How long have you known he was going to do this?" I ask her.

"Well, let's see." She looks to Andrew, calculating back, and Dad comes to give us each a hug. "Maybe two months?"

"We got the tickets in April . . ." Dad says. "So, longer than that."

"I asked your permission in February," Andrew says, laughing. "On our two-month anniversary."

Lisa comes out, and she and my mom turn high-pitched and animated with their shared happiness. Ricky, Dad, and Aaron give each other a *here we go* look and head inside, presumably to find beer in Benny's fancy new fridge. Benny greets my parents before heading down the steps with Kennedy, who's holding a book about leaves. Theo wrestles with Zachary in the living room. I miss Kyle, and I miss my brother, but I bet there's a tiny electric zap in their mood, even in the middle of their busy lives.

I catch a small tidbit of what Mom is saying: ". . . here, but before or after Christmas?" and assume that our wedding is being planned without us, that the pressure for grandchildren will start almost immediately, and that we'll have our hands full with busybodies for the rest of our days. All of that will have to be discussed, but after the moment we exchange our vows—whenever that is—luckily, we won't have to negotiate how to blend our families. They were blended long before we came along.

When we step out of the sun and back into the house, my eye is caught by a framed picture on the wall in the new sitting room. From far away it's hard to tell what it is, but up close, I realize it's an aerial photograph. Andrew puts his arm around me and then leans in, studying the photo. Finally, he reaches forward, putting the tip of his finger right in the middle. "There we are."

"What?"

He moves his finger to the side, and I see what he's showing me. It's the cabin, in the center of a cluster of other buildings, in the midst of a busy swirl of streets, in an even busier stretch of mountains. Beyond that, the world stretches out in both directions, and every single point on Earth's surface is the center of someone's universe, but this picture gets it right.

The center of my world is right where I'm standing.

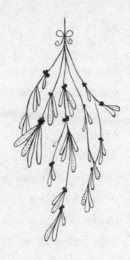

acknowledgments

J ust a little bit of magic, we said. We can totally do it, we said. It'll be easy!

It may not have been easy, but writing this novel was certainly fun. We wrote this one before 2020 arrived, before all hell broke loose, and the idea of falling into a romance time loop felt like a perfect, seasonal escape.

It feels even better now when we get to go back and read it. Mae is safe at this cabin, with loved ones and only the requirement that she figure out what path she's meant to take. If we all had something this simple to focus on, life would be so much easier.

We guess that's what romance gives us—yes, it's aspirational and wish fulfillment; it's fun and uplifting— but this year, it is also a much-needed escape. Romance is here doing what romance does, and we need it now more than ever. So we have to start this off by thanking some spectacular romance creators whose work has pulled us out of reality and into true joy this year: Park Ji-eun (*Crash Landing on You*), Alexis Hall (*Boyfriend Material*), Scarlett Peckham (*The Rakess*), Rebekah Weatherspoon (*Xeni*), Martha Waters (*To Have and to Hoax*), Kate Clayborn (*Love Lettering* and also your Twitter feed), Lisa Kleypas (hi, goddess), and Nora Ephron for, well, everything. We are deeply inspired by you, and so grateful to be able to turn to your creativity and entertainment in these weird, wild times.

Our core team is the best core team: Agent Holly Root is the consistent voice of calm, wisdom, and delightfully timed snark. Our editor at Simon & Schuster/Gallery, Kate Dresser, puts up with a lot, and we mean a lot, of U-turns. Thank you, Kate, for being the CLo enthusiast when we start, the sounding board when we're stuck, the gentle red flag when we're editing. Kristin Dwyer is our PR rep and Precious, and even when time stopped and we no longer knew what the world looked like past our own window, it was okay. We did it, we got it done: people found our books. You always do so good, girl.

Thank you to the S&S/Gallery team for hustling their hardest, as always: Jen Bergstrom (we truly adore you), Aimée Bell, Jen Long, Rachel Brenner, Molly Gregory, Abby Zidle, Anne Jaconette, Anabel Jimenez, Sally Marvin, Lisa Litwack, John Vairo, and the entire Gallery sales force and subrights groups. In the midst of a pandemic, the loss of Carolyn Reidy hit everyone hard. She will be greatly missed. It makes us doubly grateful to everyone at S&S for always being amazing and forever being on our team.

Thank you to Marion Archer for reading, and rereading,

and rereading. Your notes and feedback are always so spot-on and appreciated. Erin Service, making you swoon is our only goal. To the readers in CLo and Friends, thank you for making us laugh and keeping us company (and, of course, for loving our books). We adore each and every one of you.

To every reader out there, we hope this book finds you safe and happy. Thank you for picking it up. It is our greatest wish to the universe that Mae and Andrew's story gives you an escape that you choose, but (for your sake) one that you don't need too desperately. It's been a hard year, and we are here sending love and—we hope—a rollicking dose of magical fun.

With massive affection,
Christina & Lauren

Keep reading for a sneak peek at the next
"delightful" (*People*) novel from
New York Times bestselling author Christina Lauren.

Coming soon from Gallery Books!

CHAPTER ONE

J essica Davis used to think it was an honest-to-God tragedy that only twenty-six percent of women believed in true love. Of course, that was nearly a decade ago, when she couldn't imagine what it felt like to be anything but deeply and passionately obsessed with the man who would one day be her ex. Tonight, though, on her third first date in seven years, she was astounded the number was even that high.

"Twenty-six percent," she mumbled, leaning toward the restroom mirror to apply more lipstick. "Twenty-six women out of one hundred believe true love is real." Popping the cap back on, Jess laughed, and her exhausted reflection laughed back. Sadly, her night was far from over. She still had to make it through the entrée course; appetizers had lasted four years. Of course, some of that was probably due to Travis's tendency to talk with his mouth full, oversharing highly specific stories about finding his wife in bed with his business partner and the ensuing messy divorce. But as far as first dates went, Jess reasoned, it could have been worse. This date was better, for sure, than the guy last week, who'd been so drunk when he showed up at the restaurant that he nodded off before they'd even ordered.

"Come on, Jess." She dropped the tube back into her bag. "You don't have to make, serve, or clean up after this meal. The dishes alone are worth at least one more bitter story about his ex-wife."

A stall door clicked open, startling her, and a willowy blonde emerged. She glanced at Jess with bald pity. To this woman, she must look like a wet dog out in the rain.

"God, I know," Jess agreed with a groan. "I'm talking to myself in a bathroom. Tells you exactly how my night is going."

Not a laugh. Not even a courtesy smile, let alone camaraderie. Instead she moved as far away as possible to the end of the empty row of sinks and began washing her hands.

Well.

Jess went back to rummaging through her purse but couldn't help glancing toward the end of the counter. She knew it wasn't polite to stare, but the other woman's make-up was flawless, her nails perfectly manicured. How on earth did some women manage it? Jess considered leaving the house with her zipper up a victory. Once, she explained an entire season's worth of data analysis to a roomful of marketing executives with makeup only on one eye. This gorgeous stranger probably hadn't been forced to change outfits after cleaning glitter off both a six-month-old cat and a seven-year-old child. She probably never had to apologize for being late. She probably didn't even have to shave. She was just naturally smooth everywhere.

"Are you okay?"

Jess blinked back to awareness, realizing the woman was speaking to her. There was really no way to pretend she hadn't been staring directly at this stranger's cleavage.

Resisting the urge to cover her own less-than-impressive assets, Jess offered a small, embarrassed wave. "Sorry. I was just thinking that your kitten probably isn't covered in glitter, too."

"My what?"

She turned back to the mirror. *Jessica Marie Davis, get your shit together.* Ignoring the fact that she still had an audience, Jess channeled Nana Jo: "You have plenty of time. Go out there, eat some pasta, go home," she said aloud. "There's no ticking clock on any of this."

"I'm just saying, the clock is ticking." Fizzy waved vaguely toward Jess's butt. "That booty won't be high and tight forever, you know."

"Maybe not," Jess said, "but Tinder isn't going to help me find a quality guy to hold it up, either."

Fizzy lifted her chin defensively. "I've had some of the best sex of my life from Tinder. I swear you give up too quickly. We are in the era of women taking pleasure and not apologizing for getting theirs first, second, and one more time for the road. Travis might be ex-wife-obsessed, but I saw his photo and he was fine as hell. Maybe he would have rocked your world for an hour or two after tiramisu, but you'll never know, because you left before dessert."

Jess paused. Maybe . . . "Goddammit, Fizzy."

Her best friend leaned back, smug. If Felicity Chen decided to start selling Amway, Jess would simply hand over her wallet. Fizzy was made of charisma, witchcraft, and bad judgment. Those qualities made her a great writer but were also partly the reason Jess had a misspelled song lyric tattooed on the inside of her right wrist, had disastrous not-even-close-to-Audrey-Hepburn bangs for six depressing months in 2014, and had attended a costume party in LA that turned out to be a BDSM scene in a dungeon basement. Fizzy's response to Jess's "You brought me to a sex party in a dungeon?" was "Yeah, everyone in LA has dungeons!"

Fizzy tucked a strand of glossy black hair behind her ear. "Okay, let's make plans for your next date."

"No." Opening her laptop, Jess logged onto her email. But even with her attention fixed elsewhere, it was hard to miss Fizzy's scowl. "Fizz, it's hard with a kid."

"That's always your excuse."

"Because I always have a kid."

"You also have grandparents who live next door and are more than happy to watch her while you're on a date, and a best friend who thinks your kid is cooler than you are. We all just want you to be happy."

Jess knew they did. That was why she'd agreed to test the Tinder waters in the first place. "Okay, let me humor you," she said. "Let's say I meet someone amazing. Where am I going to hook up with him? It was different when Juno was two. Now I have a light-sleeper seven-year-old with perfect hearing, and the last time I went to a guy's place it was so messy, a pair of his boxers stuck to my back when I got up to use the bathroom."

"Gross."

"Agreed."

"Still." Fizzy rubbed a thoughtful finger beneath her lip.

"Single parents make it work all the time, Jess. Look at the Brady Bunch."

"Your best example is a fifty-year-old sitcom?" The harder Fizzy tried to convince her, the less Jess actually wanted to get back out there.

"Mrs. Brady didn't give up. All I'm saying."

"In 1969 only thirteen percent of parents were single. Carol Brady was a trailblazer. I am not."

"Vanilla latte!" the barista, Daniel, shouted over the din of the coffee shop.

Fizzy motioned that she wasn't done being a pain in Jess's ass before standing and making her way to the counter.

Jess had been coming to Twiggs coffee shop every day for almost as long as she'd been freelancing. Her life, which essentially existed in a four-block radius, was exceedingly manageable as it was. She walked Juno to school just down the street from their apartment complex while Fizzy grabbed the best table—in the back, away from the glare of the window but near the outlet that hadn't yet gone wobbly—at seven thirty every morning. Jess crunched numbers while Fizzy wrote novels, and in an effort to not be leeches, they ordered something every ninety minutes; the treats had the added benefit of incentivizing them to work more, gossip less.

Except today. She could already tell Fizzy was going to be unrelenting.

"Okay." Her friend returned with her drink and a blueberry muffin and took a moment to get situated. "Where was I?"

Jess kept her eyes on the email in front of her, pretending to read. "I think you were about to say that it's my life and that I should do what I think is best."

"We both know that's not something I would say."

"Why am I your friend?"

"Because I immortalized you as the villain in *Crimson Lace*, and you became a fan favorite so I can't kill you off."

"Sometimes I wonder if you're answering my questions or just continuing an ongoing conversation in your head."

Fizzy began peeling the paper off her muffin. "What I was going to say is that you can't throw in the towel because of one bad date."

"It's not just the one bad date," Jess said. "It's the exhausting and alien process of trying to be appealing to men. I freelance dataset algorithms and consider my sexiest outfit to be my old *Buffy* shirt and a pair of cutoffs. My favorite pajamas are a threadbare tank top and some maternity yoga pants."

Fizzy whimpered out a plaintive "No."

"Yes," Jess said, emphatically. "On top of that, I had a kid when most people our age were still lying about enjoying Jägermeister. It's hard to polish myself for a dating profile."

Fizzy laughed.

"Plus, I hate taking time away from Juno for some guy I'm probably never going to see again."

Fizzy let that sink in for a beat. "So, you're . . . done? Jessica, you went on two dates with two hot, if dull, men."

"Until Juno is older, yeah."

She regarded Jess with suspicion. "How much older?"

"I don't know." Jess picked up her coffee, but her attention was snagged when the man they referred to as "Americano" stepped into Twiggs, striding to the front precisely on cue—8:24 in the morning—all long legs and dark hair and surly, glowering vibes, not making eye contact with a single person. "Maybe when she's in college?"

When Jess's eyes left Americano, horror was rippling through Fizzy's expression. "*College?*" She lowered her voice when practically every head in the coffee shop swiveled. "You're telling me that if I sat down to write the novel of your future love life, I'd be writing a heroine who is happily showing her body to a dude for the first time in eighteen years? Honey, no. Not even your perfectly preserved vagina can pull that off."

"Felicity."

"Like an Egyptian tomb in there. Practically mummified," Fizzy mumbled into a sip.

Up front, Americano paid for his drink and then stepped to the side, absorbed in typing something on his phone. "What is his deal?" Jess asked quietly.

"You have such a thing for Americano," Fizzy said. "Do you realize you watch him every day?"

"Maybe I find his demeanor fascinating."

Fizzy let her eyes drop to his ass, currently hidden by a navy coat. "We're calling it his 'demeanor' now?" She bent, writing something in the Idea Notebook she kept near her laptop.

"Every day, he comes in here and emits the vibe that

if anyone tried to talk to him, he would do a murder," Jess quipped.

"Maybe he's a hit man."

Jess, too, inspected him top to bottom. "More like a socially constipated medieval art professor." She tried to remember when he'd started coming in here. Maybe two years ago? Monday to Friday, same time every morning, same drink, same sullen silence. This was a quirky neighborhood, and Twiggs was its heart. People came in to linger, to sip, to chat; Americano stood out not for being weird or eccentric but for being almost entirely silent in a space full of boisterous, lovable weirdos. "Nice clothes, but inside them he's all grouchy," Jess mumbled.

"Well, maybe he needs to get laid, kind of like someone else I know."

"Fizz. I've had sex since birthing Juno," Jess said in exasperation. "I'm just saying I don't have a lot left over for commitment, and I'm not willing to endure boring or outright terrible dates just for orgasms. They make battery-operated appliances for that."

"I'm not talking just about sex," Fizzy said. "I'm talking about not always putting yourself last." She paused to wave to Daniel, who was wiping down a table nearby. "Daniel, did you catch all of that?"

He straightened and gave her the smile that had made Fizzy write the hero of *Destiny's Devil* with Daniel in mind, and do all manner of dirty things to him in the book that she hadn't dared do in real life.

And would never do: Daniel and Fizzy went out once last year but quickly ended things when they ran into each other at a family reunion. Their family reunion. "When can't we hear you?" he asked.

"Good, then please tell Jess that I'm right."

"You want me to have an opinion about whether Jess should be on Tinder just to get laid?" he asked.

"Okay, yup." Jess groaned. "This is what rock bottom feels like."

"Or whichever dating site she likes!" Fizzy cried, ignoring her. "This woman is sexy and young. She shouldn't waste her remaining hot years in mom jeans and old sweatshirts."

Jess looked down at her outfit, ready to protest, but the words shriveled in her throat.

"Maybe not," Daniel said, "but if she's happy, does it matter whether or not she's frumpy?"

She beamed at Fizzy in triumph. "See? Daniel is sort of on Team Jess."

"You know," Daniel said to her now, balling the wash rag in his hands, smug with insider knowledge, "Americano is a romantic, too."

"Let me guess," Jess said, grinning. "He's the host of an LA-based sex dungeon?"

Only Fizzy laughed. Daniel gave a coy shrug. "He's about to launch some cutting-edge matchmaking company."

Both women went silent. *A what now?*

"Matchmaking?" Jess asked. "The same Americano who comes in here every day and never smiles at anyone?" She pointed behind her to the door he'd exited only a minute ago. "*That* guy? With his intense hotness marred by the moody, antisocial filter?"

"That's the one," Daniel said, nodding. "You could be right that he needs to get laid, but I'm guessing he does just fine for himself."

At least this particular Fizzy tangent happened on a Monday—Pops picked up Juno from school on Monday afternoons and took her to the library. Jess was able to get a proposal together for Genentech, set up a meeting with Whole Foods for next week, and bash through a few spreadsheets before she had to walk home and start dinner.

Her car, ten years old with barely thirty thousand miles logged on it, was so rarely used that Jess couldn't remember the last time she'd had to fill the tank. Everything in her world, Jess thought contentedly on her walk home, was within arm's reach. University Heights was the perfect of blend of apartments and mismatched houses nestled between tiny restaurants and independent businesses. Frankly, the sole benefit of last night's date was that Travis had agreed to meet at El Zarape just two doors down; the only thing worse than having the world's most boring dinner conversation would have been driving to the Gaslamp to do it.

With about two hours until sunset, the sky had gone a heavily bruised gray-blue, threatening rain that'd send any Southern Californian driver into a confused turmoil. A sparse crowd was getting Monday-levels of rowdy on the deck of the new Kiwi-run brewery down the street, and the ubiquitous line at Bahn Thai was quickly turning into a tangle of hungry bodies; three butts were attached to humans currently ignoring the sign for customers not to sit on the private stoop next door to the restaurant. Nana and Pops's tenant, Mr. Brooks, had installed a doorbell camera for the front units, and almost every morning he gave Jess a detailed accounting of how many millennials vaped on his front step while waiting for a table.

Home came into view. Juno had named their apartment complex "Harley Hall" when she was four, and although it didn't have nearly the pretentious vibe required to be a capital-*H* Hall, the name stuck. Harley Hall was bright green and stood out like an emerald against the earth-tone stucco of the adjacent buildings. The street-facing side was decorated with a horizontal strip of pink and purple tiles forming a harlequin pattern; electric-pink window boxes spilled exuberant flowers year-round. Jess's grandparents Ronald and Joanne Davis had bought the property the year Pops retired from the navy, which was around the same time that Jess's long-term boyfriend decided he wasn't *father material* and wanted to retain the option to put his penis in other ladies. Jess had packed up two-month-old Juno and moved into the ground-floor two-bedroom unit that faced Nana and Pops's bungalow at the back end of the property. Given that they'd raised Jess down the road in Mission Hills until she'd gone to college at UCLA, the transition was basically zero. And now, her small and perfect village helped her raise her child.

The side gate opened with a tiny squeak, then locked closed behind her. Down a narrow path, Jess stepped into the courtyard that separated her apartment from Nana Jo and Pops's bungalow. The space looked like a lush garden somewhere in Bali or Indonesia. A handful of stone fountains gurgled quietly, and the primary sensation was *bright*: honest to God, the most dramatic magenta, coral, and brassy purple bougainvillea dominated the walls and fences.

Immediately, a small, neatly French-braided child tackled Jess. "Mom, I got a book about snakes from the library, did you know that snakes don't have eyelids?"

"I—"

"Also, they eat their food whole, and their ears are only inside their heads. Guess where you can't find snakes?" Juno stared up at her, blue eyes unblinking. "Guess."

"Canada!"

"No! Antarctica!"

Jess led them inside, calling "No way!" over her shoulder.

"Way. And remember that cobra in *The Black Stallion*? Well, cobras are the only kind of snakes that build nests and they can live to be twenty."

That one actually shocked Jessica. "Wait, seriously?" She dropped her bag on the couch just inside the door and moved to the pantry to dig around for dinner options. "That's insane."

"Yes. Seriously."

Juno went quiet behind her, and understanding dropped like a weight in Jess's chest. She turned to find her kid wearing the enormous-eyed expression of preemptive begging. "Juno, baby, no."

"Please, Mom?"

"No."

"Pops said maybe a corn snake. The book says they're 'very docile.' Or a ball python?"

"A python?" Jess set a pot of water on the stove to boil. "Are you out of your mind, child?" She pointed to the cat, Pigeon, asleep in the dying stretch of daylight streaming through the window. "A python would eat that creature."

"A ball python, and I wouldn't let it."

"If Pops is encouraging you to get a snake," Jess said, "Pops can keep it over at his house."

"Nana Jo already said no."

"I bet she did."

Juno growled, collapsing onto the couch. Jess walked over and sat down, drawing her in for a cuddle. She was seven but small; she still had baby hands with dimples on the knuckles and smelled like baby shampoo and the woody fiber of books. When Juno wrapped her little arms around Jess's neck, she breathed the little girl in. Juno had her own room now, but she'd slept with her mom until she was five, and sometimes Jess would still wake up in the middle of the night and experience a sharp stab of longing for the warm weight of her baby in her arms. Jess's own mother used to say she needed to break Juno of the habit, but parenting advice was the last thing Jamie Davis should be giving to anyone. Besides, it wasn't like anyone else ever occupied that side of the mattress.

And Juno was a master cuddler, a gold-medal Olympian in the snuggle. She pressed her face to Jess's neck and breathed in, wiggling closer. "Mama. You went on a date last night," she whispered.

"Mm-hmm."

Juno was excited for the date, not only because she adored her great-grandparents and got Nana Jo's cooking when Jess was out, but because they'd recently watched *Adventures in Babysitting*, and Fizzy had told her it was a pretty accurate depiction of what dating was like. In Juno's mind, Jess might end up marrying Thor.

"Did you go downtown? Did he bring you flowers?" She pulled back. "Did you kiss him?"

Jess laughed. "No, I did not. We had dinner, and I walked home."

Juno studied her, eyes narrowed. She seemed pretty sure that more was supposed to happen on a date. Popping up like she'd remembered something, she jogged to her roller backpack near the door. "I got you a book, too."

"You did?"

Juno walked back over and crawled into her lap, handing it over.

Middle Aged and Kickin' It!: A Woman's Definitive Guide to Dating Over 40, 50 and Beyond.

Jess let out a surprised laugh. "Did your Aunty Fizz put you up to this?"

Juno's giggle rolled out of her, delighted. "She texted Pops."

Over the top of her head, Jess caught a glimpse of the dry-erase board next to the fridge, and a tingling spread from her fingertips up to her arms. The words *NEW YEARS GOALS* were written in Juno's bubbly handwriting.

NANA & POPS
    Get a personal trayner
    Take a wock evry day

JUNO
    Lern to like brocooli
    Make my bed evry mornning
    Try Something New Sunday!

MOM
    Try Something New Sunday!
    Nana ses be more selfish!
    Do more things that skare me

Okay, Universe, Jessica thought. *I get it.* If Mrs. Brady could be a trailblazer, maybe it was time for Jess to try, too.

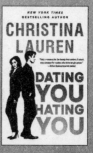